SOME CAN SEE

A NORTHERN MICHIGAN ASYLUM NOVEL

J.R. ERICKSON

🌼 Created with Vellum

DEDICATION

For Matthew P., Mattski, Cole Train, Moa Macimbe, Schnitzel

AUTHOR'S NOTE

Thanks so much for picking up a copy of Some Can See. I want to offer a disclaimer before you dive into the story. This is an entirely fictional novel. Although there was once a real place known as The Northern Michigan Asylum - which inspired me to write these books - it is in no way depicted within them. Although my story takes place there, the characters in this story are not based on any real people who worked at this asylum or were patients; any resemblance to individuals, living or dead, is entirely coincidental. Likewise, the events which take place in the novel are not based on real events, and any resemblance to real events is also coincidental.

In truth, nearly every book I read about the asylum, later known as the Traverse City State Hospital, was positive. This holds true for the stories of many of the staff who worked there as well. I live in the Traverse City area and regularly visit the grounds of the former asylum. It's now known as The Village at Grand Traverse Commons. It was purchased in 2000 by Ray Minervini and the Minervini Group who have been restoring it since that time. Today, it's a mixed-use space of boutiques, restaurants and condominiums. If you ever visit the area, I encourage you to visit The Village at Grand Traverse Commons. You can experience first-hand the asylums - both old and new - and walk the sprawling grounds.

PROLOGUE

*A*ugust 18, 1935
Sophia

SOPHIA LIFTED THE ROCK, hoping for a salamander. She kicked the black dirt crawling with ants and moved onto a downed tree branch. The previous summer she and her friend Ellen had found half a dozen salamanders at least. This summer Ellen didn't want to play in the woods. She wanted to go into town with her mama and gaze in the store windows at the new dresses on display. Or she liked to stay home and practice French braiding her hair.

"We're thirteen now," Ellen had said to Sophia half a dozen times at least - as if that explained why she wanted to sew a new dress instead of swim in the pond.

Sophia yawned just thinking about it.

Sophia had asked her brother Grimmel to join her, but he preferred to play in the cow pasture with the neighbor boys. Plus, Mama had given him new chores since Daddy died and he hardly had time to play with his friends let alone his little sister. Sophia too had new chores. She mucked the stables and fed the chickens every morning.

That day, rather than fill the wood box, she'd streaked for the woods praying mama didn't spot her through the kitchen window.

A branch snapped nearby, and Sophia tucked behind a tree

1

searching for a wandering deer. Sophia liked to lie in the downed grass where the deer nested at night. Their beds were soft and matted and she could almost imagine wrapping her body around a little fawn and stroking his knobby spine. She crept further, listening for another sound, but heard nothing.

Giving up her search, she scanned the ground for more rocks. Her daddy had told her that salamanders like dark, damp places and rocks were their perfect hideouts.

"Sophia…" she heard her name and glanced up to find Rosemary on the deer path in front of her.

Rosemary wore a pretty yellow dress streaked in mud and dark stains. Her mama would have her hide for that. Her dark curls, usually neatly arranged on her head, hung loose and wild. She watched Sophia with big empty eyes.

"Rosemary?" Sophia asked, feeling a trickle of fear light along her spine for Lord knows why. She surely wasn't afraid of Rosemary. "Your mama is lookin' all over for you. The sheriff came by our house. You better run home fast. Maybe stop at the pond and wipe off your dress."

Rosemary didn't speak or even blink. Something wasn't right with her eyes. As Sophia stared at her, she noticed other wrong things. A trickle of blood hovered just beneath Rosemary's nose and her arm seemed bent at a weird angle, like it had been broken, and now hung in a sack of skin.

Sophia wanted to take a step back, but instead she walked forward, lifting a hand.

"Are you hurt, Rosemary?"

Rosemary nodded and turned back the way she'd come. She didn't speak but walked further into the forest. She moved in a jerky limp that should have sent the girl sprawling, but somehow didn't. They came to Earl's cabin, an old hunting shack abandoned for years since the old man who lived there died in his sleep. It was only four walls with a dirt floor and a few holes for windows. Rosemary stopped at the door.

Sophia stared at it, knowing Rosemary wanted her to look inside the cabin, but her feet had grown roots and she couldn't move a muscle. The hot day grew hotter. She sleeved a sheen of sweat off her upper lip and turned back the way they'd come thinking for the first time she should run for help.

2

Rosemary hitched forward into the cabin. The door creaked on a rusted hinge. Sophia stepped in behind her leaving the glare of sunlight for the stifling darkness of the cabin. It smelled like the barn after daddy had slaughtered a pig. Sophia wrinkled her nose and stuffed her t-shirt up over her face. The door had swung closed, and she couldn't see. Her eyes hadn't adjusted to the dark and the windows offered little light. Something lay on the floor in the center of the cabin. Sophia blinked down. Where had Rosemary gone?

Sophia stepped to the door and kicked it open. It clattered against the side of the cabin making her jump. Turning back, she looked at the cabin floor trying to understand what lay there. It had been covered with an itchy looking blanket, and next to the mound lay a knife with a bone handle. Sophia bent down and picked the knife up with one hand while pulling the blanket back with the other.

Her breath caught hard in her chest as she stared at the body of Rosemary Bell. The girl lay in a pool of spreading darkness. Her face was tilted toward the door and Sophia saw her wide eyes staring vacant, the whites red and veiny. Her mouth hung open and blood trickled from her nose.

Sophia stumbled back, clutching the knife tight in her hand. When a crow called in the forest, Sophia whirled around and leapt from the cabin running hard, pausing only when she remembered that Rosemary had taken her to the cabin. How? But she didn't stop to consider. Jumping over logs and tearing through raspberry bushes that pricked her bare legs, she raced for home.

Only when her feet met the edge of her families' property, thick with black-eyed Susan's, did she slow and catch her breath. Gasping, she hurried for the house walking first into the barn and calling out for Timmy. She still clutched the knife, and she threw it hard on the floor before running to the house.

Her mama stood at the kitchen sink, elbow deep in a basin of sudsy water.

"Mama... mama," she whispered, pushing through the screen door and shaking her head back and forth as if she might clear the vision of Rosemary slumped on the floor.

"Sophia Ann Gray, if you are tracking dirt into this kitchen, I'll..." but her mama didn't finish the sentence. She whipped her hands from the sink, dried them on a cloth, and strode to her daughter, grabbing

Sophia's shoulders and bending low to look into her face. "What's happened?"

Sophia looked at her hand and wondered at the dark red streaks there. Had she cut herself on the knife? But no, it was Rosemary's blood she stared at.

"Are you hurt?" Sophia's mother took her hand and gently turned it over.

Sophia shook her head.

"Not me, Mama. Rosemary. I found her…"

Sophia's mama frowned, her eyes moving from Sophia's face back to her bloody hand.

"She's hurt? Where is she?" Her mother straightened up, yanked off her apron and slipped into her shoes. She pulled open the door and grabbed Sophia's hand smearing the blood onto her own.

Sophia pulled back, holding her ground, afraid to return to the woods and the cabin and…

"Sophia, snap out of it. This is not time for one of your daydreams. If Rosemary Bell is injured-"

But Sophia didn't let her finish.

"She's dead, mama. Rosemary is dead."

~

Twenty Years Later
1955
The Northern Michigan Asylum for the Insane

Doctor Kaiser held the framed photograph in his hand. His mother had been beautiful and terrible like a witch from a fairy tale who appeared golden and glowing until you saw her reflection in the mirror. Then you'd see her molten skin and flashing red eyes, her hands like claws reaching out for you when you turned your back.

He put the photograph in his desk, locked the drawer and stood.

He wound through the asylum's administrative floor, nodding at the doctors and nurses, avoiding the small talk. The intolerable Dr. Moore tried to catch his eye, and he turned taking an alternate route, descending a set of stairs to the patient transport tunnels.

An orderly ushered a young man down the hall. The man's eyes darted around and when he glimpsed Kaiser, he stopped in his tracks clutching the woman's shirt.

"It's okay," the attendant, a young woman, whispered, patting the patient on his back. "Good morning, Doctor."

"Good morning," Kaiser murmured.

He hurried down the tunnel and into the light of day, glancing back at the dark hole he'd emerged from. The tunnels were necessary in the northern Michigan climate. He was grateful for the enclosures when the snow piled high and ice encased the sidewalks. However, he never felt at ease moving within them. It was like experiencing burial while still alive.

He turned and stared at the Northern Michigan Asylum. His eyes climbed to the spires that rose pointed into the gray morning sky. Lights blazed in a hundred windows.

Careful that no one saw him, Kaiser ducked into a thicket of trees. He followed a path in his memory, his steps growing faster when he met the little hill that would take him to the hidden forest chamber.

The Umbra Brotherhood met six times a year in asylums all over the country, and today, an especially curious patient would be displayed.

He met Dr. Knight on his walk as he ascended the hill.

"I barely slept a wink last night," Dr. Knight admitted as they hurried down the slope into the gnarled basin of trees hidden in the forest.

"Why is that?" Kaiser asked, wishing he had made the entire trek alone. He preferred to gather his thoughts before entering the chamber and getting besieged by the voices of the others.

"I've never presented before," Dr. Knight said. "Dr. Claymore, from the Eastern Michigan Asylum, helped me bring the patient in. I had to run back to my office for an antacid."

Kaiser cocked an eyebrow, but didn't offer his sympathies. He'd presented half a dozen times. He was less interested in the doctor's nerves than his patient.

Supposedly the man could channel the dead.

"Here, I've got it," Knight announced stopping at a wall of brambles that hid the chamber door from view. He groped in the branches, fumbling until Kaiser considered shoving him out of the way and doing it himself.

Kaiser glanced at the hill behind them, checking again they weren't followed.

"There," Knight sighed, followed by a satisfying metallic click. Knight pushed through the branches and Kaiser followed.

They moved through a long rock passage lit with torches. Condensation gathered on the walls creating a slippery tunnel that reminded Kaiser distastefully of a yawning mouth.

The brick chamber opened before them. Doctors, over twenty-five in all, filled the wooden benches around a raised platform. On the platform, strapped to the bed, lay patient number six-twenty-four. His eyes stared wide and glassy. His lips moved, but no sound emerged.

The last meeting of the brotherhood at the Northern Michigan Asylum had not gone well. The patient, a young woman who could levitate objects, died on the table.

Kaiser settled onto a bench, staring intensely at the patient.

The young man cranked his head to the side and locked his green eyes on Kaiser's. A rush of unease moved through the doctor as the patient opened his mouth and began to scream.

CHAPTER 1

$\mathcal{J}$uly 11, 1955
Hattie

HATTIE'S HANDS SHOOK, her fingers trembling over the flat glass surface, callused plump ends shining back at her in the candlelight. The peach-colored candle dripped a stream of wax into its soft belly slowly caving out of sight. Her face was reflected in the glass case, but the flame distorted her image, revealing another Hattie - a ghoul version of her eight-year-old self.

If she touched the glass - the beautiful sprayed and smoothed glass, so clean it reflected the fine satiny cobwebs clinging to the chandelier - it would smudge. Smudges were fingerprints, evidence, and hers so obvious with her fat fingers that Gram Ruth called baby sausages.

Instead, she went for the shining Mahogany frame; the corners carved in neat spirals that twisted down and down. Crevices impossible to clean, Gram said, huffing and puffing with a dirty sock and a can of lemony spray that made Hattie sneeze. It was not the case itself that Hattie longed to touch, but what lay inside.

She wanted to set the candle down, but dared not soil a single piece of furniture. Gram Ruth's parlor was off limits. No playing, no pets and above all else no kids. Her mama told her that rule every time they visited Gram Ruth and Gram mentioned it three or four thousand times. Hattie's sister Jude and her twin brother Peter would moan *We Knoooooowwww* and roll their eyes, but Hattie never said boo. If she kept quiet, Gram would let her peek while she cleaned the room, let her walk carefully amongst the shining furniture, not touching anything.

Hattie switched the candle to her left hand, the hot wax giving just barely beneath her anxious fingers. "Not too tight," she whispered.

On Daddy's last birthday she'd gotten so excited placing lit candles on his chocolate cake she'd squished one and dripped melted wax all down the sleeve of the navy blue dress her mama had just made her. Daddy laughed and kissed her head, but Hattie's big sister, Jude called her a *clumsy little fool* and lit the rest herself.

The flame mesmerized Hattie, as did the sweet smell, like the oatmeal Mama made on weekdays, when a woman couldn't be burdened with some fancy meal at breakfast time.

Holding her breath, she slipped the left edge of her palm beneath the heavy glass lid, the wood pressed firmly against the flesh of her hand. It sat there unmoving, no startling screech as it gave way, no shift at all. Hattie was strong for an eight-year-old. The previous year when Ben Kinney pulled her hair at school she squeezed his fingers so hard he cried. Mrs. Updike made her miss recess for two days, but Hattie didn't care because Ben was a scuzzbucket and he got what he deserved.

Hattie bent her legs and maneuvered her shoulder beneath her palm. Her daddy did this when he had to get their cellar door open to let in some fresh air, usually after their cat Turkey Legs had pissed. Hattie wasn't supposed to say pissed, but Peter did and so did Jude. Pushing up, Hattie felt the lid give way.

She stared hard at the candle flame and gripped the smooth edge of the lid, moved its weight from her shoulder to her hand, almost losing it when the full burden took hold. The flame dulled, dipped beneath the pink-orange crater and slid back out, a serpent's tongue lighting her way. Carefully, sweat sliding like oil down her armpits, she pushed the lid up and back, slowly, slowly until it rested with a groan on its metal hinges.

The candle was no longer shaped like a neat cylinder; her chubby fingers had squashed the juicy wax into a strange sculpture, something she'd see in her mama's art books. For a moment, she forgot about the glass case, too preoccupied with imagining what the candle might now be. In clouds, Hattie often spotted puppies and airplanes, but in this candle she could see only the purple rubber sheaths on her sister's bike handlebars.

The glass on the case reflected the flame and Hattie turned gazing down. Her eyes raked over the contents. The floor of the case was covered in crisp, pink velvet, each fiber combed flat by Gram Ruth. Hattie had never seen Gram brush the velvet, but her mama had told her she did it every Saturday morning with a genuine silver brush filled with soft bristles. Her own pink fingers looked pale and ugly against the showy fabric. But it was the prize inside that mattered.

Gram Ruth's long dead cat, Felix, lived eternally in the pink velvet bed.

∾

Jude

JUDE PRESSED both hands against the window frame and pushed up. The cool night air kissed her neck, a patch of goose pimples lighting along her arms. The muscles of her thick forearms grew taut as the glass pane slid skyward, the wooden frame rubbing roughly along. She smiled at her own reflection in the glass, the bone lit moon as stark white as her gleaming teeth, her red lips almost black. Her dark ponytail had loosened and electrified flyaways stood out along her temple, erasing the two hours of ironing she had done that evening.

Swinging a bare leg through the window, she searched for the satin covered step stool she had left that evening when she snuck-out. Her red pump waved wildly, then kicked the stool which didn't tip, but bounced and settled. As she straddled the window ledge, the ridged wood pressed painfully against her pelvis, she imagined the look of horror on Gram Ruth's face if she saw Jude climbing back through the second story window after eleven pm. Such would be her grandmother's shock, Jude considered staying in place, her pelvic bone bruised by morning. Her pencil skirt was hiked around her thighs for easy climbing, exposing her left butt cheek to the dark estate.

Jude could see Gram's high bushes clinging desperately to the driveway like frantic hitchhikers trying to catch a ride out of hell. When Jude had been a little girl, she and Peter had often played in the bushes. In places, their branches grew so thick she could climb on top and crawl their length. Peter, a husky boy, born eleven minutes Jude's senior, always fell straight to the bottom.

After securing her foot on the stool, Jude slipped into the room. No lights shone, but she moved across the plush cream carpeting with ease, safe passage guaranteed by a full moon and fifteen years of familiarity.

As a baby Jude had not slept in this room. According to her father she'd slept in a raw silk bassinet that Gram Ruth bought in China when she was a newlywed. The bassinet, Jude's father said, belonged to Chinese royalty, but was sold for a bargain when the child of the Chinese couple took ill and died. Jude moaned at this point and complained that she might have died of whatever plague or pox had killed this baby, but her father only laughed. The story worked better on Hattie who found such notions romantic, suiting her strange flights of fancy.

Jude slipped her skirt to the floor and stepped out, kicking it toward a pile of wet towels clumped in the corner. Gram would have a fit if she saw the towels: *mildew and mold*, she'd say, but Jude didn't give two shits. Gram had too many rules, too many long sighs and disapproving looks.

She slid her slender fingers over her sleeveless blouse, plucking the buttons. Danny had busted two buttons, greedy and desperate as usual. He thought it turned Jude on, his frantic sucking and licking, tearing at her bra like some puppy after its mother's teat. Jude sometimes wanted to slam a fist in his head when he did that, just cock back and let one go, crack her knuckles against the hard sheet of his cheekbone.

Jude did not love Danny, hardly liked him, but he had a car and his dear old dad had a big houseboat stocked with whiskey and gin. Danny would wait at the end of Gram Ruth's long drive, his sleek blue Corvette like a heavy, haunched animal crouching in the dark. Sometimes he brought friends, other fast girls and rich boys with their windblown hair and sun ripened cheeks.

Jude would make Danny buy her a new blouse.

~

Hattie

FOR A LONG TIME, Hattie stared at the stuffed cat; its oily black fur abrasive in the pink velvet bed that held him. His pink satin collar held a heart-shaped platinum plate, Felix engraved in loopy cursive letters. A single diamond dotted the *i* on his name. His eyes were black rubies, his nose a dried crust with sunken warped nostrils. Hattie could see two pointed white fangs peeking beneath his black gummy smile that looked more like a grimace. She slid her palm over his back, the bones moving beneath her fingers like a string of pearls, down along his tail, wiry and stiff.

Her heart beat faster, a flush moving from her chest into her face as she stroked the animal, her stubby fingernails buried in fur, disappearing beneath black tufts. Felix's body was hard, like a store mannequin, not giving in the fleshy way that a body should. Just a skeleton wrapped tight with leather and covered in fur, but not really: he was a cat who had lived, a cat whose staring face hung throughout Gram Ruth's sprawling house.

Though Hattie had never met Felix, in life his eyes had been yellow, like the tiny orbs that bobbed in lanterns during the night. Gram said he was a true aristocrat, but Hattie hadn't a clue what she meant. None of it mattered really, Felix's life before the box. Hattie knew him only as this prized jewel. Perhaps in life he'd been just an ordinary house cat with an upturned nose and clumps of cat litter caked in the crevices of his padded feet. In the velvet casket, he was a Julius Caesar, a Babe Ruth, forever immortalized - in death infinitely more mysterious and grand than he'd ever been in life.

For several long minutes, Hattie stared, transfixed; petting his matted glossy fur and tracing his jeweled eyeballs with her free hand. She swayed to a music that only she could hear, a symphony of nostalgia not yet laden on her young brain, but already snaking in, leaving its slimy trail to stumble upon further down the line.

Without thought, for if she'd had one she'd never have dared, she

11

J.R. ERICKSON

plucked the cat from his velvety bed and thrust him to her chest inhaling his intoxicating scent of mothballs, castor oil and something deeper and fruity like melon. Hattie did not realize it then, but Felix would stay with her - the night a marked reminder of the end of life as she knew it.

CHAPTER 2

*J*uly 11, 1955
Jude

ONCE NAKED, Jude stood in front of her tall mirror.

She turned once, flexing her right calf forward and pointing her toe, evaluating herself from toe to hair roots and then back down again, appraising every centimeter. The way her toes spread out, thin and then widening into small square blocks, her toenails painted a deep red. Her ankles were narrow and opened into shapely calves, not too big, but a single wide line distinguishing the muscle from bone. Her small round knees became thick thighs then tapered off to her shaved crotch.

She stole razors from her father, refusing to make do with the tiny pink girl razors that barely cut the hairs, let alone scraped to her skin. She always left a single neat black line of hair, no complete baldness because it looked too juvenile and small, like an off-limits area rather than the sexy hideaway she hoped to cultivate. From the small streak of black curls came her flat belly that widened along her hips and then dove back in to stretch over her ribs and up to her plum sized breasts, small dark pink nipples pointed and severe. Her shoulders were wide, her muscular biceps hinged with thick forearms.

Her face sat proportionally on her thin short neck. Jude did not hate her face, but neither did she love it. Her upper lip was thin, barely disguising her long white teeth that Peter called buck. Her nose was small, a good feature, as were her wide almond-shaped brown eyes. Finally, her slightly bushy dark eyebrows and then her hair, just past her shoulders, chestnut, and wavy, neither straight nor curly. Her grandmother said her hair came from her great aunt Lynn, a woman she'd never met who died of syphilis - according to family legend. Perhaps more resemblance than Jude wanted to admit.

At fifteen, Jude had already entered her age of sexual enlightenment in full splendor. Though still a virgin - barely - she boasted to all of her girlfriends she'd done everything but go all the way.

Her breasts looked dented, pale finger marks creasing the milky flesh. Danny's short, hard grip imprinted on her tender skin, not that she cared, a means to an end. Tomorrow there would be bruises, maybe long red streaks, and Jude would have to wear her halter bikini to hide the marks, but she didn't mind. When she let Danny touch her, she owned him.

~

Hattie

THE CANDLE WAS NEAR DEATH, its life flickering and shuddering and threatening to cast Hattie into a dark, off limits room with no beacon to guide her out. She leaned into it, holding the candle close as if that might stop the non-existent wind from blowing out the flame, but to no avail. It gave a closing wave and then sagged sideways, the wick taking its final sleep in a bed of molten wax.

In the darkness, Hattie's eyes burned, and white spots danced in a canvas of black. Felix was nestled against her chest, his hard body comforting, his dry nose pressed into her neck, the way Gram Ruth held babies. *Suffocating them,* Jude said.

In the far corner, Gram's big grandfather clock tick-tocked the seconds away. To fight her fear, she whispered them out loud, soothed by her voice in the silence, but also afraid of waking someone, of waking Gram. After counting three hundred and thirty-two seconds, she took a step and then another.

Hattie had visited the room often, only with Gram Ruth, of course, and knew the layout well. If she walked a direct path to the door, she would leave Felix's cabinet to her left, Gram Ruth's blue crushed velvet chaise would stand to her right. The only other obstacle would be the big, round marble table that held a crystal vase of flowers. This table stood in front of the glass French doors that opened into the room.

Hattie shuffled forward, sliding each foot out and then sliding the other to meet it, a snowshoer in socks. The darkness was not whole; it slithered away as her eyes adjusted, hulking shapes staring at her, their shadowy bulk a welcome sight. Her shin brushed the chaise, the velvet scratching along her bare calf inches below the hem of her rose-colored nightgown.

The glass doors were propped open and Hattie used a single hand to slide each closed. They ghosted over the plush carpeting in silence, only a single metallic click to give her away.

If taller, she might have taken the stairs two at a time, rushing to the sanctuary of level two, a faster ascent to her child's pink bedroom. A Victorian-flavored room with curls and tendrils of pink, like the sugar plum dreams of such unfathomable innocence that only a child could stand it.

Hattie adored the room, loved it so fiercely she often cried just standing in its center, staring out across the expanse of decadence: the tall doll house carved of real wood and expertly decorated by a keen eye and tiny adult fingers. The front of the house opened, exposing the interior to any interested eyes, such a naughty privilege to peak so unashamedly into, not only the lives, but the furnishings of another. What child slept in that miniature cherry maple bed, its sky-blue lace coverlet tucked into the creases of wood, whittled for that very purpose? Hattie longed to climb into that house, to roam freely the rooms that flecked her dreams like sugar sprinkles on morning pancakes. A house so similar to Gram Ruth's, but so distant, so unconnected, impossible to imagine how one could live within the other. And this, this spectacle, took up mere feet in her opulent bedroom.

Speak nothing of the downy stuffed toys heaped on the floor, but not haphazardly, no, carefully arranged on a wide chenille throw of periwinkle color. Then the vanity, gilded with a gold powder so fine it might have brushed off when touched, but didn't, somehow clung like enchanted fairy dust to its delicate legs, to the smooth mirrored edges. The glass table was adorned with bottles of fragrance - perfume in aquamarine bottles, or amber hued, shaped as smooth round crystal balls or tall thin feminine bodies. Aromas not meant for any child and surely not meant for a child such as Hattie. A child whose own mother preferred the scents of strong ivory soap and the bitter odor of burning wood.

Though Gram Ruth lived in a mansion, it was an old mansion. *Haunted old*, Jude said. *Creepy old*, according to Peter. And it was true, all they said. Many times Hattie had stayed awake long into the night whispering with her mother about the spirits who wandered Gram Ruth's home and property, but that was their little secret.

Hattie maneuvered, like a stealthy cat, leaping with the wistful air of a floating feather, landing on the spongy front pads of her feet, defying the house in its desire to ferret her out to her heavily sleeping grandmother.

At the top of the Grand Staircase, Hattie stopped. The hall was dark, and yet at the far end, she could see the girl in the yellow dress. She stood outside Hattie's door, her eyes vacant, one hand swinging against her side like a rag doll's.

"I don't want to see you, right now," Hattie whispered, repeating the words her mother taught her.

She stared at Felix for a long time, saying it over and over again. When she looked back up, the hall was empty.

∽

Jude

JUDE LONGED TO SHOWER, her skin was smeared with the salty saliva of Danny's wandering mouth, but Gram had a hard rule of no showers after nine pm. She reigned over her grandchildren like a frigid nun supervises orphans.

Jude did not even play at liking Gram Ruth, who also did not feign at liking her. They were two opposing female forces, on such opposite ends in the world of what female meant, they could hardly be lumped together solely based on their sexual parts.

Jude fancied herself a feminist, an empowered woman, a young, hot-blooded sexualized animal intent on carving her place out in the world of men. Gram Ruth may have considered herself a feminist as well, though the kind that settled into patriarchy as if it were good manners rather than direct oppression. At sixty-five, she continued to wear girdles heavily laced up her back, tighter and tighter until the softly lined skin of her aging bosom toppled over the stiff fabric. Her panties were large, bleached white, and covered everything, including her sadly sloping ass and the pouch of curdled belly that hung below Gram's bellybutton like an alien twin. The type of secret body anarchy that besieged all aging peoples, women especially, slowly taking over their body as a final 'fuck you' to the chaos of life already endured.

Showers were not permitted after nine pm, nor was music, television, loud talking, telephone calls (unless for Gram Ruth), playing outside, playing inside, visitors and anything that might be remotely fun.

In previous years, Jude had avoided breaking the rules. She followed Gram's stern instructions, taking only minor consolations like late night reading or an occasional midnight snack after Gram had already stated, "the kitchen is closed."

However, all that had changed when Jude's parents had dropped her and her siblings at Gram Ruth's door that summer. The act did not look different from the outside; there were no teary-eyed goodbyes or strange melancholy silences. Her parents had stopped for a quick chat with Gram, pecked the kids on their already sun-burnt cheeks, and loaded back in their station wagon, bumper bruised and rust peeking from the tire wells. Nothing out of the ordinary was said that day, no slip of the tongue, or overheard conversations, but Jude knew. Something was amiss - the careful alignment of their small family had fallen off its tracks. She *knew* her parents' scowls, smiles, forehead creases, clammy hands, tone of voices, body postures. She recognized a good hug (full body contact) versus a bad hug (shoulders and arms only).

Something was amiss, had been amiss for weeks.

Her mother had changed. Her face had grown gaunt, haggard, her youthful beauty ravaged by some unseen enemy. Jude's father bounced between apathy and fervor, one moment staring in silence at some impossible puzzle and the next seeming to find the perfect piece. Jude had theories: illness, adultery, depression. Sometimes she logged them in her journal, once an emotionally charged depiction of girlish enterprise, now a scrupulous recording of her two uninformed subjects. On the flimsy pages of her dime store diary, the lock a cheap silver clasp, laid the minute details of her parents' lives.

Jude loved her parents fiercely, and sometimes considered herself their protector. They both had a dreamy quality that frightened her for their place in the big bad world. They kissed and laughed. Sometimes they lay in the yard with Hattie on her back between them looking at the stars, or the clouds, or even allowing the rain to fill their mouths. Jude rarely joined in such sensory adventures, but she secretly delighted in her parents' way of living. Her mother painted wild pictures of blazing sunsets or fields of flowers and Hattie would sit next to her smearing splotches of paint on the green grass in their backyard.

Except, that summer they had not done those things. One afternoon the fizzy lightness of their little life seemed to pop and rush into the sky allowing a darkness to slip in.

Jude yearned to talk to Peter, her twin, her second soul, but High School had severed the invisible umbilical cord that slithered between them. Peter now lived football, football, football, and girls. His hormones raged so constantly that Jude felt them within herself, and could not deny at least a portion of her fuming sexual desire was born directly of his loins. He had beat her to sex because he was a boy and would, in the course of their futures, beat her to most of the things she would claim as her own.

Peter had slipped away, into the strange world that teenage boys vanished into, and Jude could not follow.

Knowing she must forego the shower, Jude slipped on a pair of silk bottomed pajamas and matching top. They were a gift from her parents the previous Christmas. She fumbled around her nightstand, pulling open a drawer. A bible sat inside and though Jude rarely prayed, something unsettling gnawed her once the lights were out. She touched the bible, and whispered her own prayer, made up weeks earlier when the darkness had first settled on their home.

"God, please fix it. Please make my mother well if she's ill, bring my father back from the edge. Just make us whole again. Amen."

Putting the bible back, she hurried to the bathroom to brush her teeth before bed.

～

Hattie

HATTIE SLIPPED DOWN the hallway on tip toes, the home stretch, the walls rising up on either side like a vice that might begin its slow crank at any moment. Hers was the room at the end of the hall, the last door on the left. A long blank wall stretched between the kids' bathroom and her bedroom, for hers was the largest of the children's rooms and the most isolated.

The first was Peter's on the right. The heavy air could not stifle his tattered snores; she imagined his thick neck bulging with each escape of breath.

Next came the vacant room. Gram Ruth called it the playroom though it held no toys, only a big mahogany desk, long jagged scratches left in its shiny face. The drawers held old notebooks, some pages filled with stick figure drawings, others just arbitrary notes made by long forgotten hands about long forgotten tasks.

Halfway down the hall, a muted scuffling invaded her delicate ears. Hattie stopped and clutched Felix as though he were her father's firm torso, not a long dead cat taxidermied into modern existence. The sound was quiet enough, careful enough to be unnatural, not the accidental sounds that belonged to old houses - floor creaks and such. No, it struck Hattie as foreign, ominous, terrifying.

Her heart rate doubled; tripled, sped towards the red panic zone - insisted she run, scream. But she did none of those things, only cringed, her small indulgent face crumpling into the frozen O of horror she saw in Peter's horror comics. She held Felix up like a shield, a garlic wrapped crucifix for the vampiric monster waiting to devour her.

Ahead a door creaked open.

Hattie screamed loud and piercing, a sound that sliced the old house in two, that might have woken the dead, brought Felix back from cat heaven or hell. A scream Hattie felt in her muscle and her bones.

Another scream accompanied her own.

Jude's voice ripped through the previously silent hall.

She stood in front of Hattie in the darkened hallway soon to be awash in fierce yellow light. Her big sister's face must have matched her own, so twisted in shock and horror that Hattie might simply have been staring at herself, instantly aged nine years for time took those allowances. Age came not from the passage of minutes, but how much terror and strain clotted those minutes.

The hallway light flicked on, the small crystal chandelier drenching them in brilliant sparkling light.

"Whoa, cut the gas," Peter's voice joined the fray. Peter with his tousled auburn curls, his rumpled white t-shirt, his boxer shorts sagging to reveal soft white belly and the scrawny black hair of puberty's first appearance, stood in the hallway. He had stepped between the two sisters; sleep caking his squinted eyes, hands on his soft hips.

Jude pulled her hands away from her face, frozen in terror for barely a second before light cast away the demons, and her mouth became an angry red line.

"What the hell are you doing?" Jude snapped. She snatched away the cat. Hattie started to cry out, but Jude had already stuffed the cat into her dark bedroom as Gram Ruth's sleepy and worse, angry, face appeared at the top of the stairs.

CHAPTER 3

*J*uly 12, 1955
Jude

JUDE STRODE into the kitchen still flying on the previous night's activities. It wasn't a love thing; she always floated high after a night sneaking out with a boy. She never did those things at her own home, only at Gram Ruth's. At home, she didn't feel the need to rebel; her parents gave her plenty of freedom, but Gram's house was different.

"We've been robbed!" the scream pierced the early morning quiet and Jude dropped the porcelain mug of coffee she'd just poured. It shattered on the tile, shards streaking in every direction, hot coffee splattering her bare legs.

"Damn, ouch, ouch," she spat, dancing away from the heat.

Footsteps pounded through the house. The housekeeper Camille hurried into the kitchen grabbing a rag and dropping to her hands and knees to wipe the mess.

It had been Gram Ruth who screamed, and Jude heard the groundskeeper, Frank, talking to her in the parlor. Jude went to the freezer and pulled out a tray of ice, rubbing a cube on her inflamed skin.

Camille looked up as she wiped coffee from the floor.

"You okay, honey?"

"Yeah," Jude grumbled.

Peter walked in, hair mussed, and took a glass from the cabinet.

"Why's Gram having a cow?" he asked, holding it under the faucet.

Camille pursed her lips and lifted an eyebrow.

"You two don't have any idea what happened to Felix?"

Jude groaned and dropped her ice in the sink.

"Hold on." She ran up the stairs two at a time and pushed into Hattie's bedroom. Her little sister was lost in a sea of pink blankets and didn't stir. Felix was propped on the pillow at the head of the bed.

When she returned to the foyer, Gram was red-faced arguing with Frank who was showing Gram that nothing else appeared to be missing. Gram looked up and spotted Jude, narrowing her eyes on the dead cat clutched in Jude's hands.

Her grandmother was a formidable figure, standing nearly six feet tall with raven black hair and a sharp pointed face that could only be described as witchy. Her personality matched.

"You, you," she sputtered marching to Jude and ripping Felix from her hands. "No wonder your mother's gone. What kind of mother would want the likes of you?"

Peter walked in, eating an apple.

Gram spun and grimaced at Peter as if he were an ugly extension of his twin sister.

"What do you mean, mom's gone?" he asked, casting troubled eyes at Jude.

"Yeah. Mom and Dad are picking us up today," Jude snapped at Gram who clutched Felix as if he were a prized diamond and not a dead, stuffed cat.

"She's dead," Gram hissed and turned, stomping back to the parlor.

Peter turned to Frank who blinked after their grandmother.

Jude clutched the polished banister beneath her hand. She tried to make sense of her grandmother's words. Had she said their mother was dead?

"I, I hadn't heard. I..." Frank stuttered looking at the twins. Camille hurried in from the kitchen, her face pinched with worry.

"Is it true?" Jude demanded.

Camille reached for her, but Jude spun away.

"I don't know, honey. Your daddy will be here soon and... I just don't know."

Jude turned and ran out the door, letting it hang open behind her. She raced across the grounds and into the forest beyond. She didn't need to turn to sense Peter behind her.

~

Hattie

HATTIE SAT HUDDLED beneath a comforter in Gram's huge parlor. Though it was stifling hot beneath the blanket, she stayed put, watching the bodies moving about through a sliver of fabric.

Everyone wore black. Black pants and dresses and funny little black hats with spiderweb veils. Tiny black pearls studded the surface of Gram Ruth's veil. Even Hattie's daddy wore black though that morning he'd been in khakis and a blue shirt when Gram saw him walk down the stairs and practically screamed he was dressed inappropriately for the occasion. Her daddy rarely listened to Gram, but that morning he had. He walked back up the stairs, his smile gone, looking like the outdoor dogs after Frank hit them with a switch.

Gram laid out a plain black smock for Hattie which she refused to wear after she refused to take her bath. Beneath the comforter she wore the yellow summer dress with purple thread her mama had sewn for her that summer. The thought of her mama made her belly hurt. She didn't know why, just that Gram Ruth said, *Mama went to heaven and wasn't comin' back* and that made Jude and Peter cry and their daddy leave the house for long walks. Since Gram told them the news, Peter had stayed in his room and Jude stalked the house with angry red eyes and Hattie knew better than to talk to her.

"Hattie-bug?" Her daddy's voice floated down to her through the hot dark space she'd burrowed into. "I got you a piece of cake," he said, his big gray eye appearing at the hole she peeked from.

His eye disappeared, and Hattie saw a hunk of cake frosted in white sitting on one of Gram Ruth's fine china plates. The special ones piped in golden swirls that Gram only brought out at Christmas. Hattie's stomach grumbled at the sight of the cake, but she shook her head roughly.

"No, Daddy," she whispered.

"How bout I take you upstairs, Hattie-bear? Blanket and all?" he asked, reaching inside her cocoon and finding her sweaty little hand.

"Okay," she agreed.

He lifted her and carried her away. Gram tried to stop him, but he brushed past her. Hattie saw Gram's feet stuffed into her ugly pointed black shoes. Jude called them witch's shoes. In her bedroom, Daddy set her on the huge four-poster bed thick with frilly pink bedding.

He pulled away the heavy comforter and helped her onto the pillows. His face looked drawn and tired, but his eyes did not seem sad.

"It's going to be okay, Hattie. I promise."

He kissed her lightly on the forehead and left the piece of cake on her bedside table. Gram Ruth would have a fit, a shit fit Peter would say. No food was allowed upstairs.

Hattie watched her father retreat from the room, his stiff black shirt clinging to his sweaty back.

~

Jude

FOUR DAYS. Four days since Gram uttered the words *your mother is dead.*

Jude sat in the parlor in a black dress that Camille had made. She had refused the black tights despite Gram's malevolent stares at Jude's bare legs. People stood in little groups, talking, eating tiny sandwiches, patting her father on the arm. They offered Jude paper words of sympathy and gave her stiff hugs she wanted to shrug off. Peter stood with Danny who stared at her at every opportunity, gazing at her naked legs like a dog in heat. She refused to look at him, to look at anyone.

Felix, the dead cat that had spurned those hateful words from her grandmother, was tucked in his cabinet and covered with a black tablecloth. A framed photograph of her mother sat in its center surrounded by fat white roses. Her mother, Ann Elizabeth Porter, stared out from the frame in her white wedding gown, her signature gold locket suspended from her delicate neck. Her long golden hair flowed over her shoulders and her blue eyes seemed to watch Jude across the room. Except she was dead. She would never watch Jude again.

It seemed macabre to Jude that Gram Ruth had chosen her mother's wedding picture for the memorial, but her father relented. He seemed uninterested in the details. When Jude tried to get him alone, he brushed her off claiming errands and phone calls, anything to avoid her.

In a matter of days Jude's life had ceased. She still existed, a body, a set of organs, a brain, but the light - where was the light? She felt nothing, numb, and then in other moments she felt everything - her mother's soft hands rubbing her back when she fell asleep at night, the long sweet grass she and Peter rolled in at their family's farm, the warmth of the fire they sat by playing board games, eating popcorn, telling stories. Had those things died with her mother? Had they all died, but been left to walk the earth as fleshy bags void of heart?

"Jude?" She looked up to find her grandmother holding a piece of pecan pie. It was Jude's favorite and though her grandmother was smiling, Jude saw the disdain tucked behind her dark eyes.

"No, thank you," she murmured.

"You need to eat, Jude," Gram Ruth said, pushing the pie closer. "Camille made this special for you."

"I'm not hungry," Jude said, turning her gaze back to her mother's photo.

"Take the pie," Gram said through gritted teeth.

The smell wafted in Jude's nostrils and brought a wave of Christmas Eve dinners. Her mother made a pecan pie every year just for Jude.

Jude lashed out, slapping the plate from Gram's hand. It flew across the thick carpeting, the plate skidding to a stop at the feet of several people. Gram lifted a hand as if she would slap Jude, but Jude was already on her feet, pushing past Gram, shouldering through the group by the door, racing through the house. She ran out the back door and into the woods, kept running, pulling her dress over her head so she wore only her slip and bra.

A creek ran along the back of the property and Jude waded in, the water icy cold, and shocking. Her feet sank into the slippery mud and she threw her body forward letting the water swallow her whole.

CHAPTER 4

ate July 1955
Jude

"WHAT HAPPENED TO MOM?" Jude demanded to her father's back. He stood facing Gram Ruth's scrubbed granite countertop, his shoulders rigid.

"She had an accident, Jude," he murmured.

She grabbed his arm and tried to turn him. Her dad had been acting strangely since their mother's death, disappearing for hours at a time, walking the house mumbling to himself. He was like a man possessed.

"Why won't you tell us what happened?" Jude bellowed, fists balled at her sides. She wanted to hit him, to beat his chest with her fists, to run to the bedroom that was not hers, but a tomb in Gram Ruth's mausoleum, and rip the wallpaper from the walls.

He turned and looked at her with bleary, red eyes. He'd been drinking scotch, and his hands shook when he lifted one and ran it through his hair.

"Peter and I are fifteen years old, we deserve the truth. Was it a car accident?"

Her dad blinked at her as if she were demanding he solve complicated trigonometry.

"Jude, I just can't right now. Okay, honey? I don't feel well."

He patted her shoulder absently and walked from the room toward the stairs.

Jude snatched the crystal glass that stank of scotch and threw it to the floor. She didn't jump back at the sound of the shattering glass or the shards that grazed her legs.

Wildly, she looked around for something else, a piece of Gram's pristine china, but Peter peeked his head around the doorframe.

"What the hell was that?" he asked looking from Jude to the shattered glass. He sighed and walked toward her, stepping carefully around the slivers strewn across the tile floor.

Jude cried when he touched her, huge gulping sobs that Peter liked to tell her sounded like bleating sheep.

"Oh dearie." Camille's voice interrupted them. She swept into the room in her stiffly pressed white smock. "Had a little accident, did ya?"

Jude shook her head, crying.

"Why won't anyone tell us? Camille, do you know? What happened to Mama?"

The word Mama created a wave of grief so strong it threatened to pull her under.

"Come on Judes," Peter mumbled. "Sorry about the mess, Camille."

He pulled Jude from the room and out the front door.

In their treehouse, quickly growing too small for the two to sit comfortably, Peter watched her with sympathetic eyes.

"I'm sad about Mom, too. I am. But she's gone, Jude. She's up there now," he gestured toward the sky.

Jude snorted.

"And you're okay with that? Some bullshit story about an accident?"

Peter rubbed his big hands together. He'd definitely make varsity football that year. Jude guessed he'd gained twenty pounds that summer.

His eyes welled up, and he shook his head.

"I don't know. I mean, no, of course not, but maybe it was gruesome or something and they don't want to upset us. Hattie's already falling apart, and you've seen Dad. It's like everyone's eatin' grape's off the wallpaper. I just want it all to be over."

"Don't you realize it will never be over, Peter. Mom is dead!"

Peter closed his eyes, but Jude could still see the tears flowing over his red cheeks.

"It's more than Mom being dead," Jude continued, sitting up on her knees. "It's like, when Dad first told us, he acted as if it wasn't real, you know? He said he'd tell us all soon, but then he stopped saying that and he's not just moping around. He's acting kooky. I've seen him walk in and out of Gram's barns like a hundred times. Why?"

Peter shrugged and threw up his hands.

"I don't know, Jude. Are you writing a book? You're Sherlock Holmes, right?" he rolled his eyes. "Every thing's a big conspiracy with you. Maybe it's not. Maybe Dad's sad. End of story."

Jude glared at her brother wondering how they could share the same genes and still be so different. Did he not see it? How everyone was skirting the truth?

∿

Jude

"GIVE ME THAT." Jude snatched the bottle of whiskey from Danny's hand where he'd been ready to drink.

"Hey," he sputtered when some sloshed onto his wrist. The smell filled the car.

Jude tilted her head back and took a long drink, grimacing at the taste, but savoring the burn as it roared into her belly. She leaned her head against the leather passenger seat and wiped her mouth on her arm.

"Come on," she said gruffly, pulling her dress up over her thick thighs, past her waist so that Danny had a view of her black-clad bottom as she climbed over the seats into the back of his car.

"Whoa," he breathed, taking a drink. "You're bitchin' hot, Jude."

"Don't talk," she whispered when he climbed back and lowered his face close to her own. He kissed her and when he slipped his tongue into her mouth, she thought of biting it, but instead grabbed his shirt and pulled it over his head. He fumbled with his pants, finally getting them off.

"Are you sure?" he murmured, kissing her neck, trying to look into her eyes, but Jude didn't want to look in his eyes.

She didn't answer, just reached down and grabbed him, forcing him into her. It hurt, and she gritted her teeth until he broke through her unopened body and sank into her. They both gasped, him in pleasure, her with release, some sensation that abated her rage.

The moments after were less fulfilling as Danny mumbled and whispered and pumped into her. He finished with a strangled groan and collapsed onto her, dripping saliva down her neck. His weight felt oppressive and the temperature in the car seemed stifling and unbearable.

"I have to go," she huffed shoving Danny off her. He fell to the floor, surprised, but she was already up, turning the door handle and pushing the car door open, falling out into the cool grass. She scrambled up to standing, the moonless night welcome as she pulled her dress back down.

"Hey, wait," he whispered.

She watched him in the lit backseat shuffling into his pants, his face red, welts on his shoulders where she'd sunk her fingernails into him.

"Just give me my shoes," she muttered, looking toward the dark estate. They had parked at the end of Gram Ruth's property where Danny was dropping her off.

"Are you okay?" he asked, stepping from the car holding Jude's Mary Janes.

She snatched them and turned, running into the dark woods that edged the property. Her bare feet sank into the grass. The sobs she'd been holding hostage burst forth. She doubled over and dropped to her knees, pressing her face into the ground as she wailed. She wanted her mother, needed her mother so badly she thought her body might split open from the pain.

"Please, please, please," she murmured, crying, begging whatever god existed to bring her back, to restore her family to whole.

Eventually her eyes ran dry, her head throbbed from the effort and she stood, not bothering with her shoes as she tromped through the woods back to Gram Ruth's house. The veranda was lit and as she left the shelter of the trees, she saw her father standing near the rail smoking a cigarette. She had never seen him smoke before.

He turned when he heard her, stubbing the cigarette on the ground.

"Jude?" She watched his eyes take in her puffy face and rumpled clothes. "Oh dear, we've messed everything up. Your mother was right."

His words barely registered beneath her haze of alcohol and grief. He strode from the porch and wrapped her in a hug.

"I have something to tell you," he said into the top of her head. He tilted her chin up and wiped her face with a kerchief he pulled from his pocket.

"Jack?" Gram's sharp voice sliced through the quiet.

Gram stepped onto the porch.

"I need to speak with you," Gram announced, leaving no room for argument.

"We'll talk tomorrow," her father whispered, giving Jude a peck on the forehead.

He walked away, following Gram into the house. Jude wondered what he'd been about to say.

Jude never heard her father's confession.

Twenty-four hours later he was dead.

.

CHAPTER 5

*1*932
Sophia

THE FIRST TIME Sophia saw the woman, she thought she was selling bibles. Course, who in their right mind went to someone's barn to sell bibles instead of their front door? Furthermore, who sold bibles in a white linen dress on a dusty country road? But being nine years old, Sophia didn't bother with such rationales. Her child's mind was like a dream mind - anything could make sense.

"You lost?" Sophia asked her when she didn't see a stack of bibles clutched in the woman's pale hands.

The woman tilted her head to the side and stared at Sophia with eyes like the little ice crystals that formed on the pond in winter. They glittered in the sunlight, and for an instant seemed to vanish all together, replaced by a bright whiteness that slid into eternity, no bottom to speak of.

"Sophia!" she had turned at her mother calling from the kitchen and when she turned back the woman was gone. Sophia ran deeper into the barn, peered behind the old milk crates, but no sign of her. She would have scoured the woods, but her mother's call came again, shriller this time and Sophia knew if she kept lunch waiting, a switch might be in order. She ran back to the house, breathless and asked her mom and her two brothers if they'd seen her.

"Who?" Grimmel asked, spooning more pickle relish onto his plate.

"The lady in the white dress," Sophia told them, grabbing extra strawberry jam for her toast when her mother turned back to the stove.

"I didn't see anyone," Grimmel shrugged.

Sophia's brother Timothy ignored her all-together as was his habit. Since turning fifteen the previous February, Grimmel and Sophia had been reduced to children, and Timothy elevated to their father's farm hand - in other words an adult. He rarely spoke to Grimmel and never spoke to Sophia except to boss her around.

"Sophia, I don't have time for child's play today. I've three pies to bake for women's garden club tomorrow, a whole load of wash thanks to your mud antics last week and a year's worth of cucumbers to jar. Eat your lunch and then you're to go down to Hilda's farm to collect apples."

"But Mom, I talked to her. I'm not makin' it up. I swear."

Sophia's mother turned and gazed at her daughter with a stare bordering on frustration. She pursed her lips and sighed.

"Timothy, when you're done with lunch, check the sheds and the barn for this woman."

Timothy looked up from his lunch, surprised. He started to argue, but his mother silenced him with a look.

"Yes ma'am," he told her.

Satisfied, Sophia scarfed down her lunch and set off for Hilda's. She was not keen on picking apples, but Hilda's barn cat Gray had birthed a litter of kittens three weeks before and Sophia jumped at every opportunity to play with the little furballs.

THAT NIGHT, when daddy returned from town, he tucked Sophia into bed. In the summer, she and Grimmel slept on the screened porch. At night, the heat of the day settled into the land to feed the plants, and the air came alive with the sounds of darkness.

"I hear our good friend the Barn Owl," Sophia's dad whispered, his eyes twinkling in the light from the kerosene lantern at her bedside.

Sophia listened and sure enough the familiar screech greeted her.

The cry rose amidst a melody of night song. Crickets and tree frogs and night birds all had their voices in the mix. The scent of grass and hay and the mossy smells from the pond mingled together. Years later Sophia would find herself transported home to nights on the farm when any of those sounds or smells found her.

"Mama says you saw a woman on the farm today?" her father chided her, gently.

Unlike Sophia's mother, her father treated his only daughter with a tenderness that revealed their secret bond. Since birth, Sophia's father doted on her. Not as his princess, but as the special child. The child who appeared in their life as a gift after they believed only Timothy and Grimmel would grace their home. She stole into the world like the quiet mist that floats across the pastures every morning, sliding from her mother's womb with barely enough time for Heather to sit up in bed and announce that her water had broken. Daddy delivered Sophia with his own two hands. He still told the story of the caul that sheathed her face and neck and how he and Mama were afraid to cut it away. Finally, for fear that Sophia might suffocate, her daddy ripped the milky red veil from her face and welcomed the first wild cry of his baby daughter.

"Yes, she wore a white dress, and I thought she was selling bibles, but then she didn't have any bibles."

"Did you talk to her?"

"Yes, well," Sophia paused. "I tried to anyhow, but Mama called us for lunch."

"Hmmmm...." her daddy scratched the stubble on his chin and looked into the night thoughtfully. "Not a neighbor then? Hilda's granddaughter, maybe, Sarah?"

"Daddy, Sarah is hardly a year older than me and we've only played a thousand times. I think I'd know if it was Sarah."

Her daddy chuckled and shook his head. He kissed Sophia lightly on the forehead.

"Well if you encounter her again, you ask her name and then you come straight to me, okay?"

Sophia nodded, but when she saw the woman again, her father was dead.

∼

J.R. ERICKSON

September 1934

HER DADDY DIED on a beautiful autumn day when the leaves fell long and soft and piled in great heaps of copper at the edges of the road. Sophia remembered the blue ribbon that her mother tied in her hair that morning, insisting that Sophia look fine for the Sunday brunch that the Church of Nazarene held every September. She remembered the chalky smell of the old woman who hugged her close when they led her mother away from the picnic to a shadow at the side of the church. She remembered most of all the look on her mother's face as the joy drained out. First the light left her eyes and then the soft rise of her mouth fell and turned down and her chin quivered. Sophia could not hear her cry, but for years, her memory would conjure a stream of fat tears rolling over her mother's cheeks.

A farm accident, they called it. Daddy suffered a heart attack and fell off his tractor. He was run over by the disc-harrow - the part that chopped up the weeds. At twelve years old, Sophia understood what that meant - pain. When a boy at school told her that detail, Sophia kicked him in the shin as hard as she could and ran the four miles home.

She didn't go to the farmhouse, but to the barn where she hid in the little loft and wept until dusk. When she finally peeled her tired body from the dusty floor, she saw the woman for the second time.

Somehow, without making a sound, she had climbed into the loft. She sat on her knees, her legs tucked beneath her in the same white dress. Sophia looked first at her startling gray eyes, and then she took in every detail of the strange woman who had not spoken a word. Her long auburn hair was loose and flowed over her shoulders, and her face looked soft and pale. Sophia thought if she touched it, the woman's skin would feel like milk does when you dip your fingers in it. Her features were small as was the shape of her body from her breasts to her hips, but she was not a girl. Sophia knew girls, and this was a woman. She thought of her daddy then and cried.

The woman moved to embrace her and Sophia held out her arms, longing for a real hug. Her mother grew stiff when embraced and though she tried to comfort her children, her own grief had turned her

34

body to stone. Sophia sighed as the woman wrapped strong arms around her. She pressed her face into the woman's small chest and she felt the wetness of her tears on the soft linen cloth. And then the warmth and the comfort dissolved and Sophia's arms held nothing. She opened her eyes to the empty loft. The dust moved, unsettled, in the place where the woman had sat, but the woman herself had disappeared.

∾

AUGUST 18, 1935

SOPHIA CRAWLED BENEATH HER BED. She stared up at the springs flecked with dust and traced her finger along the iron frame. Outside wheels crunched over the stony driveway and a door slammed. She turned her head and watched her mother's bare feet pass. The screen door opened and slammed shut.

"Hi Heather, how ya doing?"

"Busy, Sheriff," her mother said shortly, and Sophia imagined her wiping flour on her apron. Her hair would be tousled with flyaway strands sticking from her messy ponytail. Her mother was beautiful, everyone said so, but never more beautiful than mid-day when the housework left her dishevelled. Then she transformed from the rigid woman who longed to put everything in its right place to the flesh and blood person who wasn't afraid to hug and let you lick the cookie dough spoon before she washed the dishes.

"I'm looking for Rosemary Bell. Lives down by Moores Hardware, about Sophia's age?"

"Well she's not here as far as I know, but Sophia run off this morning so who's tellin' if they're together. Sophia's thirteen now and should be doin' chores, but some days I don't have the heart to scold her."

Sophia lay perfectly still wondering if she ought to reveal herself. Instead, she listened.

"Rosemary's been missin' since last night actually," the Sheriff continued. "Her ma called me up this morning when she still hadn't come home. They thought she might have walked across town to stay at her grandma's, but no sign of her there either so I'm checking with all her little friends…"

"Summer makes vagabonds out of most our children," Sophia's mom murmured.

"That it does. Well if you see Rosemary, tell her to high-tail it home. I'd say it's gone too long to avoid a lashing, but it will be lesser the sooner she shows up."

"Will do, Hal."

Sophia watched her mother's feet pass by a second time - the bottoms dirty and hard looking. She returned to the kitchen where Sophia hoped she was making blueberry dumplings with the blueberries she and Grimmel had picked the day before.

Sophia crawled from the beneath the bed, made sure her mama's back was turned, and sprinted for the woods. It was her turn to fill the wood box, and Sophia's mama expected her to clean the chicken coop too. But summer was fading fast, and Sophia woke that morning desperate to search for salamanders. She glanced behind her a final time and slipped into the trees.

CHAPTER 6

September 1965
Hattie

HATTIE SLUMPED onto the couch with a groan. Her back ached from shoulders to hips and a sticky sweat made her white t-shirt cling to her skin. She surveyed the apartment and smiled despite the chaos that greeted her. Yes, boxes stood waist high in nearly every inch of the space. Yes, the walls were mustard yellow, the carpet threadbare, and the bay window's bench was rotted clear through, but it was all hers.

She could hear Mrs. Bowers, the woman who owned the house and lived downstairs, trying to coax one of her cats in from the porch.

For the first time in her life, Hattie lived on her own. She played with the tiny charms dangling from the gold bracelet around her wrist, meditatively rubbing her thumb over the shapes.

She leaned back and closed her eyes and again conjured a vision of her future apartment. A blue suede couch, just like Coco Chanel's, stretched over thick burgundy carpet. On the couch, Hattie's future cat Edgar lounged sleepily with his long white fur fanning around him in a sunlit halo. The ornate gold side table held a sleek black telephone, a tall Tiffany lamp and a stack of art books. Across from the couch, two wing backed leather chairs courted the sofa. A new bench had replaced the bay window seat with a thick pad and a black coverlet, piled high with throw pillows. On the window ledge a steaming cup of cocoa fogged the window. From the street, a melancholy song drifted in the air and carried with it memories of dancing beneath twinkling lights. Most important of all would be the little balcony containing her easel, a stack of fresh canvas and a whole case full of paints.

In her vision a figure appeared. A little girl in a bloody yellow dress stood just behind Hattie's easel.

A loud knock at the door startled Hattie from her reverie. She snapped her eyes open and frowned at the chipped coffee mug adorning the pale wood coffee table she'd taken from Gram Ruth's barn.

She had not seen the girl in years. Unlike other ghosts Hattie had encountered, the girl never spoke. Hattie would no longer be able to daydream about her future apartment without placing the little girl in it.

The knock came a second time and she sighed, pushing the image from her mind.

"Hi," she said, opening the door and smiling cautiously at Mrs. Bowers holding a pie.

"Peach. Baked it myself this morning. I'm so happy to have another lady in the house." The woman shuffled across Hattie's doorstep, moving aside a box to set the pie on Hattie's little kitchen table.

～

Jude

"NOT TOO CLOSE," Jude called to the group of women staggered in front of the historical museum. There were five women aging from seventeen to eighty-five years old. They represented a photo journalism piece for Radical Feminism, a magazine devoted to covering real women neutralizing gender stereotypes.

The seventeen-year-old wore a pretty yellow sun dress. Her wavy strawberry blonde hair sat in a pile on top of her head, held there by sparkling barrettes. In her solo shot, she would wear overalls, and sit on the tire of the enormous combine she drove at her father's farm. The others, a mechanic, a carpenter, a banker, an attorney and the oldest woman, Janice, a professor, all looked the part of the perfect lady. They smiled with red lips, and jutted their hips out, admiring patent leather high heels. It was the comparison photographs that excited Jude. The pictures that blew their first impression out of the water. Jeans and suits, oil streaked hands, leather briefcases, all truths that most people preferred to ignore.

"Interesting shot," a man spoke behind her, but she ignored him.

No stranger to the attention of men, Jude rarely gave them first priority. She lowered her gaze to the camera, clicked the shutter several times and stood back, surveying the position of the sun.

She could feel the man continuing to hover behind her.

"Can I help you with something?" she quipped, turning to face him.

The man, tall and broad with golden hair that curled beneath his ears, smiled, and offered Jude his hand. Unnervingly handsome, Jude thought, gazing back at gray-blue eyes that reminded her of Petoskey stones.

"I'm Damien," he told her, waiting patiently, hand extended.

Jude considered snubbing him. Some part of her wanted to. Anyone that handsome deserved a little rejection now and then, but the way he looked at her caused something to stir. She was curious.

"Jude," she told him.

"I'm sorry to interrupt," he began when she didn't say more. "I was having a coffee over there and saw you setting up the picture. I need to hire a photographer, so I thought..."

"For what? A portrait?" she sneered.

"No," he grinned. "I'm terribly un-photogenic so that's the last thing I'm looking for. Actually, I'm a doctoral student of psychiatry and writing my thesis on the motivations of people who become homeless."

"The motivations?" she asked wryly. "Probably not to starve or freeze to death."

"I'm studying a different motivation, actually. I didn't mean to bother you though. I'm sure I can find someone else." He didn't sound offended, but he turned and began to walk away.

"Wait," Jude called, cursing his good looks. "I'll be done with this set of shots in a half hour. If you're still at the coffee shop, we can talk about it."

He smiled, two rows of straight white teeth, and his face lit with apparent joy, and perhaps relief.

"I'll be there."

~

"I'M STILL NOT sure why you need a photographer," Jude admitted after Damien explained his thesis in more detail.

He cocked his head and looked out the window, thoughtful.

"I guess it helps me to study them better. I work with patients face to face and want to pull up a photograph each time I'm reading an interview and put a face to a name," he said, pouring more sugar into his coffee.

She looked at his cup and grimaced.

"Are you drinking coffee or a milkshake?"

He widened his eyes and then looked at the sugar canister in his hand as if he didn't know how it had gotten there.

"I don't like coffee," he admitted, grinning. "But it's become a necessary evil. This is how I force it down."

"Seems you're taking a spoonful of sugar to an unhealthy level," she said, pushing the sugar across the table.

Damien's lips were heart-shaped with a tiny divot in his upper lip. His eyelashes were long and blond, his hands large and fine-boned. Jude had never been drawn to photographing men for the sake of their beauty, but found herself wanting to take shots of his body in parts, a single flexed forearm, the spirals of his ear, the tapering of his lower back.

"It's an interesting project," Jude admitted. "But if you want photos for your personal use, you can use an instant camera. I'm a photographer, Damien. You'd be throwing away money if I took your pictures."

"I appreciate your honesty." he said. "But I'd prefer a professional take them. Maybe I'll publish my findings someday, even put them in a book."

She cocked an eyebrow considering whether she'd want her name attached to those photos. She thought yes, an existential examination of homeless people was interesting if nothing else.

"Okay, sure," she said. "Listen, I'm done for the day. Do you want to get a drink?"

Damien smiled and sat back in his booth. They stared at each other for a long moment, long enough for Jude to know the attraction was mutual.

"Yes," he said. "I'd love to."

~

Hattie

HATTIE FOUND a hammer in the shoe-box she had taken from Peter's old room at Gram Ruth's. It contained the hammer, two screwdrivers, a pack of nails, duct tape, batteries and a flashlight. She tugged a bit of colored plastic from the bottom, recognizing an old key chain that used to hang from Peter's bike handlebars. It showed an orange Detroit Tigers logo. Hattie traced her fingers over the plastic, rough on the edges likely from a few scrapes on the road.

They had deployed Peter to Vietnam seven months before. Hattie had cried when she hugged him goodbye, Jude told him he better watch his ass, and Gram Ruth had given him a crisp twenty-dollar bill and said not to blow it on alcohol. He sent Hattie a letter, once a month, describing the glossy ferns and endless rains of the jungle. He didn't tell her about death and dying though she saw the newspapers and knew he faced it daily. Jude was his twin. If he told anyone the harsh realities of his life as a soldier it was her. Jude could hear those stories and not cry a tear. Hattie, on the other hand, cried if she saw a squirrel dead in the road.

She slipped the key chain into her pocket. Using a screwdriver, she pried the lid off the musty crate she'd retrieved from Gram Ruth's loft. A billow of dust blew into her face and she sneezed, waving at the air until it settled. Hattie pulled out a wad of tissue paper sprinkled with mouse poop and tossed it into a paper garbage bag. Beneath the tissue, she found the albums and lifted the first one out, smoothing her fingers along the yellowing fabric. She had not looked at the photo albums in years.

In the months after her mother died, followed by her father only weeks later, Hattie slept with the albums every night. Many of the photos were dull, their images worn away by Hattie's needy fingers. One picture of her mama and daddy holding their family's cat Turkey

41

Legs on the porch of their farmhouse had been so tattered after Hattie's touching, Gram Ruth had thrown it away without even asking. Hattie still remembered the picture, the way her mama looked to the left gazing at Daddy while he grinned holding a wriggling Turkey Legs in place as Jude, even then loving photography, snapped the shot.

Jude would laugh if she saw the stack of albums Hattie brought into her new home. She pulled each one out, wiped a layer of silt from their covers and stacked them neatly to the side. She wanted the wedding photograph of her mama that had been displayed at her memorial, but found the bottom of the crate filled with straw and no more photos.

She'd have to return to Gram Ruth's.

∼

Jude

"PSYCHIATRY?" Jude said, eying Damien through increasingly drunk eyes. "What compelled you to become a head-shrinker?"

Damien took a shot and laughed, grimacing at the bitter taste. His blond hair settled over his eyes and he swiped it away.

"I like to help people."

"Oh come off it," she badgered. "Don't go one-dimensional on me now. We just spent twenty minutes talking about why you're conflicted about living in the suburbs. You can do better than, 'I like to help people.'"

"Another round?" he asked, waving at their empty glasses.

Jude gauged her level of drunkenness and knew she should say no. "Yeah, but first an honest answer."

He squinted and puckered his lips.

"I'm curious about people and why they do what they do." He waved to the bartender to refill their drinks. "My father's a religious man and he believes the devil is behind the dark things in this world. I tend to think the opposite. Perfectly good people do terrible things. Case in point." He pointed at the line of empty shot glasses.

Jude rubbed the back of her neck, the familiar urges of her body imagining unbuttoning Damien's shirt.

"I don't think the devil's behind this," she laughed. "What saint doesn't love a little holy wine?"

He grinned.

"Nor do I, but it's against my better judgment. I have to work tomorrow. You too, I bet. Yet here we are." He winked at her and held his shot glass high after the bartender refilled it.

"Maybe we better call it a night then," she said, clinking her glass against his. "There's a motel across the street."

He paused with his glass almost to his lips, studying her.

For an instant, Jude saw his face darken, and she thought he might say no. Then he slammed the shot and stood, holding out his hand.

"I'll absolve my sins tomorrow. Tonight the devil wins," he told her.

She took his hand, the sensation buzzed up her arm and streaked through her body.

They'd be lucky to make it to the room.

CHAPTER 7

*A*ugust 18, 1935
Sophia

"TELL the sheriff you were playing in the woods and found Rosemary in the barn," Sophia's mother said, meticulously cleaning the blood from Sophia's cuticles.

Sophia's mama had called the sheriff and told him to come right away. Then she'd gathered all her children at the kitchen table.

"But Rosemary found me," Sophia started. "She led me to the cabin, Mama."

Timothy sputtered and threw up his hands in exasperation.

"Aren't you listenin', Sophia? You can't tell the Sheriff that or he'll think you're stark-ravin' mad!"

"Tim!" Sophia's mama gave him a stern look.

"It's true, Mama. If Daddy were here, he'd say the same thing," Timothy argued.

"No, he wouldn't," Sophia wailed, tears pouring over her cheeks. "Daddy'd believe me, and he'd want me to tell the truth."

Grimmel watched Sophia with wide, frightened eyes, but didn't offer his two-cents.

Sophia's mama took her hands and examined them, sighing and shaking her head.

"Honey, we do believe you. Okay, sweet pea? But people get real scared when someone dies, especially someone young like Rosemary. We don't want to make things worse."

Sophia sniffled and looked at each of their faces. Timmy was looking pointedly away from her. Grimmel seemed to be fighting tears. And Sophia knew from the sag in her mama's shoulders she was exhausted, her dogs were barkin', and she probably wanted to lie down or take a bath.

"But mama, I don't ever go to Earl's cabin. It's spooky. None of us kids do. Nobody's gonna believe I went in there."

"They will, Sophia. They won't have any other choice. Okay? Let's keep it simple. You found her body in the cabin."

A knock sounded on the screen door and they all grew silent. Sophia's mama stood, brushed invisible dust from her dress and strode to the door.

"Hal," she said, smiling and opening the door wide so the sheriff could step inside.

"I've been out to the woods," he told her, shoving his hands deep in his pockets.

"And?" Sophia's mother asked, but they already knew. After Sophia's confession, Timothy had run to the cabin and peeked in just to be sure. He confirmed what Sophia had said.

Rosemary Bell was dead in Earl's cabin.

"She's passed on," he said thickly. "Got a few officers out there lookin' around, but I wanted a quick talk with Sophia. On her own, if I might."

Heather shook her head.

"No, I'm sorry, Hal. You can speak with her, but I'm going to stay. She's real shook up as I'm sure you can imagine."

Hal fiddled with his belt buckle, and Sophia's eyes hovered on the revolver at his hip. It gleamed black and heavy looking. Finally, he nodded.

"Yeah, okay. Shall we?" he gestured outside, and Sophia's mama nodded curtly.

"Come on, honey," she told Sophia, taking her hand and pulling her from her chair.

Sophia's legs trembled as she followed them to the dirt drive. The day was still hot, but the sun had begun its slow transition to the west.

A few more hours and the stars would poke holes in the darkening sky.

"How ya doin', Sophia?" the Sheriff asked scanning her as if searching for clues.

Sophia looked at her mama who nodded at her to answer.

"Okay," she said.

"Can you tell me what happened?" he asked.

Again, she dared a glance at her mama, but this time Heather stayed focused on the sheriff.

Sophia swallowed the lump gathering in her throat.

"I was playing in the woods and um... looked in the cabin and um... I saw Rosemary in there."

The sheriff nodded.

"Did you touch anything, Sophia?"

Sophia nodded, pulling at her hair until it fell out of the loose braid her mother had made.

"There was a blanket."

"There was a blanket covering Rosemary?"

"I took it off."

The sheriff nodded.

"Why were you in the woods, Sophia? Had you planned to meet Rosemary there?"

Sophia shook her head.

"I was just looking for salamanders under logs."

"And you figured there'd be salamanders in the cabin?" the Sheriff asked skeptically.

Sophia felt sweat gathering beneath her arms. She wanted to pull off her dress and wade into the pond or the stream. She wanted to wipe off the gritty feeling in her hair.

"No, I was following a deer trail and then-"

"And then she saw the cabin and peeked inside," her mama finished. "Sheriff, she's clearly upset. I don't think this is the best..."

But he interrupted her.

"It is the best time, Heather. Sophia found Rosemary's body, and I'm sure you can gather from what she told you that Rosemary didn't slip and fall out there. Someone murdered her. That means a murderer killed a little girl not a half a mile from your property. I'm sure you understand the urgency."

Sophia's mother had gasped at the word murdered and she clutched Sophia's shoulder so hard it hurt.

"I... I guess," she stammered. "Of course, yes, go ahead."

"Did you see anyone walking in the woods, Sophia?"

"Just Rosemary," she whispered.

The sheriff lifted an eyebrow.

"You saw Rosemary walking in the woods?"

Sophia looked at her mama, alarmed, and then shook her head.

"In the cabin. I just saw her in the cabin."

The sheriff cocked his head to the side, but didn't probe further.

"You didn't hear anything? Someone running away? Anything like that?"

Sophia shook her head.

"You were friends? You and Rosemary?"

Sophia shrugged.

"We haven't played this summer, but last summer we went swimming together sometimes."

"At the pond in the woods?"

Sophia nodded.

"But not this time? You weren't meeting her out there?"

Sophia shook her head, reaching for her mother's hand. It was as sweaty as her own.

"Did you ever know Rosemary to play in the woods alone?" he asked.

Sophia wrinkled her brow, considering. She hadn't ever thought about it. Didn't everyone play in the woods alone?

"I do, so she probably did too, right?" she looked at her mama who nodded.

"Most kids who live near woods play in them, Hal. You know that as well as I do. Rosemary wasn't a tom boy like this one here," she nudged Sophia. "But she liked to play like the rest of them. Maybe she was picking flowers out there. Or berries. The raspberries are in season..." she trailed off.

"Yeah. Her mama said somethin' like that. But she's wandered a long way off gettin' to Earl's cabin. That's a good three miles from her place."

"Maybe she didn't walk there..." Sophia's mother said, but couldn't seem to finish the statement.

"Yeah," he sighed and looked toward the woods.

～

"She did it," Margaret Bell, Rosemary's mother, screamed, clawing at the pearl necklace hanging from her slender neck. The necklace broke and pearls fled down her cream dress and across the dirt driveway. Red welts appeared on the pale skin of her chest.

Margaret was not an uppity woman, but for Sunday's church service she always wore a neatly pressed cream dress and the pearls that had passed through her family for generations. Now the men chased them along the dirt and stones. Her husband Paul swore under his breath as he watched the most valuable item in their household vanishing into the dust.

Heather squared her shoulders, her chin high, as Sophia cowered in the barn behind her. Watching her mama staring down all those towns-folk made her knees clack together so loud she clamped them shut with her hands.

"Margaret Bell, our girls have grown together. My Sophia has been haulin' fresh tomatoes and pumpkins from our garden to your house for ten years. You're going to stand here and accuse my little girl of murder?"

Margaret's eyes narrowed, and she leaned forward.

"She was born with the devil's mark. Everybody in town knows it!"

Sophia frowned. The devil's mark? She slid deeper into the barn as the voices outside grew louder. When she reached the back of the barn, she opened the door a crack and found Grimmel standing just outside.

"Go up in the tree, Sophia," he whispered.

"Where's Timmy?" she asked, using her older brother's pet name, which he hated.

"He's headin' out there to meet the mob."

Sophia heard Timothy's voice join the fray. She ran into the forest, finding their climbing tree and crawling to the highest branch. From there she could no longer hear the voices. If she looked toward home, she could see her mama and Timothy amidst the crowd, but she didn't look, instead tilting her face into the afternoon sun. A dry, hot breeze blew in from the south. Her daddy had called those sandstorms and said rain would soon follow. When the sand got agitated, it needed a bath to calm down. The thought of her daddy sent a spasm of pain through Sophia's belly.

A shriek came from the crowd of people, and Sophia turned straining to see. Someone strode from the barn holding something high. It agitated the other townspeople. Margaret Bell collapsed onto the ground.

Sophia could not see what the man held, but cold wet fingers seemed to reach deep inside her and grab hold of her heart.

They had found the knife.

CHAPTER 8

eptember 1965
Hattie

"HI CAMILLE," Hattie kissed their aging housekeeper on the cheek. "I'm going to run out to the barn and see if I can't find a picture I want."

Camille kissed back and caught Hattie in a half hug.

"Ain't the same without you Hattie Girl," Camille told her, catching her with those big sad eyes. Jude nicknamed Camille Ms. Cow Eyes. "Your Gram Ruth's like a ghost haunting her own house."

"Now don't make me feel bad Camille," Hattie scolded, teasing. "I do miss you and your cinnamon cookies though. Gram will be fine, she just needs a bit of time to get used to things."

"Well, maybe you're wise beyond your years, my little lamb," Camille murmured. "I sure hope so. I have a plate of those cinnamon cookies waitin' for you in the pantry."

Hattie promised to stop back in and hurried out to the barn, running to catch a green maple leaf as it drifted down from a tree.

She put all her weight into the heavy barn door. The rusted hinges groaned, but gradually gave way and the door slid open. In the bright light of day, the interior looked ominous. The skin along Hattie's arms prickled, and she rubbed her hands over her biceps to cast away the foreboding. She dug out the oil lantern that Camille had given her and lit it, stepping into the darkness before good sense told her not to.

The fire cast a soft circle of light and Hattie held the lamp in front of her as she walked. On the ground floor, the barn held her grandfather Andy's antique cars. Covered in sheets, once white, now thick with gray dust, the cars felt like something loved and then forgotten. She remembered her daddy once asking Gram Ruth if he could drive the cars out and tune them up. He would take their mother on an old-fashioned date, he'd said, so excited that even Hattie, only four at the time could hear the enthusiasm in his voice. "Absolutely not!" Gram had told him with such a sour look on her face he dropped the subject.

Hattie surveyed old farm equipment and tools. The barn had mostly belonged to her grandfather. He tinkered, her daddy told her, much to Gram Ruth's dislike. Gram prided herself on being upper class and she expected her husband to behave in the way of wealthy, sophisticated men. Cigar lounges and golf games, not greasy hands and oil stained britches.

After her grandfather died, before Hattie was born, Gram Ruth left the barn to the elements and time. Hattie once overheard her daddy say Gram crammed everything she wanted to forget in the barn.

The ladder into the loft hung in a pocket of gloom. As Hattie climbed she craned her head back and looked high where the roof steepled and a thousand cobwebs hung like shimmering gauze. The lofts were the only part of the barn still in use, kind of. Gram sent Frank to the barn once a month to store unwanted furniture, old paperwork, and anything else she had tired of looking at.

The summer Mama died, Hattie's daddy stored some of their things in the loft. In a blink they transitioned from living in their farmhouse in the country to living in Gram's cold mansion.

In the beginning, before the deaths, Hattie loved staying in the house. Every room held secrets - old trunks and hat boxes, locked drawers and deep closets. She explored tirelessly, prowling the house and the grounds, in a perpetual state of wonder.

Gram Ruth, despite her stony demeanor, coddled Hattie. Sometimes she even opened her bed and allowed Hattie to climb onto the high mattress, covered in an antique silk coverlet. She would not tell Hattie stories, but would sit patiently as Hattie told her own. Every day Hattie offered a new story about chasing a red squirrel or capturing a minnow in her palm. Jude and Peter didn't have time for her stories, and that summer, with her parents away, Gram Ruth had been her most avid audience.

Hattie had assumed they would move home at the end of the summer, but then Daddy died - fell from the loft she now climbed into. Hattie barely remembered the months after the deaths of her parents. When she tried to look there, a dark veil of sorrow coated her memories.

The loft floor was littered with holes from broken planks. Furniture and boxes were stacked on the solid areas. Hattie could see footprints in the dust and mouse droppings. She walked carefully, avoiding the soft boards that gave when she placed her weight on them. The furniture stood along the barn wall, and Hattie smiled noticing that Frank had even hung some of her family's pictures. She saw a picture of a moon rise that her mama had painted for her daddy as a gift. Another, a photograph, showed her mama cradling her baby twins, Jude and Peter, in her arms and laughing at the ground where their family dog Howdy stood staring up at her. Hattie had never known Howdy, a black and white mutt that her daddy found on the side of the road. He died of sadness Jude told her after their pet cat Boots ran away.

Hattie took both pictures and stacked them on the floor. She would have to fight the urge to take most of their stuff. A collector, a pack rat maybe, Hattie's love of material items could quickly overwhelm her new apartment. It was not value she coveted, at least not the monetary kind, but nostalgic value. She wanted to wrap up in an afghan her mama once draped over her shoulders. She longed to smell her daddy's cologne on one of his old sweaters.

"It will bury you," Jude once told her, when Hattie was begging Jude to tell her stories of their mama. "Spend too much time in those memories and they'll just heap on top of you until you can't breathe."

Jude never liked to talk about their parents. She insisted that the only way to look was forward. Peter would tell Hattie if she prodded enough, but he didn't remember the things she wanted to know. He didn't remember how their mama's laugh sounded when she heard a really funny joke or what their daddy used to wear when he took Mama on a date.

Hattie looked at her watch and frowned. She'd intended to help decorate the food pantry for autumn and had been looking forward to it, but now, steeped in the past, she wanted to sit on the floor and spend days sifting through the history of her family. Tragic. That's what Camille called it. Their history was tragic.

An accident took her mama. Hattie didn't even know what kind. How funny, she thought, that no one ever mentioned what tragedy stole their mother. Funny too that she never thought to ask. Only eight when she died, it barely mattered that her mama died of something, only that she died. *Dead, dead, gone forever.* Her daddy broke the news, Hattie balanced on his knee. He said Mama went to heaven to live with Grandpa Andy. Hattie thought she cried though her memory of that time seemed frosted and blurry. Like she looked through glass thick with steam. More than a memory, she remembered a dark hole opening and falling into it. Falling and falling and never hitting the ground.

A muffled cough startled her, and she reeled back nearly falling over a stack of boxes. Deeper in the gloom before her, a man started to hum. She recognized the song, but not the voice it belonged to.

"Sweet dreams till sunbeams find you
Sweet dreams that leave all worries behind you
But in your dreams whatever they be
Dream a little dream of me."

Hattie's heart thudded in her chest and she held the lantern up peering into the darkness where the sound emerged.

"Who's there?" she called, but the humming took on a familiar ghostly quality, moving further away.

She walked forward and saw the young man clearly before he dissolved into the dust motes around him.

Hattie took a trembling step forward, the lantern bobbing in her shaky hands.

She looked at the place the man had been. A maroon curtain covered a pile of stuff. Tucked beneath the curtain, Hattie found a wooden crate. Someone had nailed the crate closed, perhaps in a hurry. The nails stuck at odd angles. The hammer, likely used, lay on the floor nearby. A strange sensation settled over her. She experienced a sudden desire to leave the loft and drive home.

She picked up the hammer and started prying.

∾

IT TOOK LONGER than Hattie expected. Mostly because the odd angle of the nails made them hard to remove. As she grabbed them with the hammer's claw, she wiggled and pulled, even putting her feet against the crate for leverage. Finally, one whole edge was nail free, and she pried the top open and peered inside, disappointed at the contents. The crate contained old newspapers. Reaching inside, she grabbed one from the top of the stack. Yellowing, but still crisp and intact, Hattie studied the name: Lansing State Journal. It was dated July 13, 1955.

She scanned the headlines, glancing over the articles about record production in the automobile industry and water shortages. On the second page, a grainy photograph caught her attention. She leaned closer, holding the lamp near the page, careful not to let the flame too close.

A woman peered out from the backseat window of a black car. Her eyes were wide, her mouth open in a little o of confusion. She wore a scarf over her hair, and she'd lifted her hand to her throat where Hattie saw a heart-shaped pendant.

Justice for Rosemary Bell, the headline read.

Hattie scanned the article, eyes flicking back to the picture again and again. The reporter spoke of an unsolved murder of a young girl, Rosemary Bell, from the year 1935. At the time of the murder, the police believed another thirteen-year-old girl - Sophia Gray - had committed the murder, but disappeared before charges could be brought against her.

A long quote from Rosemary's mother lamented their years of grief and their belief that justice would someday come for little Rosemary. The accused murderess, Sophia, had maintained her innocence; however, her knowledge of the murder at the time evidenced her guilt. Sophia Gray whose whereabouts for the past twenty-five years remained a mystery, had been remanded indefinitely to the Traverse City State Hospital, also known as the Northern Michigan Asylum for the Insane, a facility for those suffering from mental illness.

Hattie looked again at the picture. She studied the woman and felt a growing unease. Though the woman's face was blurry, Hattie stared at the familiar heart-shaped pendant set against her throat.

"But my mom wasn't Sophia," Hattie told the empty room. Her

voice echoed in the space and she shuddered as it reverberated back to her... Sophia... Sophia... Sophia.

Her mama's name was Anne. Still the picture unnerved her.

She pulled out another paper.

Again, the story did not appear until the third page.

Hattie gasped when she saw the photo above the story.

The photo revealed two young girls, arms linked standing in front of a pen of horses.

"The girl in the yellow dress," Hattie whispered touching the picture. Though the girl did not wear a yellow dress in the picture, there was no mistaking her. Hattie had been seeing the girl her entire life.

The other girl was equally unnerving. Hattie might have been staring at her own reflection. The second girl had Hattie's same long straw-colored hair, wide-set eyes and rosebud mouth. She wore a plain looking dress and her feet were bare.

"Rosemary and Sophia," she said, leaning closer to the image.

The room seemed to lurch, and Hattie closed her eyes, pressing her hands against the floor to steady her. The newspaper fell to the floor in a whoosh and cast a cloud of dust into the air. Hattie opened her eyes and watched the lantern's flame flicker and dance wildly despite the stillness in the air.

"Daddy?" she asked, strangely sure he spoke to her through the fire. The flame grew still, jerked once, and went out.

CHAPTER 9

ugust 19, 1935
Sophia

"BE A GOOD GIRL, SOPHIA," her mother said, wrapping her arms around Sophia.

Her mother's face was wet with tears. She'd pinned up her hair and put on a clean dress, but already long tendrils fell free and clung to her damp face.

"I don't want to go," Sophia whispered glancing at the man who stood in their kitchen.

He wore a dark suit, his shiny black shoes foreign against the scratched, wood floor.

Tim leaned against the counter, his arms crossed, watching the man with suspicious eyes. Grimmel slouched beside him, his face streaked in tears.

"She's in good hands, Heather," the man said. "We've got a great big house." The man shifted his attention to Tim. "My son is a couple years younger than you, Tim. Your father and I had grand plans for our sons to play together. At least two of our children will get to do that," the man continued, gesturing at Sophia.

Sophia found it hard to breathe.

Her little suitcase sat near the man's feet.

"When can I come home?" Sophia asked, as her mother pulled away.

Heather blinked at her, more tears streaming down her face. She seemed unable to speak.

"Best if we get on the road, Sophia," the man said. "We have a long drive."

"And the sheriff may be back," Tim grumbled.

He grabbed Sophia and hugged her hard.

"Be strong, Soph," he murmured.

SOPHIA HOVERED in the doorway staring into the huge veranda. A maroon carpeted staircase curved up from gleaming marble floors. Above the foyer hung a glistening chandelier, sparkling with hundreds of tiny lit bulbs. It reminded Sophia of a giant spider with a thousand glittering eyes.

The man, Andrew Porter, turned toward her. He offered her another smile of encouragement and beckoned her onward.

"It's okay, Sophia," he said kindly. "Your father was my best friend. We go all the way back to your age. A shame he passed, and I'm right sorry to have missed his funeral. Might have made this a little easier." He gestured to the house. "I want to welcome you to my home, to your new house."

"This is a house?" Sophia whispered. Her huge eyes tried to take it all in, walls climbing into dark crevices, vases and paintings and the aroma of overripe flowers. White statues with twisted faces and blank eyes watched her.

Sophia burst into tears before she could clamp the emotion back.

Suddenly she understood. Her father was dead, and her mother and two brothers were gone. She would never run her hands along Jasper the barn cat's smooth back or feed breakfast scraps to their six chickens. Gone were humid nights on the porch listening to the crickets and the hoot owls and the bull frogs sing her to sleep. She would no longer feel her mother's warm, callused fingers carefully brushing through the tangles of her hair while she sat in the wash basin. Sophia's little alcove behind the wash room where she snuck off to read books would sit empty. Gone was the closet that still held her daddy's clothes where she laid and smelled the sweat and work of his days in the field even though he'd been in the ground for nine months.

Her legs trembled, and she spun toward the door, ready to run, but Andrew surrounded her with thick arms and the scent of some foreign cologne that made her eyes water. His stiff suit pressed close to her face, the fabric strange and dark. He shushed her and picked her up as if she were a baby and not a thirteen-year-old girl.

He carried her into an adjoining room and laid her on a stiff little sofa. She cried against an itchy pillow as the man, the stranger, rubbed her back and told her again and again that it would be okay.

～

SOPHIA SAT in Andrew and Ruth Porter's enormous parlor and tried to look anywhere except at Ruth, Mrs. Porter. Hands tucked beneath her thighs, palms sweating a halo into her dress, she stared out the giant window to the grounds beyond.

If she cupped her hands around her eyes and blotted out the room, she would only see the rolling expanse of trees and bright flowery bushes. Then she could almost believe she had walked into town to sit by the mail office or the library.

She had not been whisked away in the night by a strange man she'd never met, laid wide awake in a huge bed listening to the creaks and groans of the house, and cried an endless stream of tears for her mother, her father and her brothers.

Ruth watched her with a pinched, unhappy expression that made Sophia question the state of her dress and the dirt beneath her fingernails. It was her best dress, Daddy's funeral dress, but the day of travel followed by a night sleeping in it left it slack and wrinkled. Her blonde hair, in braids when she left, hung mostly unravelled on her shoulders.

Ruth, Mrs. Porter, sat stiff like a broom with her hands in her lap. Her fingers, laced together, appeared to be clenching so tight that her knuckles looked white and hard.

Andrew walked into the room holding a clear glass filled with amber liquid. He took a sip, kissed Ruth lightly on the temple, and sat in a chair near a small table that held an ivory chess set. Ruth narrowed her eyes at the chair, as if she'd expected him to sit next to her, but he appeared not to notice.

Sophia smiled at Andrew, Mr. Porter, and then abruptly at her feet when she felt Mrs. Porter's eyes boring into her.

"I know this is a big change, Sophia," Andrew started.

"A change!" Ruth scoffed. "An intrusion!"

"Ruth," Andrew warned in a voice that silenced his angry wife. "Should I speak to Sophia alone?"

Ruth glared at him but shut her mouth.

"I won't bore with you the adult stuff," Andrew began again. "Only that your mother and I agreed it was in your best interest to leave your farm for a while."

"How long?" Sophia asked, praying he would say a few days, a week at most.

"A pretty long time," he said. "Small towns have long memories, Sophia. What happened to that little girl…"

"Rosemary," Sophia interrupted.

"Didn't your mother teach you not to interrupt your elders?" Ruth snapped.

Andrew glowered at her.

"It's okay, honey," Andrew told Sophia. "You have questions and that's okay. Yes, her name was Rosemary. What happened to Rosemary was a horrible tragedy, but it wasn't your fault."

"And how do you know that?" Ruth interjected, nearly rising out of her chair with the admonition.

Andrew stood and strode angrily to his wife.

"Please join me in other room. Excuse us, Sophia."

Ruth sprang from her chair as if ready to attack Andrew, but composed herself at the last moment and followed him out the door.

Left behind, Sophia stood and drifted around the room, eyes darting again and again to the parlor doors. Small stiff furniture covered in strange fabrics that Sophia had never seen spread across the room accompanied by shiny tables holding vases and crystal bowls. A gold framed painting of a severe looking man astride a horse took up one entire wall.

In the distance, she heard muffled angry voices, but gratefully could not make out their words.

A sharp knock on the window startled her, and she nearly raced back to her chair, fearing that Mrs. Porter had caught her snooping. A face peered at her through the glass. The boy, older than her, had dark close-cropped hair and big, inquisitive gray eyes that sparkled in the morning sun. He knocked again and waved.

"I'm Jack," she heard his muffled call through the glass. She smiled back.

~

JUNE 1938

"YOUR MOM HATES ME," Sophia said, reaching up and running her fingers through Jack's hair. It had grown long, much to Ruth Porter's horror, but Sophia loved the dark curls he tucked behind his ears.

Jack leaned over Sophia, propped on one elbow in the grass that had once been a horse pasture before the Porter's estate had been scrubbed of its animals at the insistence of Ruth, the matriarch.

"My mom is..." he paused, frowning, "severe. But she doesn't hate you. You've been here three years, Sophia. You're part of us, now. Honestly, I think she always wanted a daughter and maybe you just remind her of what she never had."

Sophia traced her finger along Jack's jaw. He dipped down and kissed her.

If Ruth knew Sophia and Jack had fallen in love, she'd probably burn the estate to the ground.

In the three years Sophia had lived at the house, Ruth had never warmed to her. Andrew took her under his wing and treated her kindly, but it was Jack who loved her. Two years older than Sophia, Jack was worldly in a way Sophia couldn't fathom. At first they were friends. Jack showed her the property, the woods, took her to town and introduced Sophia to his friends. He made sure that Sophia didn't merely exist at her new home in Cadillac, but also had a life.

"Do you think I can ever go back?" Sophia asked looking beyond Jack into the clear sky.

"Where? Home?"

"Yes. I miss my mother and my brothers." In the first year, Sophia had asked Jack a hundred times if he thought she could go home. He even helped her create elaborate plans to ride in the backs of hay trucks and sneak onto train cars, but every time the date for her departure grew near, he insisted she stay for a bit longer. It had been over a year since she'd even posed the question.

Jack sat up.

"I never want you to leave, but that's selfish, isn't it? How about this? In a couple more years we can get married and then we'll go visit them together. I'll drive and you can lie in the backseat so that no one sees you. It will be an adventure."

Sophia smiled.

"After we get married?" Sophia looked into Jack's dark eyes, his mother's eyes, which often unnerved Sophia, but oh they were beautiful, deep and gray with tiny streaks of light moving towards the black mystery right in the center.

"Of course! I mean you want to marry me, don't you?"

Sophia sat up and snuggled into Jack's lap.

"I've never wanted anything more."

July 1941

MANY TIMES in the years to come, Sophia would remember that conversation.

They never went on that adventure. Jack's father, Andrew Porter, died less than a year later, and a year after *that*, at eighteen-years-old, Sophia gave birth to Peter and Jude, twins.

Life transformed and Sophia often struggled to keep up with the constant changes.

When Jack bought the farmhouse, Sophia rejoiced. They were finally free from the watchful eyes of Ruth Porter. After Andrew's death, Jack's mother became unbearable, undermining Sophia at every turn.

The final straw had come when Sophia discovered Ruth feeding the babies formula after Sophia and Jack had both made it clear she was breastfeeding only.

Sophia looked up from her painting and watched Jack in the backyard. He was tilling the soil for her new garden. Jude and Peter were on a blanket, not yet crawling, but both on the verge. Their dog Howdy trotted by and Jude, trying to pet him, flopped on her side. Peter followed suit and soon both babies were rolling on their backs, feet wagging in the air.

As Sophia painted, an image emerged, and she realized she was capturing a memory of the little pond behind her childhood home. The pond where she'd nearly drowned one summer and been saved by an angel. As she painted, the ghostly image of a woman reflected in the water appeared.

"Soph." Jack's voice startled her, and she looked up. The sun had begun its descent.

"Anne," she reminded him. Only Jack spoke Sophia's true name, but as their children grew, it would be important that he always call her Anne. "I lost track of time," she murmured, setting her brush down and turning in her chair.

"That's beautiful," he said, coming to stand behind her. He placed his hands on her shoulders, pressing into the knotted muscle, smoothing the tension away.

"Where are the babies?" she asked, seeing the empty blanket in the yard.

"Asleep. I put them in their cribs. I'm sure they'll need to eat soon, but first..." he trailed off and Sophia felt his hands slide to the front of her dress and slip down beneath the light fabric. He grazed her milk tender breasts and leaned down kissing her neck.

"Mmmm," she murmured. "Yes."

Jack guided her from her chair, her back giving a little groan, her feet tingling from sitting, and led her to the bed. She fell back marvelling at the man who never ceased to amaze her.

"How did I get so lucky?" she murmured as he leaned over her on the bed, pressing his unshaven face into her neck as he kissed her.

"I'm the lucky one, Sophia."

CHAPTER 10

eptember 1965
Hattie

HATTIE SAT in the last pew of the little church she visited every Sunday. She went alone. Hands clasped in her lap, she stared at the serene figure of Jesus Christ suspended from his wooden cross. His downcast eyes seemed to peer into another world, a peaceful world, where love ruled supreme.

That Sunday, she felt especially drawn to the tranquil space. The night before she had dreamed of the girl in the yellow dress. In her dreams the girl had been alive running with her friend, Sophia. Sophia - who was later accused of Rosemary's murder.

Hattie had attended church since she turned ten years old. On her tenth birthday, a Sunday, she asked Gram Ruth's cleaning lady Marcy to take her to the Sunday service.

Marcy, a skinny mother of three, had looked at Hattie in puzzlement. She waited for Hattie to explain and when she did not, Marcy told Gram Ruth that they were off to run errands and she drove clear across town to her own church and they attended together. After that, they attended church every Sunday.

Hattie listened rapt to every sermon and committed to memory the most important pieces for her own life. Pastor Greg told his congregation that love, acceptance, and forgiveness solved all things. He prayed for the ailing in the community and in the world. He passed the collection plate, while earnestly demanding that you only give if you could spare the money. Marcy put five dollars in every single week, even though Hattie knew her three young children often wore shoes with soles flapping, and homemade pants that were too tight. Hattie saved her candy money to put in the plate on Sunday morning.

Nine years later, Hattie still went every Sunday. Pastor Greg, graying now, continued to inspire her and draw out the glimmer of light that Hattie often lost sight of. As she perched on the edge of her seat, hands mindlessly knitting together and then breaking apart, she saw Greg nod toward a young man who entered the nave and took a seat near the back of the room.

After the sermon, Hattie slipped around the crowd bidding farewell to Pastor Greg and took the back stairway into the basement. She walked to the nursery where the mothers plucked children from playpens and bouncer seats. Ansel sat in the corner clumsily stacking wooden blocks. He stared at the small tower with such focus that Hattie stopped, not wanting to interrupt him. His two-year-old hands were pudgy and uncoordinated. As he set the top block down the structure collapsed and he squealed in frustration.

"Antsy Pants," Hattie called squatting down. Ansel turned and a drooly grin replaced the grimace from moments before. He stood and rushed over to her, nearly tripping over his scattered blocks. She caught him as he barrelled into her and kissed his head through his thick mop of black curls. He smelled like talcum powder and bananas.

Hattie watched Ansel every Sunday after service. His mother, Katherine, met with Pastor Greg for guidance and Hattie had volunteered to care for the toddler during their meetings. Katherine was Marcy's oldest daughter, only seventeen years old, and Hattie had often thought of her as a younger sibling. Though Hattie saw Marcy's children less as they grew older, their younger days of playing together at Gram Ruth's left a lasting bond. When Katherine became pregnant at only fifteen, it devastated Marcy and she turned to Pastor Greg and to Hattie for help with her wayward child and now grandchild.

The nursery emptied, and Hattie settled into a rocking chair, plucking a copy of *The Giving Tree* from the little bookshelf. Ansel scrambled into her lap and she rocked, reading the story as he pointed at the pictures and shouted his version of words.

"Twee, twee," he said enthusiastically as she turned the page.

"Yes that's the Giving Tree isn't it? And there's the little boy."

Hattie read the words, but her mind flicked repeatedly to that aged newspaper and the two little girls.

The door creaked open and Hattie looked up to see the young man who'd arrived late to the service that morning.

His tall frame filled most of the doorway and his shaggy blond hair fell past his ears. Eyes the color of a lake when a storm is gathering watched her beneath long golden lashes. He dressed casually in dark jeans and an olive sweater.

"Hi," he told her smiling. "I'm looking for Pastor Greg's office, apparently this is not it."

He cocked an eyebrow, and she stumbled through her mind looking for words.

He walked into the room and shifted his attention to Ansel. "Hey there, little man, what'cha reading?"

"Twee!" Ansel shouted and pointed to the picture of the tree.

"Ahh the Giving Tree, one of my favorites too."

"His office is at the end of the hall," Hattie told him finally swallowing the lump in her throat. "There's a little plaque on the door with his name."

"Great, thank you." He held out a hand. "My name is Damien. I'm sorry to interrupt your story."

"Not at all," she said, wondering at the fluttering in her stomach when her eyes met his. "Hattie, that's my name."

The man left and Hattie returned to the story, but she found it hard to concentrate.

Hattie had rarely considered boys. They existed, sure, but she noticed them in the same way she noticed spider webs or wall clocks. They took up space and sometimes she might bump into one, but otherwise they held little interest.

She often marveled at her older sister's preoccupation with the opposite sex. Jude did not just notice boys, she lived and breathed them.

Hattie, on the contrary, had no time for boys and, honestly, not much time for girls either. As a child she played alone. She traipsed through the woods and built rock villages, hunted for salamanders and spent weeks coercing squirrels to eat from her hand. She played with other kids when they were thrust upon her, but she did not seek out friendships or feel their absence once gone. Hattie preferred writing stories and painting elaborate pictures of the thoughts in her head.

She also talked to ghosts.

The first had been the girl in the yellow dress, though Hattie never spoke with her.

Later she encountered Kitten. A little girl with red frizzy hair who sometimes appeared by the stream on Gram Ruth's estate. Hattie would wade in the water searching for shiny pink stones and suddenly the girl would be staring back at her. Hattie only saw her in the water's reflection. When she looked up, the girl was nowhere to be found, but return her gaze to the water and she stared back, as if caught in the surface of the rippling stream. She called her Kitten because her small dark eyes reminded Hattie of a kitten she'd once seen in a children's book.

David visited her in Gram Ruth's house. He hung himself there a century before in the cellar after his daughter died of pneumonia. He talked to Hattie about hunting elk in Canada, fighting in the war, and how to shine your shoes. He asked Hattie questions, but he never listened to her answers unless they reminded him of his daughter and then he would interrupt her and tell her about his daughter's doll collection, or how she liked to braid her mother's hair. Hattie did not enjoy talking to David, but he would pester her until she listened to him, sometimes pacing around her room in the middle of the night if she tried to ignore him during the day.

Her favorite ghost was Amelia. Amelia was a young woman who rode horses as a girl. She told Hattie about her horse, Francis and how her black coat gleamed like molten silk. She played with Hattie too. They ran through the forest together, hiding behind bushes and racing to the tops of the trees. Amelia told Hattie secrets about Gram Ruth and Jude and Peter. Amelia was the first to refer to herself as a ghost.

"I'm dead, silly," she had told Hattie one day while they hunted for wild raspberries. "So of course, I'm a ghost."

After that, Hattie went to church. Not because she believed the ghosts were bad, but because she wanted to be closer to the other side. She spoke to Pastor Greg about the ghosts only one time. He responded in a kind, but bemused sort of way, and Hattie understood that for too many people seeing was believing.

"Hattie?"

Hattie startled and looked up to find Katherine standing in the doorway, holding a small casserole baked for her by one of the congregants. Ansel had fallen asleep on Hattie's lap and his bottom lip quivered with his baby snores. Hattie yawned and blinked, trying to clear her mind of the memories.

"Sorry Katherine, I was drifting."

Katherine smiled knowingly. Anyone who grew up around Hattie knew her tendency to slip into her thoughts, sometimes for hours at a time.

"Thank you for watching him, Hattie," Katherine told her, scooping Ansel up with her free arm. She adjusted him so that his head drooped on her shoulder.

"Can I help you?" Hattie asked gesturing toward the casserole.

"No, my mom's upstairs," Katherine reassured her. "And Pastor Greg wanted you to stop by his office on your way out."

Katherine backed out of the nursery, and Hattie took an extra moment to get her bearings. She thought again of Amelia and wished that she still saw her. Amelia had stopped visiting her after Hattie's sixteenth birthday. No reason, no farewell, she just never appeared again.

Hattie stopped at the drinking fountain and let the cool water flow across her forehead. She wiped her face on her sleeve and then knocked lightly on the Pastor's door.

"Come in," he called,

She pushed open the door. Pastor Greg sat on a little couch. Damien was perched on the edge of the Pastor's scarred desk.

"Damien tells me the two of you have met?" the Pastor asked, beckoning Hattie towards a vacant chair.

She flicked her gaze at Damien where those startling gray eyes followed her with interest.

"Yes," she agreed, focusing on the Pastor's face.

"Damien is a doctorate student in psychiatry at a Christian University. He needs help with his thesis and I believe you might be the ideal young person to assist him," the pastor told her, beaming.

"Psychiatry?" Hattie mumbled, at a loss for what the word meant let alone how she could help him. "Insane people?"

Damien smiled, but Pastor Greg nodded.

"We at the church tend to believe such individuals have merely lost the path. Though I do support what you do, Mr. Ross, or is it Dr. Ross?" Greg asked.

"Damien, please. I'm not quite ready for formal titles just yet. I still have a year of rotations left in addition to my thesis."

Hattie looked at the floor, allowing her eye to follow the dark carpeting to the base of the wall where tiny hairline cracks ran into the plaster. A million different pathways for a wayward ant.

"What do you think, Hattie?" the pastor's voice broke through her thoughts and she snapped up, looking at him.

"About what?"

Damien stood and grabbed a battered-looking leather briefcase. He pulled out a sheaf of papers.

"I'm studying existential psychology in the homeless population," Damien told her, crossing the room and settling into the chair next to hers.

She looked at him vacantly.

"Existential psychology?"

"Yes, I'm studying in particular the idea that our concept of aloneness creates a sense of meaninglessness in the world and in life."

Hattie waited, assuming there must be more.

"I figured you might be able to help," Pastor Greg chimed in. "Because you volunteer at Helping Hands and therefore know many of the homeless people in our area."

Hattie nodded. She had been volunteering at Helping Hands for over five years. She helped organize the food pantry, worked with area churches to provide temporary shelter, and sometimes just talked with the men and women who needed a listening ear.

"It's not invasive," Damien quickly added. He handed Hattie a sheet of questions. "I just need to sit with them and ask these questions. I'm writing my thesis on the topic. It's completely anonymous and confidential."

Hattie studied the questions.

What catalyst occurred that caused your homelessness?
Do you believe in God?

Do you have a purpose in your life?

Hattie imagined working with Damien. For a moment, she saw them together. They sat in a park and interviewed Henry, a man who slept near the rose bushes. Damien's shoulder was pressed against hers. He smelled of cloves and pine and rested his hand on Hattie's knee in a knowing way. He touched her easily and delicately. His hand was warm through her wool skirt.

In the pastor's office she shivered and looked into Damien's face. Those eyes again, searching her.

"Sure," she said at last. "I can help you."

∽

Jude

DAMIEN. Jude settled deeper into the couch with her glass of sherry and said his name out loud.

"Damien."

Her stomach lurched and her spine tingled at the thought of him. She took another sip, and lifted her forearm, inhaling. He had kissed her there - kissed her arms and hands and lips and belly. He had kissed nearly every inch of her body and his kisses felt like warm rain and his laughter when she sunk her hands into his hair sounded coarse like grating seashells in the surf.

"Damien," she said again, and her dog Gram nipped at her foot lovingly.

Gram's wiry hair tickled her, and she laughed and batted him away, regretting for the zillionth time naming him after Gram Ruth, whom she loathed. In truth, she thought she would loathe the dog as well with his wiry hair and ugly long face.

She took him home in an act of guilty weakness after the man she'd been seeing presented him to her as a token of love. A puppy then, she had planned on taking the mutt to a shelter the very next day for a more sentimental fool to cherish. However, the next day she spent twelve hours on a photo shoot and fell into bed too exhausted to worry about the little devil. The following day she slept to make up for the long shift. The day after, she had lunch with a girlfriend and then a hair appointment and so on. Until suddenly Gram was five months old and Jude begrudgingly enjoyed their morning walk. In fact, when she finally slowed long enough to consider giving him away, something within her cried out in such despair she immediately closed the topic and never brought it up again. Gram, four now, having far outlived the suitor who purchased him, was Jude's most beloved friend and like the dog itself, his name had become endeared to her and she could not change it.

"Oh, but Damien, now that is a name I wouldn't even think of changing," she purred aloud to the room.

Gram barked a seeming agreement and regarded her with his typical toothy grin. Jude scratched his head and then cringed when she realized she'd wiped some of Damien's scent from her palm.

"Okay Jude, you've gotta come down, honey or this guy's gonna throw you for a loop." She spoke again to the empty room and considered her advice for a moment. Had she ever felt so head over heels for anyone in all her life? No. It was easy to find that answer. No, in the hundred or so men she'd chatted with, dated, slept with; Jude had never fallen for a single one. They all presented with a thousand flaws from cheap tippers to married with kids. Many had professed their own love, but Jude never returned the ardor. A flirt she might be, but a liar she was not.

And then Damien appeared and in twenty-four hours everything changed. Everything. The smell of her morning coffee brewing and the taste of fresh strawberries in yogurt and the press of a silk shift beneath her dress transformed into explosions of sensation that all took her back to Damien. Every bite of melon felt like his soft, satin lips. The song on the radio had her whirling in his arms.

She downed the last of her sherry and jumped off the couch. She knelt, hugged Gram fiercely and fled to the door where his blue leash hung next to her key ring.

"Come on Gram, I need a dose of reality."

CHAPTER 11

 une 1955
Sophia

"Sophia?" She heard her name and whirled toward the voice before remembering she wasn't Sophia Gray. She was Ann Porter and had been for fifteen years.

The woman who stared back offered a hesitant smile, but Sophia saw pain in her expression. She looked to be in her seventies, but no, younger. Time had not been kind and deep grooves etched her once pretty face into a map of worry and sadness.

Sophia tried to place her but found no memory to match the tired woman before her.

"I'm sorry, do we know each other?" Sophia started, but the woman cut her off.

"Margaret Bell. I must admit I'm shocked that you do not remember me."

And the name, like the chime, sounded an alarm in her mind - Bell, Bell, Bell. Her friend Rosemary, dead now twenty years and Margaret, her mother, standing before Sophia with a look transforming to suspicion and then to something darker, hatred.

"Yes, oh my, of course." Sophia searched for words, but only little murmurs and grunts emerged. In an instant, she traveled back to 1935. No longer was she a grown woman with three children. Instead, she stood before the accusing glare of Margaret Bell - a weeping child promising that she did not, could not, hurt Rosemary.

Sophia turned abruptly and walked away. She grabbed Hattie's tiny hand in her own, ignoring Hattie's cry of protest as the apple she held fell from her grasp. She left her cart filled with groceries and walked faster. In the parking lot, she scooped Hattie into her arms and ran. She yanked open the back door of her station wagon and pushed Hattie inside. Hattie's head bumped the door frame, and she cried out. Sophia looked up, wildly, like a mouse caught in the cat's paw. Her heart lurched as she saw Margaret standing in front of the store. She held a paper and pen and wrote furiously, glaring at Sophia. Her lips moved as if she spoke.

"Mommy," Hattie wailed from the backseat. "You left Gator."

Her tiny daughter's desperate cry woke her from her temporary reverie. She looked at Hattie's eyes filled with tears.

Gator. Hattie's favorite stuffed animal. A plush alligator her daddy had gotten in Florida when he was a child. Sophia could imagine the toy staring from between the shopping cart bars where Hattie placed him so he could watch them shop.

Sophia clenched her eyes shut. Overhead a perfect blue sky showed dark rolling clouds accumulating on the horizon.

"I'm sorry, baby," Sophia whispered. She moved into the driver's seat, slammed the door, and squealed out of the parking lot.

"It's too late, honey," Sophia told Jack, smoothing the lock of dark hair curling down his forehead. She pursed her lips to bite back the tears that threatened.

Jack looked as beautiful as the day she first laid eyes on him now twenty years past. His gray eyes caught the morning light and set off a firework display of gold and steel and slate that helped her, for a moment, forget she had to leave him.

"No." He shook his head and furrowed his brow. The fine wrinkles along his forehead and around his eyes did not leave when he straightened his face. Somewhere over the years, Sophia and Jack grew up.

Whatever happened going forward, she had won the lottery when she met Jack Porter.

"There has to be a way. You were a child for Christ's sakes and innocent!" he muttered.

She fingered the gold heart suspended on a chain around her neck. Her mother had given it to her for her thirteenth birthday. The night Sophia fled her childhood home, her mother had tucked a tiny rose petal inside the locket.

"My mother has money, Sophia. She plays the pauper, but we know that's not true. I'll steal it if I have to."

"No." Sophia shook her head and clutched Jack's hand to her mouth. "Don't ruin anything with your mother, Jack. We need her now. The kids need her. And someday when I'm out, I need to show my face around there. Even if I'd rather not walk the grounds at the Porter estate ever again."

Jack smiled and lifted a brow. "Not even the cedar grove?"

She laughed and flicked his ear. He pretended to howl with pain and fell into her lap.

The cedar grove that lay at the far north end of the estate was the place that Sophia and Jack first made love. She was sixteen and Jack was eighteen. They crept across the dewy grass beneath an eclipsing moon. A wool blanket tucked under one arm and Sophia snuggled beneath the other, Jack had guided them through the dark trees into a small clearing. Drunk on apricot wine and unexplored desire, they touched each other carefully and then ravenously. After they made love, they had lay curled together and listened to the night telling its stories.

"Maybe the cedar grove," she murmured, leaning down and kissing his temple.

~

JULY 11, 1955

"I'M NOT sure about this, Jack."

Sophia sat on the edge of their bed, her suitcase open beside her. She'd done as he asked and packed only the necessities and a handful of nostalgic items: pictures, jewelry, baby blankets for all three of her children

"I am," Jack said kneeling before her and looking earnestly into her face. "Soph, I will not let you go. You're innocent and I won't lose you to a witch hunt. What do we have here, anyway? This will be a new start. How exciting! You've never even left Michigan, honey. There are mountains in Colorado. There's a whole unexplored world just waiting for us."

Sophia touched his cheek and smiled.

When Jack first suggested they fake her death and move away, Sophia laughed at the notion, but he was relentless. He became so fixed on the idea it took on a life and now she too couldn't seem to turn away from it.

"What about your mother? She's accepted us leaving?"

"It was her idea, Sophia. She's going to help, said she might even move out to Colorado in a year or two. She dotes on Hattie; she'll follow us."

"Great," Sophia said trying not to roll her eyes and wishing she shared Jack's faith in his mother.

He smiled and shook his head.

"I get it. She's difficult, but she's volunteered to help. She'll pick you up here in the morning and take you to my dad's hunting cabin. It's rustic, but you'll only be there for a week and I've stocked it with food. There's a well out back and an outhouse."

"I remember, Jack. I've been there in case you've forgotten. Our third child was conceived there, after all."

Jack grinned and brushed a hand through his hair, a move so reminiscent of the boy she fell in love with, she nearly pulled him on top of her. And then the weight of the moment returned, and her breath caught in her diaphragm.

"I'm worried about the kids," Sophia murmured, touching the gold locket at her neck. "Why do we have to tell them I've died? It's going to traumatize them."

Jack sighed and sat on the bed next to her.

"They'll learn the truth a few days after, and we need them to act the part. If they don't seem sad it will look suspicious. And think how happy they'll be when they find out you're alive. Jude and Peter will love it, they're always pulling pranks."

"I'd hardly call this a prank."

"It's a bid for your freedom, Sophia. There's no lie I won't tell to protect you."

Sophia looked at Jack for a long time, and then pulled her wedding ring from her finger. She stared at the diamond, an heirloom that had belonged to Andrew's mother, Jack's grandmother. It had not been passed to Ruth because she insisted on a modern ring when Andrew proposed, but Sophia loved the platinum ring with its small diamond set in a bough of intertwining vines. She put the ring into a little velvet pouch and slid it into the compartment within the suitcase.

"You don't have to take that off," Jack said, reaching for the bag.

"Just in case," she said. "It's distinctive. Better if I'm as plain as possible."

"Five days," Jack said, eyes glittering. "Five days until our new life."

CHAPTER 12

$\mathcal{S}$eptember 1965
Hattie

"OKAY, WHERE'S THE FIRE?" Jude asked, walking into Hattie's apartment without knocking.

Hattie frowned at her older sister but said nothing. Fighting with Jude about guest etiquette was the last thing she felt like doing.

"I don't think Mama died in 1955," Hattie let the words out in a rush.

She watched for Jude's reaction, but Jude merely continued into the apartment running her hands over furniture and inspecting pictures.

"Love what you've done with the place," she joked, gesturing to a stack of unpacked boxes taking up most of the living room floor.

"Did you hear me?" Hattie asked, annoyed. She and Jude had never been close. The age gap combined with different personalities, world views, and perceptions of reality put them at odds from the beginning. Hattie tried over the years to connect with Jude, but Jude always pushed her away. "I'm not your mother," she'd say.

"Oh, Hattie," Jude murmured inspecting the scarred coffee table in Hattie's living room with a grimace. "I hope you're not listening to ghosts again."

"I'm serious, Jude," Hattie said, fighting her growing upset.

Somehow Jude always reduced her to tears, but today she would not allow it. She squared off against her older sister. Hattie stood over five inches taller than Jude, but she was like a reed and Jude an oak tree. "Listen to me, damn it!"

Jude turned to her in surprise.

She started to say something, likely a jab about Hattie's dirty mouth, and then stopped. She took a seat at Hattie's little kitchen table and patted the chair next to her.

"Okay, I surrender," she told her, smiling. "Tell me, little sister."

Hattie walked to the bureau by her door and lifted the first newspaper from the stack. Already folded to the article about her mother, she dropped it on the table in front of Jude. She watched Jude glance at the picture and then lift it toward her face for a closer look. Her eyes scanned the article. She pursed her lips, frown deepening, and returned the paper to the table.

"Our mother's name was Anne," Jude said, but Hattie saw the question in her eyes.

"It's her, isn't it?" Hattie asked, already knowing the truth.

Jude lifted the paper again, studying the image.

"Yes, it's her. I recognize her. Even with the scarf. And that necklace..." she trailed off, but Hattie understood. Their mother always wore the gold locket and though a gold locket was not unique, the way it rested on their mother's chest was.

"She had an accident," Jude said, talking to herself. "That July, they dropped us at Gram Ruth's and then Mama died."

Jude rarely said mama, always mother, and Hattie could see her working back through the years in her mind.

"He never said what it was, the accident," Jude continued. "Dad, he was acting so strangely and then-"

"He died too."

Jude nodded, frowning at the newspaper.

"The Northern Michigan Asylum? Mom was not crazy. Why would they...?"

Hattie showed her the second paper that depicted two young girls standing in front of a horse pen. She considered telling Jude about the girl in the yellow dress, but bit her tongue.

Jude whistled, shaking her head and glancing at her baby sister. Hattie knew she was noticing the resemblance.

"There's more. A whole crate of stuff nailed shut. I didn't take much, but I'm going back. I need to see what's in that crate."

Jude nodded, eyes fixed on some place far away. "In the loft? Where Dad died?"

Hattie nodded. She had considered that too. Had Daddy put the crate there? Or someone else? Had the guilt from the lie killed him?

"Fucking Gram Ruth," Jude spat. "She has to be behind this." Jude stood angrily from her chair, knocking it to the floor. She paced to the little window that looked over the street below. "How could Dad have lied?"

Only eight when their mother died, Hattie had lived in a haze of grief and loneliness. She barely remembered the stories they were told.

"Let's go right now," Jude said, turning away from the window with a wild expression.

Short and muscular, Jude looked like an animal cornering her prey. Even her caramel colored pencil skirt and red sweater gave her the appearance of a brightly colored jungle cat.

Hattie shook her head.

"No, Gram will be there, and I don't think we should tell her."

"Confront her, you mean? That's exactly what we should do."

Hattie's stomach turned at the thought of facing off with Gram Ruth. She had always done her best to stay on Gram's good side. Unlike Jude who intentionally riled her at every opportunity.

"Don't tell me you're still scared of her?" Jude demanded.

Hattie shrugged and fiddled with the edge of the newspaper, looking again at the picture of their mother.

"Not scared, but, I don't know. I have a bad feeling, Jude."

Jude rolled her eyes. "Don't go all woo-woo on me now. This isn't the time to flake out."

Hattie bit her tongue, tempted to tell Jude about the man who led her to the crate. She knew Jude would only laugh and write it off.

Hattie had confided in Jude, more than once, about the apparitions she'd met over the years, hoping Jude would share she too had seen the ghosts. Jude only looked at her like she was nuts and told her she better keep that crazy to herself or Gram Ruth would have her locked away.

"How will you sleep tonight, Hattie? Knowing half the truth? Will you lay in bed thinking about that crate?"

"Tonight then," Hattie said, resigned. "Gram goes to bed at nine."

"Deal." Jude lifted the paper one more time and then shook her head angrily. "I'll pick you up at eight-thirty."

~

DAMIEN

DAMIEN STRAIGHTENED his tie and knocked on the door. He wished he'd foregone his second cup of coffee. Meeting Doctor Kaiser made him nervous. He didn't need the additional caffeine to worsen the experience.

Kaiser opened his office door and gestured that Damien take a seat. The shades were drawn, blotting out the sunny day. Though the office was meticulously kept, Damien often felt claustrophobic in the room.

"Tell me about the girls," Dr. Kaiser asked Damien quietly. Damien's skin crawled, and he shifted away from the man, standing to examine a book on his fastidiously organized shelf.

"They're great," Damien told him. "Jude is a fireball, all attitude, sexy as hell, a little rough around the edges. Hattie is her polar opposite, sweet as vanilla ice cream with a heart of gold."

"Beautiful?" the doctor asked, and Damien barely caught the question, almost a whisper.

The doctor stared at a file in front of him, his eyes burning into the page, but his mind clearly elsewhere.

Not for the first time, Damien questioned working with Doctor Kaiser. Unconventional was one thing, but the man gave him the creeps. However, Damien needed the recommendation.

"Yes, both beautiful," Damien wanted to hold back, but he knew the doctor would probe for details. "Jude is short, muscley, like a gymnast and Hattie is..." Damien searched for the words, "angelic."

Dr. Kaiser looked up sharply and rested his pointed gaze on Damien. His eyes, sharp blue flecks, bore into him and Damien tried to hold his stare. After seconds that felt like minutes, Damien looked away, face growing warm. The Doctor had looked at him with knowing as if they shared a dirty secret that lived in the deepest stratum of all men. A primal urge, born of a lesser consciousness, that

79

needed only a glimpse of flesh, a brush of fingertips to awaken from its slumber.

"Any news of their mother? Sophia?" The doctor spoke her name with relish, his mouth forming the O and spreading it into a long sigh.

"I didn't want to rush into those questions," Damien told him. "I want to know them first, approach the topic carefully."

"Yes, as you should," the Doctor agreed, returning to the file on his desk with actual interest. "I expect a full report as soon as you've broached the subject."

Damien left the office and immediately shrugged out of his blazer. Sweat grew in circles beneath his armpits and the tie encircling his neck appeared to be strangling him. He stumbled into the bathroom and fought it off, whipping it onto the floor like a live snake. He splashed cold water on his face and peered at his reflection. Water ran in rivulets over the thick ridge of his brow and dripped from his chin. His eyes looked vacant and, if he were honest, scared.

The doctor terrified him.

Damien remembered a dream from his boyhood. A hideous witch chased him through the woods behind his house. He would always escape her, rush into his bedroom and close the door, only to turn and find her waiting by the window.

Dr. Kaiser reminded him of the witch from his nightmares.

Hattie

HATTIE STARED at the silhouette of the trees rolling by. Her stomach growled. Since finding the newspapers, she had been unable to eat. She tried to force down a piece of dry toast before Jude picked her up but took only two bites before throwing it in the trash. Even painting had done little to soothe her. After an hour staring at a blank canvas, she'd given up and taken a walk instead.

Jude cranked her music loud. Hattie's teeth vibrated in her head. She thought about asking Jude to turn it down but preferred the music over Jude's hateful diatribes about Gram Ruth. Hattie could tell that

Jude spent her afternoon working into a greater and greater frenzy over the lies.

By the time she arrived at Hattie's apartment, her mouth was set in an angry line and every other word out of her mouth was 'fuck.' Hattie stopped listening to her and Jude turned up her music to release some of her fury through song. Rather than sing "I can't get no satisfaction," she screamed it.

Jude parked the car on the edge of the estate in a thicket of dark ash trees, barely perceptible beneath the cloud covered moon. Jude wore black pants and a black turtleneck, her hair drawn into a tight ponytail. Hattie, less adept at sleuthing, had thrown on a pair of jeans and a loose-fitting blue sweatshirt spotted with little yellow daisies. Jude had stared at Hattie's sweatshirt when she first got in the car but refrained from the insult clearly on her face.

Jude jumped out and pulled a duffel bag from her backseat.

"Flashlight," she said gruffly, thrusting the heavy light into Hattie's hand. She flicked on her own and cast the beam through the forest before returning to her bag.

"What else do you have?" Hattie looked over Jude's shoulder, squinting into the bag.

"Just in case," Jude said tucking a revolver into the waistband of her pants.

"What? No." Hattie shook her head, dismayed at the small black weapon. "Where did you get that?"

"Peter," Jude said, pulling it out and smoothing her hand along the oiled barrel. "Safekeeping while he's in Vietnam."

Hattie grimaced and shook her head.

"I'm not going to use it," Jude argued.

"I will not go with you if you have that," Hattie protested.

Hattie hated guns. In fact, they terrified her. She had held one only once in her life. It belonged to her father, and she came upon it in his old bedroom at Gram Ruth's house. It felt heavy in her hand and alive. She nearly dropped it and when she caught it, she knew if it hit the floor, it would have exploded a bullet into the room, maybe into her body. She placed it back in the bureau and went to her bedroom where she hugged her stuffed bear, Groucho, and tried not to cry.

Jude frowned, but took the gun and returned it to the backseat.

"I swear Hattie, if we end up needing this…"

"On who, Jude? Gram Ruth? Frank? Think about what might happen if you get spooked in the dark with that stupid thing in your hand?"

Jude cocked an eyebrow and smiled.

"Well I'm happy to see you get mad about something. I was starting to think you were a porcelain doll."

Hattie shook her head and looked away, fighting tears.

Jude started into the forest, flashlight beam weaving between the trunks of trees. Somewhere far off a pack of coyotes shrieked and howled. Hattie remembered Daddy telling her they were the tricksters of the forest. He said, "Never trust a man who suddenly appears in the trees, he is probably a coyote in disguise."

Branches snapped beneath their feet and leaves crunched. To Hattie's delicate senses, they sounded like a troop of elephants in a stampede.

Through a break in the trees, the back of the barn loomed before them.

"We can go in through the old chicken coop," Jude said, gesturing towards a mostly boarded-up back entrance.

Gram Ruth and Grandpa Andrew never had chickens. Long before they developed the estate, a wealthy farmer owned the land and raised chickens, cows, and had a stable of horses. Hattie remembered her daddy telling a story about wanting chickens as a small boy. His mother, Gram Ruth, refused and then made him go to a local farm to watch the beheading of chickens so he understood the chicken's fate.

Hattie's mind was overrun with thoughts of her daddy and like earlier that day, she felt his presence as they moved toward the barn.

Jude hesitated just outside the chicken coop opening. She stared into the inky dark and Hattie knew she thought of Daddy's death. She doubted that Jude had entered the barn since his fall.

"Now or never," Jude whispered and pushed through cobwebs into blackness, holding her flashlight out to illuminate the few steps ahead of them.

They moved slowly, careful not to trip over discarded rakes and rusted farm equipment. Far in the front of the barn, Hattie could see the ghostly silhouettes of Grandpa Andrew's antique cars.

"What a waste," Jude muttered, seeing them as well.

Hattie held her flashlight up as Jude climbed the ladder. At the top,

Jude's face appeared grotesque and misshapen in the strange orange glow. She shone her own light back down and Hattie climbed quickly, listening for sounds from the house.

She led Jude deeper into the loft. They navigated gaping holes in the floor. Each groaning board caused them both to pause and hold their breaths, as if that might keep the floor from falling through.

Hattie walked to the space where the crate had been but did not see it. She moved further in, and then circled back looking for the maroon curtain which she'd draped over the crate before leaving.

Jude stood with her hand on her hip, her own flashlight dancing across the boxes.

"Where is it?" she hissed.

"I don't know. I swear it was right here." But the spot held only bits of furniture and stacks of framed pictures. She walked back and forth across the loft and then along the perimeter, returning again and again to the space where the crate had been. It was gone.

CHAPTER 13

*L*ate 1950s
The Northern Michigan Asylum for the Insane
Sophia

SOPHIA COULD NOT SLEEP. She never slept anymore, only lay tossing and listening and longing to race back through the years and make another choice.

Sometimes, she replayed that fateful morning when Ruth Porter arrived to whisk her to an isolated cabin where she would wait for her family and escape persecution by Margaret Bell. Instead, she fell into a deep, likely drugged, sleep. She woke as a prisoner in an insane asylum.

Through the window the pale moon smiled from its wide lonely face. She couldn't imagine the grounds beyond the walls. Out there the moon would not feel sad, but wild. It would race across the lush grass and disappear into the thicket of forest that surrounded her like the cage it was. Beauty was therapy, they said. But nature alone could not cure madness. Not when even nature had been manipulated to control them.

There were patients who escaped the asylum and ran into the woods. They were brought back days, weeks later. Sometimes they were naked, shivering, terrified. What slept in those woods? Some creature of the forest or was it merely the demons in their own hearts they met out there in the emptiness?

"Sophia." The whisper came from everywhere and nowhere and she thought about ignoring him. She had done it before when a spirit made contact. Eventually they went away. The room grew warmer in their absence and the thick, stagnant air dissipated. But here, she dared not turn them away. She preferred their company to loneliness.

"I hear you," Sophia whispered.

"Sophia..." the voice said again draining from the room.

She started to sit and felt a shock, bucking violently in her bed, a sharp wave of pain sliced through her head. She rolled over and fumbled to sitting, clutching her head. Her heart beat fiercely beneath her hands and she heaved for breath. It came to her slowly, and she looked around the room for the apparition, but saw only bare walls.

"Sophia..."

"I hear you," she said again. The man had died of a brain trauma, maybe an aneurysm. She had felt it in her own body and not for the first time. Sometimes the spirit could communicate a sensation.

The first time, Sophia had been thirteen and less than a month living with the Porters. By then she knew Jack, but he was still the tall, handsome son of her warden and Ruth had made it very clear he was off limits to the unruly barefoot Sophia.

One morning as she climbed into one of the many barn attics, she felt a sudden hot slash across her throat. Sophia fell from the ladder and sprawled on the dirt floor feeling a rush of hot sticky blood flowing into her throat and down her shirt. She started to scream, assuming that somehow, she had cut her throat except the sensation had left her. Only a dull aching where her head hit the floor remained.

Sophia had gingerly touched her intact throat and known someone had murdered a woman in that barn. Decades, maybe centuries earlier, but a man had cut her throat and left her to bleed to death on the dirt floor.

She shook the image from her mind and concentrated on the man in her room.

"How can I help you?" she asked.

"It is I who will help you," the voice said, and the most wonderful sensation of warmth settled over her as if he had wrapped her in a blanket and hugged her through it. She closed her eyes and bit back the tears.

Every ounce of her body ached. Tied down the day before with cold, wet sheets, she'd lain for hours shivering until Dr. Kaiser's nurse Alice released her, gave her a white paper-thin nightgown, and sent her to bed without supper.

At some point, she had lost track of the years and the other patients were of no help. One might say 1962 and another 1948 and yet another 2073. No one knew except the staff and the doctors told them to keep the date and the time of day to themselves. *It disturbs the patients,* they justified.

Sophia once watched a woman ask an older nurse for the date. She thought it might be her son's birthday, she said. When the nurse refused, the woman grew upset, resorting to begging. Finally two orderlies, burly men with mean eyes, rushed into the room and removed the young woman. Sophia did not watch further, but she heard the woman scream and cry for her son, Jeremy.

Sophia thought of her own children every day, every hour, every minute. She imagined Hattie's delicate hands drawing pictures and Jude's infectious laughter. Peter had loved to play scrabble, for hours he could string together letters - docile, celestial.

Hardest of all were thoughts of Jack. Jack who had not written, called, or visited - ever. Jack whose plan to fake her death could not fail, his confidence sweeping her into another monumental mistake.

Jack who was dead.

Sophia knew because she saw him. He did not come to her in the institution as other apparitions had.

She saw him in a dream. They walked along a deserted country road. A stream of black crows followed them landing in the trees above, spitting angry shrill cries. Sophia clung to him, but Jack unwound his fingers and when she looked into his face, she saw most of his flesh had fallen away. White gleaming bone protruded from his chin, his eye sockets, the cavity of his nose. She had awoken at the asylum, screaming. Her beloved Jack had left her forever.

DR. KAISER CLOSED the door behind him. Sophia listened to the sharp click as the lock slid into place. He sat on the end of her bed and regarded her through eerie blue eyes.

"I am hearing interesting stories about you, Sophia," the doctor said, pulling a black pen from his pocket and rubbing his thumb along the pricked point.

Sophia blinked and pushed deeper onto her bed though the small cot left little space for retreat.

The latest treatment, administered two days before, had left Sophia exhausted and terrified. She remembered Kaiser with his latex gloves and long needle. Sweating and sick, but ravenously hungry, she had clawed at the restraints placed across her arms and legs. Eventually she fell into a deep sleep, a coma, she overheard the nurses say after.

"The insulin therapy may not be strong enough for your psychosis," Dr. Kaiser continued. His eyes shone, and he smiled hungrily as he continued to massage his pen.

"I won't tell the stories anymore," Sophia said, willing to tell the doctor anything to avoid another dose of insulin. "I got carried away."

It was a lie. When she had told Ellen her dead husband never left her side, it had been an enormous relief for the troubled patient. Sophia knew Ellen would keep her secret. But there were other patients. Patients who sat and drooled and stared into nothingness, but they listened and heard and told. They played the part of the fool to gather information, which they passed to the doctors for lenience and favors.

Sophia knew better than to speak in the presence of other patients, but that day Ellen suffered. She chewed her fingers and screwed her eyes tight whenever a loud noise sounded. Sophia only wanted to soothe her, to offer her a bit of hope from the other side.

SOPHIA WOKE to darkness and groped for the bedside light. Her arms felt heavy and her legs, like bags of wet sand. She tried to turn her head and peer into the room, but something rigid held her head in place. Breathing rapidly, she attempted to blink the darkness away, noticing that her straining chest also felt confined. Slowly, agonizingly, the memory of her whereabouts returned. The State Hospital - The Northern Michigan Asylum for the Insane.

Still, that did not explain the straps and the vice around her head. Who had bound her and why? She thought back to the previous night and remembered the nurse Alice arriving with her pills. She took them, crawled into bed and then nothing. A sedative then?

Minutes crawled by. She listened for voices, dripping water, footsteps - any sound at all. Someone had moved her to solitary. It was the only explanation. In her own room, light, even on the darkest nights, crept through the window. Only in solitary were all the senses deprived. Her heart rampaged within her inert body and she wiggled her fingers and toes to have some sense of autonomy.

She blinked and felt tears stream from her eyes. Her mouth felt gritty and dry and she longed to direct a tear toward her lips. She tried again to turn her head but found no give in the thick leather that drew across her forehead and chin.

"Somewhere over the rainbow," she began to sing. It hurt her throat and made her desire for water almost unbearable, but she did not stop. "Way up high, there's a land that I heard of once in a lullaby. Somewhere over rainbow the skies are blue. And the dreams that you dreamed of, really do come true."

As she sang, she cried harder. The song transported her back to early motherhood. She sat rocking Jude in a chair that Jack had salvaged and refinished for her. It stood beneath the window in their bedroom, softened with a checkered quilt. Jack would hold Peter in bed while Sophia, Anne then, nursed and rocked her beautiful baby girl. Jude's awe-filled brown eyes would watch her mother with that all-encompassing love that makes motherhood both so divine and so fragile.

"Yes." A voice - honeyed, yet venomous - slithered across the room and turned Sophia's body to stone.

She stopped singing and crying at once.

"Get it out. Release the demons within you Sophia. I hear their strangled cries, they want to be free."

She could not see Kaiser, but knew he sat close. She had not heard his breath or detected even a trace of him when she first woke up, but he had been there for some time. Not watching her in the darkness, he too must be blind in the blacked-out room. What then? Waiting for her to wake up? Waiting to see what she would do or say if she thought herself alone and confined?

Sophia clenched her eyes against the tears that continued to flow. She hated him then more than ever before - hated him for polluting the memory of her daughter - hated him for whatever sickness drove him to hurt those he had been entrusted to care for. Every muscle in her body drew taught against her restraints and she knew that if he released her in that moment she would do her best to kill him with her bare hands.

However, he did not release her. He stood, placed a cool, damp hand on her forehead. Then he leaned down and pressed his slimy lips against her own. She tried to bite him. She opened her mouth and jerked her head towards him, but he had already pulled away.

"So much work left to do," he sighed. For a moment, she glimpsed a sliver of the light from the hallway as he slipped from the room and then darkness returned.

CHAPTER 14

eptember 1965
Jude

JUDE SLAMMED her front door and threw her purse clear across the room. It smacked the back of her couch and landed with a thud. Startled by the noise, Gram leapt up from where he'd been sleeping, and barked anxiously.

"Shut up, Gram," Jude snarled, kicking off her shoes and marching across the room to her answering machine. The little red light blinked that she had messages. She hit 'play,' frustrated at the rush of hopefulness that coursed through her.

One after another she hit delete. Two messages from strangers looking for photography services, and one message from the vet reminding her Gram was due for his annual check-up.

Seething, she picked up the machine, yanking it from the wall and held it over her head. She stood and breathed and imagined throwing the machine onto the floor and watching it splinter on the hardwood. She would stomp on it, again and again, until only tiny shards of plastic remained. Two more breaths, three and she felt a tiny pinprick in the anger ballooning inside her, just enough to allow her to return the answering machine to the table.

She ignored Gram's whining and went to the kitchen, grabbing a large round glass and filling it to the brim with Merlot. She tilted the glass back and drank half before refilling it and going to her couch. As she sat, Gram jumped onto the cushion beside her. She considered scolding him for climbing on her furniture but ran her hand over his soft ears instead. At least he wanted to sit with her.

Damien. Days had passed and not a single call. Not even a call to ask about the pictures. Clients always called. *When will the photos be ready, how did they turn out?* And she hadn't fucked those clients!

She unconsciously squeezed Gram's ear, and he whimpered, pulling away.

"Oh Gram, I'm sorry. It's not you I'm mad at. It's him. Damien. A devil's name. I should have fucking known. Isn't that right? Some demon named Damien sent to earth to turn us all towards sin?"

Gram blinked at her with soulful black eyes and then rested his scraggly head on her knee.

"You know who else I'm mad at?" She told the room. "Hattie! Hattie and her insane stories. A giant crate full of evidence, what a load of bullshit. What is she playing at anyhow?"

She said the words with intensity, but all the while she pictured those yellowing newspapers. Jude saw again the photograph of her beautiful mother, face turning away from the camera as they carted her off to a nut house.

"Gram Ruth. That's who deserves this hate," she muttered, downing her glass and standing up. "Come on, Gram. Let's go walk off some rage."

≈

Hattie

HATTIE HICCUPPED and wiped the sleeve of her blouse across her eyes. She had not intended to cry when she met with Damien, but the moment he walked into the church's little kitchen and asked how she was doing, she burst into tears.

Damien grabbed a dishtowel from the oven. It was stacked with casseroles left by the church ladies who donated dinners every week for Hattie to take to the shelter.

"Patti French made this," she murmured, smiling at the towel embroidered with little ducks and pressed it into her face. The ducks reminded Hattie of her mother and she started to cry again.

"How can I help, Hattie," Damien asked, leaning over and squeezing her knee.

His hands, large and fine-boned, felt sturdy, grounding. She turned watery blue eyes toward him and shook her head.

"You can't. I'm just..." Silly was the word hovering in her mind. Jude would have called her silly, but what was she truly? Lost, betrayed, and desperate to know the truth.

"When I was a little boy, my mother had a ritual when I was upset," Damien said, taking the seat beside her. "First, she'd let me pick out my favorite pair of pajamas. I'd put them on and she'd pack us a treat, usually cookies, and we'd go out to the horse stables. My older brother's horse was Roland, and I wasn't allowed to ride him, except on those days," he smiled at her and winked. "On those days, it was a secret between me and my mom. I would ride Roland and she would ride her horse, Sunny. A huge oak tree, perfect for climbing, stood in a pasture not far from our house. We'd ride out there, lay a blanket under the tree, and eat cookies until I thought I'd explode. Then she'd knit or read while I ran all over that tree like a squirrel."

Hattie laughed.

"I love that story," she murmured. "Is it terrible that it also makes me feel so sad and empty? Like where are those memories with my mama?"

"Not terrible at all, truthful," Damien told her. "It's refreshing how honest you are."

"Ha," she scoffed. "One of my greatest weaknesses, according to my sister."

Damien stiffened beside her.

"Then she's a fool."

Hattie turned a grateful smile on him.

"A fool I love. Though I'm not always sure she loves me back."

"If I've learned one thing from working with people, it's that families are some of the most complex, agonizing and yet amazing relationships that exist. Your sister loves you, Hattie. I try not to make declarative statements, but you're not a patient after all." He squeezed her knee again. "Love is always there, deep and everlasting, it just gets hidden by the faces we show to the world."

Hattie cocked her head and watched him. He had looked away, staring toward the beige carpet as if he could see through a crack into the future, or maybe the past.

"Listen," he blurted. "I have a friend with a stable outside town. Go with me? We'll stop and get a package of cookies?"

She smiled, a little shyly.

"Yes, I would like that."

∼

Jude

JUDE WALKED through the shadowy barn. Unlike her baby sister, she had never been fond of the large, creepy tomb-like lofts where Gram Ruth tucked her past away like it never existed. Old furniture, clothes, cars - all of it boxed and shoved beneath the sheets that spent decades collecting dust. Somewhere in those piles, Jude knew her mother's belongings lived. Not only her mother's but also her father's, Peters, Hattie's and even Jude's.

After their mother died, they returned to their farmhouse for only a week before their father announced they were moving in with Gram Ruth.

The strain of life without their mother had gotten to him. He paced a lot. Jude remembered finding him at night whispering hurriedly into the phone which he'd dragged outside. She would follow the cord from the kitchen, through the living room, onto the big porch. He'd be sitting on the porch swing, tapping his foot and shouting in a whisper. Once Jude watched him scream and fling the phone into the porch rail where the mouth piece cracked off.

Jude shone her flashlight along the dirt floor. She wasn't a reporter. Not in the typical sense anyway, but she noticed things others missed. Through the lens in her camera, Jude learned to study the details. The man standing off to the side of the crime scene, his hands shoved so deep into his pockets his forearms were invisible. Or the doll stuck in a tree after a tornado ripped through town. The little details that turned a story into real life.

Shafts of sunlight filtered through cracks in the old barn wood, but only illuminated strips in the darkness. Jude shivered and pointed her flashlight at the ladder that led to the lofts. Peter liked to play in the lofts as a child and later Hattie did too, but never Jude. Everything about the lofts reminded her of a graveyard. When their father fell to his death from that space, it only confirmed her good sense to stay the hell out of there.

She stuck the flashlight in her mouth and grabbed the rungs. As she climbed, her camera swung against her back, hanging from a leather strap around her neck. She glanced back at the dirt floor and tried not to imagine her father sprawled there, his neck broken.

At the top, more shafts of light lit the barn, and she clicked off her flashlight, lifting her camera up instead. The tiny lens seemed to magnify every object, shadow, and footprint. When she looked through the camera, she no longer viewed the world as Jude, everything fitting into her version of reality, but instead as an all-seeing eye, no biases, no expectations, truly able to see every nuance and texture.

Furniture draped in sheets, cobwebs, sagging cardboard boxes, stacks of yellowing books, mouse poop (ugh!), a tall grimy mirror, stacks of paintings not preserved, a tarnished soup pot-

Jude continued to scan and then paused, shifting back to the soup pot, she had a memory of her mother lazily stirring a pot of chicken soup for a sick Hattie. The handle had been missing. Sure enough the handle on the pot before her was broken off. Jude let the camera rest against her chest and moved toward the pile of stuff concealed behind the pot. She ripped off a dark drape covering the boxes. Dust flew into the air and she pulled her blouse up to keep from inhaling it.

The boxes were haphazard, but Jude recognized her mother's green suitcase. The clasps stuck and then popped with a loud click. Neatly folded clothes greeted her, and she sighed, disappointed. Stuffing her hands into the clothes, she searched for anything tucked further into the suitcase. Her hand struck something hard, and she wiggled out a small wooden jewelry box. Nestled in the velvet interior, she found a jumble of tangled gold and silver chains, and beneath those a tiny silk pouch. She lifted it and dumped the contents into her hand. A diamond ring landed on her palm, her mother's wedding ring.

Jude blinked at the ring, frowning. Her father would have buried her mother with her wedding ring. There was no doubt in Jude's mind that the ring would have gone into the ground with her.

Jude slipped the ring onto her pinkie. Her fingers were thicker than her mothers had been and shorter. Her mother's fingers were long and slender like Hattie's.

"Why is it in this suitcase?" she whispered, touching a pink silk nightgown her mother often wore. Something else was bothering her, too. The clothes in the suitcase were perfectly arranged, silk and soft fabrics on top, jeans at the bottom. Her mother had packed the suitcase. Her father would have thrown things in, barely folded. Jude knew the difference. For the first fifteen years of her life, Jude's mother packed her suitcases and the rare occasion her father did it, her mother laughed at the chaos of their stuff. But how could her mother have packed the suitcase? She died unexpectedly. Obviously, she didn't have time to pack her things first.

～

DAMIEN

DAMIEN'S HORSE, Luna, trotted amiably along. He ran his fingers through her long mane of white hair and watched Hattie riding in front of him. She said she had never ridden but took to the horse naturally. Long and willowy, her body moved and swayed with the animal, the wind, his breath. Her long blonde hair whipped out behind her, caught by the breeze and he imagined running his fingers through the silky strands, turning her face to his and staring into her eyes, blue and bottomless.

He squeezed the leather bridle and blew out a long, hot breath. He couldn't afford to be thinking of her in those terms, and yet... he couldn't seem to stop.

They veered off the pasture onto a dirt path that wound through the woods. The path circled an old rock quarry, flooded years ago. Damien's friend Fiona, who owned the horse stable, had once told him that local teenagers used to swim in the quarry until a girl drowned at one of their parties.

The sun glinted off the flat mirrored surface. Along the water's edge, huge weeping willows swept over the surface of the water.

Damien trotted up to Hattie and motioned toward one of the willow trees set further back. Beneath the tree an old rock fire pit stood on a hard, sandy ridge.

"Cookie picnic over there?"

"I love weeping willows," Hattie said dreamily. As they rounded the quarry, she shielded her face against the sun's sharp reflection.

Her horse, a muscular steed named Halo, nuzzled Damien's horse playfully. She nipped him, and Damien urged her toward the willow.

He dismounted and helped Hattie from her horse. She seemed weightless, like he could toss her in the air.

"Thank you," she said breathlessly, massaging Halo's neck and ears. "They're so beautiful."

"Yes, his rider is too."

Hattie blushed and turned away. Looking across the water, Damien saw her eyes take on the distant gaze that so often formed her features. Lips parted, topaz eyes sparkling, seeing into another world, he thought.

"Where do you go?" he asked her.

She closed her eyes tight and opened them, glancing at him.

"Everywhere, and nowhere."

Damien had a sudden urge to tell her everything about Dr. Kaiser, Jude, his many untruths. Hattie had a forgiving nature. She would not hate him for his deception, but would it change the way she looked at him?

"How's your project going?" she asked, smoothing her fingers through the grass.

Damien paused almost thinking she referred to his work with Kaiser and then remembered why he had originally approached her, or why she thought he had.

"Good, I've met a couple of guys who have been insightful." Which was true. Although he'd used his thesis as a ruse to meet Hattie, he intended to write about existentialism in the homeless population. Most of the homeless in Cadillac knew and loved Hattie. She was a familiar face at the food pantry and the overnight shelter.

"They're good men," Hattie said. "My Gram Ruth calls me a lover of fools and thieves." She smiled but didn't laugh. "She doesn't know them though. They're kind, gentle, and their stories will break your heart."

"Your Grandma raised you?"

Hattie nodded.

"My sister and brother were older when my parents died. But I was only eight." She paused and stared hard at a field of wildflowers beyond the trees. "I loved Gram. I love her, but…"

Damien waited, wondering about the sorrow in Hattie's eyes. Dr. Kaiser had told him almost nothing about the girls' family, but he had implied their mother was dangerous and unstable. Strangely he had not gotten that impression from either of her daughters.

"Gram was unkind to our mother. Jude and Peter still blame her for that. It's all so confusing." Hattie closed her eyes and put her face in her hands. She didn't weep but sat hiding her eyes for a long time.

"Would you like to talk about your mother?" he asked, for his own sake. In his mind he insisted he would tell Kaiser nothing of what Hattie confided to him.

"I dream of her sometimes. She's sitting at her easel painting a canvas completely black, just adding layer after layer of black paint."

"Wow."

"Yeah," Hattie shrugged. "I found something in Gram Ruth's barn. It's a newspaper clipping of Mama getting sent to the Northern Michigan Asylum. The summer we believed she died, she was actually sent away."

"And your family lied to you? To your siblings as well?" Damien shivered, wondering why Dr. Kaiser had not mentioned the secret.

"For most of my life, she was dead and now…"

"Do you know where she is?" he asked, knowing if she said yes, he would not tell Doctor Kaiser.

"No. In the asylum, I hope because then she's still alive. I only found out yesterday."

Damien wanted to rub her back, whisper soothing words into her ear. He wanted to watch her sit and paint the wildflowers.

As he looked at the delicate bones of Hattie's shoulder's an image of Jude rose into his mind. She had straddled him, her muscular arms glistening with sweat and her face tilted back in a moan of pleasure.

How had he lost control so completely? He'd been so focused on school and later his future career as a psychiatrist he'd rarely slowed down to indulge his emotions. Something about Jude had triggered him. That night as they drank and talked he found a desperate desire for her body building within him. He had acted upon it and now a similar desire arose for Hattie. But it was not Hattie's body that drew him, though it was beautiful. He wanted all of her, to wrap her in his arms and carry her home, to wake up every morning to her sleepy face on the pillow beside him.

"I need the help more than my patients," he muttered.

Hattie looked up from her hands, her eyes dry but her face splotched and red.

"What?"

"Nothing." He shook his head. "Listen, I have to get back to the university. I'm sorry to do it, but I have a patient coming in..." He didn't finish. He didn't have a patient coming in, but he couldn't trust himself in that grove for another moment.

Hattie dropped the rest of her cookie on the ground and stood, brushing off her pants.

~

Jude

JUDE STOPPED COLD, staring at her Grandmother who sat at the head of her long dining room table. The table gleamed in the flickering lights of the two polished gold candelabras. Gram had not seen her, but Jude watched the long dark shadows that played over her Grandmother's pallid face turning her into a ghoul hunched over her dinner plate.

Jude held the diamond ring clutched in her hand so tight the stone bit it into her palm. If she did not want so desperately to keep the ring she would have flung it at her Grandmother's face. Instead, she took a loud step forward, revealing she had not removed her boots when she entered the house. Gram's head snapped up and her eyes narrowed on Jude's face. Her mouth pressed into a grim line of displeasure.

"Good evening, Jude. You might have called rather than creeping into my house like a common burglar."

Jude said nothing, stepping to one of the tall wooden chairs and pulling it out with a scrape on the floor.

Gram's eyes opened wide and her nostrils flared.

"If you've scraped my floor young lady, you'll be on your hands and knees with sanding paper."

Gram glared at Jude and then stabbed a piece of chicken on her plate, taking an angry bite, but still chewing with her mouth closed, never one to break etiquette, even when her temper flared.

"What happened to my mother?" Jude shouted. She had intended to speak calmly, not lose her cool. Apparently, she'd overestimated herself.

Gram cocked an eyebrow and took another bite.

"She died in a car accident, as you well know. Why on earth are you bringing this up now?"

Jude snorted and squeezed the ring tighter. Liar hovered on her lips.

"I can't believe I thought you'd tell me the truth. After a lifetime of lies, I actually told myself before I walked through that door that this time you'd be honest."

Gram's face darkened, and her chewing became slower, more controlled. Her eyes had shifted for only an instant, darting to the side and Jude recognized the look. Gram was wondering how much her granddaughter knew.

"Where did the accident happen, Gram?" Jude asked, standing and allowing her chair to fall back with a clatter. It smacked the hardwood floor.

Gram didn't jump, just continued her chewing, staring at Jude with eyes like a snake's.

"In town? In the country? Where was she going, Gram? What street did it happen on? Who was in the other car? I'd love to talk to them."

Gram slammed her fork onto her plate and stood.

"I won't have you behaving this way in my house!" she shrilled.

Jude slammed the ring onto the table feeling the stone bite into the Mahogany - satisfied with the gouge it would leave behind. The diamond flickered rainbows in the candlelight.

Gram snarled, pulling her thin lips back as if the mere sight of the ring enraged her.

"What does that prove?" Gram snapped. "Your father kept the ring to pawn it. God knows we weren't putting a diamond in the ground."

Gram shook her head as if disappointed in Jude's weak confrontation. "Silly girl."

Gram turned, but Jude ran towards her stopping at the last minute inches from her grandmother's face. Gram Ruth stumbled back, grabbing her chair to keep from falling. Her eyes flashed furiously.

"How dare you? I raised you," the old woman seethed.

"I know," Jude hissed. "I know everything."

Jude turned, snatched the ring from the table, and stormed from the house, allowing the heavy front door to hang open behind her.

CHAPTER 15

The Northern Michigan Asylum for the Insane
Early 1960s
Sophia

SOPHIA SAT in the common area watching snow fall beyond the windows. Though it was day, the sun was muted by a thick cloud cover, and snow had been falling in droves for hours. Other patients milled about, some anxious, others determined. Agnes, who claimed to have once been a nun, sat at the grand piano plunking on the keys and occasionally belting out song lyrics.

"Pistol packin' mama, lay that pistol down," she shouted.

Candace, the short red-haired woman who bit the orderlies when they refused her canteen privileges, told Agnes to shut up and clamped her hands over her ears.

Sophia had heard good things about other floors in the asylum, but she never left Hall Five, the troubled women's hall. She spent more time in her room than in the common areas to avoid conflict with other patients.

She had made a friend or two, but noticed they were always transferred to another floor within a week of their conversations. Sophia knew Kaiser was behind it. He wanted to keep her isolated, all to himself, and had succeeded. He told stories about her violence, her delirious claims, the things she'd done before entering the hospital. Who would question him? He was a doctor after all.

Another patient, Jennifer, had given her a book about Michigan farming, and Sophia flipped through the pages, her eyes lingering on the colored drawings of green and vibrant plants. Oh, how she hungered to walk barefoot in the grass. It had been years. She rarely received ground privileges at the hospital and when she did, Kaiser nearly always appeared to usher her back inside for treatment.

In another life, she might have thought the hospital beautiful with its soaring brick walls and lush grounds. But no setting was beautiful when you were trapped inside.

∼

"I don't understand why this patient, excuse me resident, is in Hall Five." Sophia heard Kent - a new orderly on her floor - asking the question in the hall outside.

Another orderly, Debbie, answered him.

"She's Dr. Kaiser's patient, and he calls the shots. I'd cool your chops about it too. I heard another attendant ask that question last year and Alice just about flayed her alive."

"But she's not dangerous or disruptive," Kent continued. "How can they justify keeping her in here? Why doesn't she tell her family?"

"No family to speak of. Least I've never seen any. She's been here going on eight years and never had a visitor."

"You're kidding me?"

Sophia curled into a ball and thought of Jack. Jack was dead. He would never visit her. Had it really been eight years since that fateful day Ruth pulled her car down the long asylum driveway?

Sophia had only hazy memories of the day. Her mother-in-law had given her a drink before they left, a sedative likely dissolved in the bitter tasting tea. She had no memory of being admitted, of being placed in a room. One moment she was sitting in Ruth's black Chevrolet Fleetline and the next she woke in a stiff little bed, her clothes stripped away, her life gone.

"She's spoken of children and a husband," Debbie continued. "But they're probably all in her head. You know how some of these people are."

"Except she's not that way," Kent argued.

"Look Kent, you've only been on this floor for a few months. You'll hear the stories. She... she tells people weird things."

"Like what?"

A long silence lapsed, and Sophia wondered if they had moved away from her door.

"About dead people, about spirits and such. I've never heard it first-hand, but it's not only the patients that talk about it. She's told the nurses and orderlies things about their dead parents, siblings - all kinds of nutty stuff. Keep your distance, okay? The residents are manipulators. Don't let her in your head."

Sophia heard Debbie's rubber-soled shoes move off down the hall, but Kent stood outside her door for several more minutes.

Near the door, Kent's mother stood holding a dripping box of Popsicles that pooled orange on the floor. She had died twelve years prior, the day before Kent's tenth birthday.

SOPHIA SAT on the stiff white cot tucked against the concrete wall. Her room was square with a single, barred window looking over a grand courtyard. The grounds sloped and rolled, thick with towering oak trees. The flower beds burst with huge delicate peonies. When she looked out the window, she felt like Alice peeking into Wonderland, but her two-way mirror was blocked by a crisscross of cold steel.

Kent knocked once on her door and then turned the door handle. It would not matter if she sat naked on the cot, many of the patients did, or if she preferred a moment of privacy. The knock was a courtesy that many of the attendants didn't offer, and Sophia warmed to Kent for that small acknowledgment of her humanness.

"Your mother doesn't blame you," Sophia told Kent as he started toward her with her medication.

She reached to take the little paper cup that held her pills, but Kent unfurled his fingers and it fell to the floor.

"What did you say?" he asked, alarm in his eyes.

Sophia bent to pick up the pills that had rolled beneath her cot.

"It wasn't your fault, Kent," Sophia told him, popping the pills into her mouth and swallowing them dry.

The young man still did not seem to notice he had dropped the pills to begin with. He walked a few paces backwards, stopping at the closed door.

"My mother is dead," he whispered, and Sophia noticed how young Kent looked - no older than twenty-five. Only a bit younger than her own Jude and Peter.

"Yes, I know." Sophia patted the space next to her. The metal edges of the frame bit into the backs of her legs and she could feel the springs poking through the mattress, but she didn't exactly have a settee to offer him. "Denise visits me sometimes, Kent. She wanted me to tell you that you couldn't have prevented her death. It's true. She was going into town that day. She planned it before you asked for the Popsicles."

"Begged," Kent whispered, his voice strained. "I begged for the Popsicles."

He had backed against the door, but something in his features softened. A look of sadness turned his dark blue eyes paler, they glistened with unshed tears.

"I've heard the patients talking," he said. "But I thought, I thought..."

"That they were insane," Sophia laughed and patted the bed again. "It's okay honey, some of them are. Maybe we all have a little madness in us."

"I'm not supposed to talk about these things. Dr. Kaiser..." Kent's face darkened when he spoke the doctor's name.

"Is evil," Sophia finished, though he had not been about to use the term. She fought back the tremors that tried to steal over her at the mere mention of the doctor's name. "Evil, and I don't use that word lightly."

Kent swallowed and glanced behind him at the slit in the door, perhaps expecting Kaiser's blue eyes to stare back at him. Reassured they spoke alone, Kent crossed the room and sat next to Sophia. The cot sagged beneath his weight.

"Did you see her? Is she happy?" The desperation in Kent's voice made Sophia's heart throb with painful memories of her own family. Did her children lay in bed at night asking those same questions about their mother?

"Yes. Sometimes I can only hear her, she speaks to me, sings to me, Dream a Little Dream."

A stifled sob escaped him, and he pressed his hands to his face.

After a moment, he began, "Stars shining bright above you, night breezes seem to whisper I love you." He sang the lyrics low, in a whisper, and shook his head as if trying to deny the memories. "She had a record of Ella Fitzgerald singing that song, she loved that song. Almost every night, I fell asleep to those words."

"It's a beautiful song," Sophia told him, tentatively taking his hand in her own. Touching staff at the hospital could result in punishment.

He squeezed her hand back, wiping his eyes with his free hand.

"She looked beautiful, Kent. The two times she appeared in form, I saw long silver blonde hair and the most sparkling gray eyes. All smiles, no sadness in her face. I believe her only regret was you taking the blame. It hurts her."

Kent nodded and squeezed her hand again as if a door that had been closed his whole life suddenly swung open.

"I begged for those Popsicles and she gave in. A drunk driver hit her head on, at two in the afternoon!"

"She intended to go anyway, honey. Death comes for us when it's time, it's that simple. We choose long before we come here when we will die."

"But why? Why would she leave us all behind?"

Sophia smiled and tried to answer as best she could.

"Before this life, beyond this life, there is no end. So, it's easy to choose death because we know there will be growth for those left behind. And no one is left for long. We all come together again. It is only here in these physical bodies, bound by the laws of our physical world, that we forget that."

Kent nodded, but Sophia saw a hint of turmoil in his eyes.

"Why doesn't she come to me? I've prayed every night since she died for a dream, anything, a hint of her, but nothing."

"I don't know. I have come to believe after a lifetime of seeing those who have passed that we are not all meant to talk to the dead. We are meant to stay in the land of the living, to be present to what is now. But to see the bigger picture, we need people who can see beyond the trivialities of this life. This gift has ruined my life here on earth in many ways, but it has liberated, taught, and enlightened others. It has brought peace." Sophia lifted his hand, kissed it and placed it back in his lap.

A sharp knock on the door startled them both. A face moved into the slot and Sophia cringed away, expecting to see Dr. Kaiser. Instead Alice's familiar brown eyes peered in. Alice, a nurse on the ward, known for her strict adherence to rules, clicked the door open.

"You're needed in Block B, Kent. Mr Hanson..." she trailed off eyeing Sophia wearily.

Though Alice did not appear to like Sophia, she offered her a grudging respect and kept her distance. Sophia had never imparted Alice guidance from the other side, she suspected that the stiff nurse knew her abilities and feared them.

"Thank you, Kent," Sophia told him, as he hastily stood, avoiding eye contact with Alice. "If the headaches get worse, I'll tell Dr. Kaiser."

SOPHIA SAT OUTSIDE beneath a high oak tree, resting her back against the rough bark. It was a warm spring day, and Kent had pulled strings to help her get outdoor privileges.

The winter had been long and icy with snow drifts that often covered the windows. The early darkening days that lasted late into the morning left everyone - patients and staff - with moods to match.

Sophia braided strands of yarn into a rope that would be taken from her when their outdoor reprieve ended. Despite her frustration at being in the hospital for years, every spring she marveled at the beauty of the grounds. The limestone buildings rose monolithic against the blue sky, but even their grandeur was dwarfed by the soaring trees.

Sometimes patients or orderlies wandered over to her and said hello. Others lingered nearby hopeful she might offer them some insight into a loved one they had lost.

She had become the asylum medium despite her best efforts to keep her sight hidden. For the first year in the hospital she'd done rather well at melting into the world unseen, unnoticed. But eventually the spirits grew more urgent in their whisperings. They pleaded with Sophia to remedy a misconception or comfort a bereaved family member left behind. How could she deny the living the tiniest glimmer of the person they'd lost? Especially now, when she too longed for a message from her beloved? From Jack?

A tear slipped from her eye and landed on the colored braid. She had not spoken his name aloud in years. She would wait for the perfect moment because when she finally called out to him, he would come to her.

Somehow through dimensions she could not fathom despite her gifts, he would arrive, but like all sightings of spirit he would be transitory, a momentary phantom. She would wait until she no longer stood encased by thick, white walls. She would stand in an open meadow of flowers, the kind they ran through as young lovers, their hands clasped as if they truly believed they would never have to let go. In that space, with her long hair flowing like silk in the wind, a dress billowing around her legs, she would reach out to him a final time.

"How are you today, Sophia?"

The voice startled her, and her hands froze on the braid.

Dr. Kaiser stood over her, his white jacket stiffly pressed. His white blue eyes studied her hands that stopped braiding and began to shake.

"Tisk, tisk, Sophia. You forgot our appointment today, didn't you? Kent shouldn't have let you out."

Like a caged animal, she thought.

She looked across the yard where Kent squatted next to another patient, Dorothy. Dorothy suffered from paranoia. She spoke often of the mafia coming to the hospital to kill her. She claimed they already killed her family. Dorothy was clutching at Kent's white shirt and Sophia knew the woman would soon go into a fit and have to be carried back to the ward.

"He can't help you, Sophia," Dr. Kaiser whispered, reaching out with his too-soft fingers and caressing her wrist before jerking the braid from her hand. He stood and tucked it into his pocket. "You could use this to hurt someone or worse, hurt yourself. I must put this in your file."

Sophia ignored the emotion bubbling in her chest and allowed her eyes to become unfocused. Go numb, she thought. As she had a hundred other times when Kaiser appeared.

"Come with me, please," he told her, stepping away and pretending to be a doctor. He called himself that, some patients and staff even believed it, but Sophia knew the truth. Doctor Kaiser's spirit was dark.

He had become a doctor - not to help those who ailed - but to use the power his title afforded him to experiment on and torture his patients.

Sophia shot a final longing glance at Kent and then stood, following Kaiser through the asylum doors. As the doors swung closed, the sunny spring day disappeared, and Sophia blinked into the eerie gloom of the hospital.

.

CHAPTER 16

eptember 1965
Jude

"CLAYTON, my love, I need your help." Jude swept into the office of the Wexford County Gazette and spun Clayton in his chair to face her.

"Whoa, watch it," he squeaked, nearly dropping his Styrofoam cup of coffee onto his pleated khakis. "Jude, you almost scalded me."

"We both know you only drink lukewarm coffee," Jude told him, taking the cup and sipping the gritty office coffee that tasted like worm dirt. "Ugh, how do you drink this?"

He took the cup back looking at it lovingly and gave her a wounded look.

"It's my life support, as you well know. Now stop insulting my coffee and explain yourself. I'm on a deadline."

Jude glanced around the office. Two other reporters sat at their scarred desks, the keys on their typewriters clacking. Neither of them paid her any attention.

"I have a few questions about an old murder case. It didn't happen here though."

"Getting into some true crime work?" Clayton joked.

"Not exactly. And it's personal, so I'd like you to ask on the down-low."

"Down-low?"

"Yes, without raising suspicion."

"Did you kill someone, Jude?" he cocked a bushy eyebrow and narrowed his eyes in mock suspicion.

"Yes. You - if you don't help me."

"Oh, come on, when have I ever told you, no?"

True enough. Jude probably leaned on Clayton a bit too much at times. He called her for all freelance photography that the Wexford County Gazette commissioned. It wasn't any secret he had a crush on her, and occasionally she exploited it. She also just liked him. Unlike many of the men in her life, Clayton always acted the gentleman. He had only asked her out one time and when she politely declined, he simply smiled and said, "I had to try."

"Her name was Rosemary Bell, and someone killed her in 1935 in Mason - a little town downstate. She was thirteen."

Clayton jotted the information down on his notepad.

"Long time ago. I'm sure I can get access to newspapers in the area, but I doubt the same reporters will be around, assuming they even had reporters. This was a small town?"

"Yeah, from what I know, which isn't much. I'm actually hoping for more information about the girl accused of the crime. Sophia Gray."

"A girl accused? A little girl?"

"Yes. She was also thirteen."

"Want to tell me why you're interested in this case?" Clayton asked, removing his glasses and rubbing them on his shirt. He slid them back onto his face and blinked rapidly. "Guess it's in my eye." He took them off again and rubbed his left eye.

Jude considered him. She had no reason not to tell him but found the words wouldn't come.

"Not today. But call me when you get some information and I'll tell you everything."

His eyes lit up.

"Over dinner?"

She frowned and slid off his desk.

"Over coffee. I'll buy you a cup that won't burn a hole in your intestines."

Hattie

A POUNDING on Hattie's door made her jump and nearly drop the porcelain cup of tea in her hand. A splash of peppermint tea scalded her wrist, and she cried out. She placed the cup back on her kitchen counter, grateful she had not dropped it. It was one of her mama's cups. Not part of a set, her mama wasn't the kind of woman who liked things to match.

"We're all one of a kind," she used to say. "Every pebble of sand, every leaf on the tree has its own distinct self. Never forget how special every breath is, Hattie."

It was funny what Hattie remembered of her mama. Fleeting moments, bits of wisdom, the light spinning through her golden hair. Sometimes Hattie sat for hours, staring out the window, trying to conjure those memories back to life.

She opened the door to find Jude waiting impatiently on her little porch.

"What took you so long? I almost peed my pants!" Jude raced passed her.

Hattie heard the rush of pee through the open bathroom door.

"Don't you want some privacy?" Hattie asked Jude who sat on the toilet with an expression of relief, her skirt bunched around her waist.

"If I can't pee in front you, my little sister, the world really has gone crazy."

Hattie smiled. Honestly, she liked when Jude left the door open to pee. Though sisters, the years between their births had often caused a rift of sorts, as if the threads of family grew further apart over time.

"I needed that," Jude told her. She walked to the kitchen table where she had discarded her purse and a paper sack. "Breakfast," she announced.

Jude pulled out a small box of donuts and a glass container of apple cider.

"My favorite," Hattie stammered, hardly believing her eyes.

As children, their daddy had a Sunday ritual of buying donuts and cider or milk, and taking the kids fishing so mama could sleep in. After his death, Gram Ruth insisted that donuts were trashy food full of sugar. Jude, focused on staying fit, also scoffed at anything chocolate covered. Hattie hadn't eaten a donut in years.

"Don't cry," Jude growled, opening the box and handing Hattie a cherry donut with chocolate frosting. She took a glazed for herself. "I'm sorry about the other night. I wasn't mad at you."

Hattie took the donut and stared at it. Cherry with chocolate, her absolute favorite. A tear rolled down her cheek. She sat in one of the little wooden chairs next to Jude.

"Oh Hattie, what am I going to do with you?" Jude asked, handing Hattie a paper napkin. "Take a bite. A good blast of chocolate will have you speeding toward reality in no time."

Hattie ate part of the donut and savored the sweet confection. She loved sugar. In her mind, or maybe her heart, a thousand memories contained the gossamer drifts of sugary happiness: pancakes with her parents and Jude and Peter - cupcakes on her birthday. The dark chocolate torte that her daddy made Mama for their twenty year wedding anniversary - a laughing Peter had said it looked like one of Hattie's mud pies.

Jude took a sleeve of paper cups from her bag and poured them each a glass of cider. She slipped a copper flask from a garter on her thigh and added a shot of whiskey to her own. She held the flask out to Hattie and cocked an eyebrow, but Hattie shook her head no. Alcohol made her dizzy and the few times she had imbibed, she fell into a deep sleep shortly after drinking.

"So, you're not mad at me anymore?" Hattie asked, taking a sip of her cider.

"No. I was never mad at you. I mean, don't get me wrong, a late night barn raid only to find a bunch of moth-eaten clothes was not exactly my idea of a good time, but I knew it wasn't your fault. I get angry. You know how I am."

Hattie nodded. Jude made her opinion known, yelled, a time or two she even threw things. Hattie remembered Gram Ruth once running from the kitchen in shock when Jude threw a serving ladle at her.

"I have other stuff on my mind too," Jude added. "And seeing that article about Mom. I wanted to hurt someone. I still do, but I'm trying to play it cool, at least for now."

"You want to hurt Gram Ruth?"

"She's at the top of my list, but let's not forget all the scumbags who put Mom away. I mean, seriously? Our mother would not crush an ant. Remember? She used to let them crawl onto her hand so she could release them outside."

Hattie smiled and took another bite. She remembered and understood. Hattie killed nothing. If the monks could do it, so could she.

"I have a friend at the newspaper looking into the murder."

"Do you think Mama is still alive?" Hattie asked, avoiding Jude's eyes.

Jude sipped her cider, her face thoughtful.

"Because I do," Hattie added quickly. "I feel her. I never thought about it before. I always assumed she was dead, but now, when I think about her, I feel her."

Jude pursed her lips, but gave a slight nod.

"Not that I'm buying into your moony visions, but maybe. There's something," she spoke slowly as if trying to put her finger on a feeling that raced into the shadows every time she tried to look at it. "I don't know if it means she's alive and if she is," -she balled her fists on the table and a look of fresh bitterness turned her face dark- "I don't know what I'll do."

Hattie stood and retrieved her tea. She traced her fingers on the delicate yellow flowers that decorated the cup.

"I just want her back," Hattie said. "Nothing else matters. I want her back."

Jude

THEY ARRIVED at the hospital after dusk. The immense grounds rolled with fragrant green grass. Soaring oaks and maples stood in rows along a small stream. The Northern Michigan Asylum rose, monolithic, out of the surrounding nature. Massive and sprawling, the buildings of white brick towered over the long paved drive. Lights blazed in the windows casting long menacing shadows across the lawn.

"It's gigantic," Hattie whispered, staring in awe at the beautiful, and eerie, property.

"It's a prison," Jude said. She experienced a sudden, and strange, desire to rub a lucky rabbit's foot or sign the cross. Squashing the sensation, she hit the gas and her little car shot forward along the winding road that led to the asylum.

"Let's go over the plan one more time," Jude told Hattie who continued to stare out the window with huge glassy eyes. "Hey," she snapped her fingers and Hattie turned, blinking. Jude fought the urge to criticize her.

"We are students at Michigan State, studying psychotherapy. We are here, on our professor's orders, to interview several patients. He already cleared it with Dr. Staten."

"Who's Dr. Staten?" Hattie asked.

"I got his name from the staff directory. I made two patient names up, the third is Mom. You," Jude pointed at Hattie, "hang back and let me do the talking. If we run into an issue, you create a diversion."

"A diversion," Hattie agreed, her eyes already wandering back toward the window.

"Hattie, I need you to come back to earth for this okay? I need you with me."

Hattie blinked and returned her gaze to Jude, checking back in.

"Yes, of course. I'm sorry. It's just so…"

"I know," Jude acknowledged. "It's freaky, but this is about Mom. If we're going to get her back, now is our moment."

Hattie's eyes widened in what Jude figured was hope and a bit of desperation.

Jude and Peter had both struggled to accept the death of their mother, but Hattie took it far harder. She abandoned the living world in lieu of her fantasy realities. Even their father, during the few weeks he lived after their mother died, could not bring Hattie out of the oblivion she vanished into.

The asylum was a maze of buildings. Jude finally found a visitor's entrance and pushed the door open. An older woman clad in a white smock sat at a small wooden desk. She looked up sharply when they entered.

"Visiting hours are on Sunday only," she declared.

"Hi," Jude said brightly. "I'm so sorry to bother you. We're not visitors, actually. We're students at Michigan State University. Professor Humboldt sent us here to interview several patients for a research project. He said he cleared it with Dr. Staten."

The woman frowned and opened a binder on her desk.

"Dr. Staten?" she asked gazing suspiciously at what Jude thought was a calendar. "I have no record of that here. Such activities must have an authorized signature with explicit instructions. I see none of those things."

Jude grimaced and tried to appear confused.

"Really? Can you check again? We drove almost four hours to be here." She pulled a sheet of paper from her purse. "My note from the Professor says right here September eighteenth at six pm. I can't believe he'd get it wrong. I mean, he's spent months planning this. I'm not sure when we'd even be able to come back."

She waited, fingers crossed in her mind. Behind her she heard Hattie walking around the room, likely touching the walls for some energetic vibe from their mother. Jude nearly turned and told her to stop pacing.

The woman sighed and tapped her pencil on the calendar.

"Let me see the names of your patients. I can't promise anything. If they're in treatment, they won't be available."

Jude wanted to jump in the air and click her heels.

"Thank you. We appreciate it," she said instead. She handed the woman her note.

The woman read the first two names, brow wrinkled, but on the third, she stopped cold.

"Sophia Gray is no longer a patient here and I do not recognize the other names on your list. Sorry girls." She handed the page back, but neither Jude nor Hattie had missed the expression on the woman's face.

"Was she discharged?" Jude asked.

The woman did not look up from the appointment book on her desk.

"I'm not at liberty to say. Patient information is confidential."

"Something bad happened to her," Hattie squeaked, and now the woman did look up eyeing Jude and Hattie suspiciously. "Which professor sent you?"

Jude considered standing her ground, and then decided against it.

"Professor Humboldt, but that's fine. We'll come back with an updated list. He must have made a mistake."

Jude turned, grabbing Hattie's arm, and pulled her out the door.

CHAPTER 17

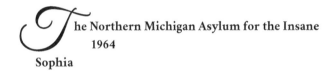

he Northern Michigan Asylum for the Insane
1964
Sophia

DAYS PASSED IN SOLITARY CONFINEMENT. Sedated, but conscious, Kaiser or his primary nurse Alice would unstrap Sophia, wash her, change her bed clothes and return her to confinement. At some point she stopped crying. Her body felt hollow and dry. Even her brain hung suspended in her skull like a wrung out sponge. Her head ached constantly.

Kaiser arrived with new treatments. He dripped water into her eyes, taped open. He tickled her. He touched her breasts and between her legs. He encouraged her to climax. He said orgasm was another pathway to release evil spirits. He administered medication that caused her to see whirling patterns of light and huge, hideous faces. He watched her for hours, often in the dark so she never knew if she was alone.

After days or maybe weeks, Alice arrived with a gurney to return her to her room. She undid her straps and helped Sophia to sit up. Sophia tried to stand, but her weakened legs folded beneath her and she sunk to the floor. In Kaiser's presence, Alice treated Sophia with disgust. Alone with her, she moved carefully, as if afraid.

She pushed her hands beneath Sophia's armpits and hauled her up, shoving her awkwardly onto the gurney. Sophia curled into the fetal position and shoved her fingers into her mouth.

Her body hurt everywhere. The skin around her lips had dried and then cracked and bled. Her hands and feet tingled with a thousand pin pricks as the blood, cut off by the restraints, fought back into her limbs. Her head, raw where Kaiser had yanked her hair, throbbed with greater intensity as they moved into the hallway beneath fluorescent lights. She closed her eyes and tried to go somewhere else in her mind.

"Where has she been?" the wheels of her stretcher halted at the sound of Kent's voice.

"In solitary. Violent thoughts. Dr. Kaiser wanted to ensure she could not harm herself or others."

Kent did not speak, but Sophia heard the sharp intake of his breath.

"She's been in solitary for eight days!"

"I suggest you take it up with Dr. Kaiser if you have an issue with his therapeutic recommendations."

Sophia heard Kent scoff and the slap of his tennis shoes as he stomped away.

She opened her eyes and watched his retreating form, wanting to call him back.

SOPHIA WOKE DROWSY AND NAUSEOUS. She tried to move her arms and then her legs, but leather straps held her pinned to the bed. They had placed something rubbery in her mouth to keep her from biting her tongue, or perhaps from biting her doctor. The only light emanated from a single bulb so bright it pierced through her eyes and reverberated in her brain.

Closing her eyes, Sophia heard the voice of Dr. Kaiser.

"No, a lobotomy is the last thing we want here," he argued. "At least until we've thoroughly researched her claims."

"Her claims?" A woman's voice asked. It sounded familiar. "You sound as if there could be some validity to her stories."

"Of course not," Kaiser snapped. "It's nonsense, the devil's work. But once the lobotomy is performed, there's no reversal."

"But if, as you say, the devil is at work in your patient, shouldn't you take steps to close the gateway? It is in her best interests. Just last week Dr. Lewis performed a lobotomy on patient eight-seven-four."

"The boy who claimed to be channeling his dead grandmother?" Kaiser asked.

"Yes. And since that time he's been perfectly normal. No midnight writing sessions, no paranoia. It's practically a miracle," she said.

"Except miracles are exactly what we refute, aren't they, Doctor? We live in the world of science, not miracles," Kaiser hissed.

"Yes, of course," the woman sounded flabbergasted.

Sophia cracked her eyes and tried to get her bearings. She'd undergone electro-shock therapy. She'd had it enough times to know the after-effects. Her head ached, and waves of nausea rolled through her. Restrained, she could not turn to throw up. She focused on calming the dizziness by staring hard at a tiny crack in the ceiling overhead.

The woman moved to Sophia's bedside. Her hands were cold and clammy as they grasped Sophia's face. She used her thumb to press one of Sophia's eyelids high, leaning close to her face. Sophia recognized her as a doctor from another floor in the asylum.

"Perhaps another treatment altogether. Consider the lobotomy, Dr. Kaiser. We don't want to release these sick minds back into the world. If she's still speaking of spirits, then she's far from cured."

"Mmmhmmm," Kaiser murmured. His fingers moved toward Sophia's face and his forearm brush against her breast. She wanted to roll away from him but couldn't move.

The woman trained her beady brown eyes on Sophia, her thin lips pursed as if she studied an especially nasty rat. Sophia's cheeks flushed, and she experienced an uncharacteristic shame beneath the woman's gaze. She clenched her eyes shut and her insides rolled. Her mouth opened a spew of vomit rose and splattered both doctors' coats.

"Ugh." The woman backed away, pulling her white coat off and dropping it on the floor.

Dr. Kaiser also removed his coat, watching Sophia through angry, hard slits of blue.

The stink of her vomit filled her nostrils. She looked at Dr. Kaiser, her eyes pleading and reluctantly he unlatched the leather straps around her head. She was not free, but able to turn her head to the side.

"You'd best call Alice to come clean this up. I'm expected in therapy in a half hour," the woman doctor said stalking from the room. Her rubber-soled shoes slapped on the cement floor.

Alone, Kaiser took a wet washcloth from a basin by the bed and wiped Sophia's face. His eyes moved up and down her body. The cool washcloth was a relief, but his touch made her recoil.

"How are you today, Doctor?" a man asked from the doorway and Sophia saw another doctor, his white coat pristine, filling the doorway.

"I'm well, Dr. Knight. And you?"

"Fine, fine. Though I saw the insufferable Dr. Moore leaving your room. More wisdom to impart?"

Kaiser did not turn, but cocked his head to the side, and roughly wiped the cloth over Sophia's cheek, smearing the vomit more than cleaning it.

"The Lobotomy Queen wanted to recommend I render this patient as brain-dead as all of hers."

"Surprise, surprise," muttered Knight. "This is the patient who speaks with the dead?"

Knight leaned toward her, unfazed by the smell, and peered into her face studying first one eye and then the other.

"Yes, patient seven-twenty-two, Sophia Gray," Kaiser replied.

"We're meeting on the 10th this month. Can Sophia be present? The other doctors don't have a suitable patient for the Umbra Brotherhood?" The man continued, reaching a hand out to wave it in front of Sophia's face as if her eyes weren't open wide watching him.

"I prefer if you don't speak that name here," Kaiser uttered, casting a dark look at the man. "I had hoped to be further in her treatment when I presented her," he continued dropping the soiled rag on the floor. "She's not as foggy as I would like after the electro-shock. I wonder if a higher dose is in order." He seemed to be talking more to himself. "Yes, let the others know. I'm willing to present her."

CHAPTER 18

eptember 1965
Jude

SOMETHING SNAKED from the darkness and grabbed Jude's sleeve.

"Ahhh...!" She screamed and jumped back scrambling in her bag for a weapon.

"Sshhh-" A woman's voice snapped.

The woman stepped from the trees. She wore a plain gray dress and her hair was tied in a severe-looking bun at the base of her neck.

"You want em' comin' out here?" she hissed, gesturing at the asylum and stepping closer to Jude.

Jude saw the woman missed several of her teeth. Her eyes darted toward the asylum.

"You knew our mama?" Hattie asked, stepping between Jude and the woman.

Jude stifled an urge to push her baby sister behind her.

The woman nodded.

"Lucy," she said pointing at herself. "And you're the daughters. You look just like her," she said to Hattie.

"Do you know where she is?" Hattie asked.

The woman nodded and pursed her lips.

"Meet me at Grady's Diner."

"In town?" Jude asked, incredulous. "Don't you have to...?" she gestured to the hospital door.

The woman let out a shrill cackle and slapped her thigh.

"I'm not a patient! I used to clean in there." She laughed again. "They don't like me hanging around, but I have a right to be here. They kept my supplies," she growled, glaring at the lit windows on the second floor. "And I'll get 'em back, too. Meet me in fifteen minutes?"

"Yes, yes," Hattie gushed grabbing Jude's sleeve as if this woman might have their mother sitting at home in her parlor.

"Sure," Jude grumbled. She wanted to talk to the woman but preferred to do it alone. She worried about Hattie's reaction if they received bad news about their mother's fate.

LUCY ORDERED a cup of black coffee and sipped it, nervously drumming her fingers on the white porcelain cup. Jude couldn't shake the feeling she'd been a patient at that hospital. The woman's paranoia was palpable.

Hattie asked the waitress for a cup of ice tea with packets of sugar, and Jude opted for a coffee to which she added a dash of whiskey. When Lucy saw the flask, she tilted her cup and Jude added a shot to hers.

"You're the older girl," Lucy said, wagging a finger back and forth. "Your mama said you were a willful thing, wild. I can see it."

Jude didn't respond. She wasn't interested in this woman's two minutes analysis of her character.

"How did you know her?" Jude asked.

"I told ya. I cleaned in there for twenty years. Till they hired some ferners undercuttin' the good local people."

"Ferners?" Hattie asked.

"Foreigners," Jude told her, trying not to roll her eyes.

"Anyway, about our mom..." she said taking a drink of her coffee and wishing she'd just gone straight for the flask.

Hattie was practically bouncing up and down in the seat beside her. The fluorescent lights seemed to burrow holes in Jude's skull, and the man at the counter's ears reminded her of Damien. Damien who still hadn't called. Damien's whose pictures sat in a pile on Jude's kitchen table and when she got home, she had half a mind to burn the lot.

"Sophia was a gem," Lucy told them, smiling her toothless smile.

"Was?" Hattie asked, her blue eyes growing wide.

"Is," Lucy corrected. "It's only, well I haven't seen her in a while, but I'm sure she's livin'. She only escaped nine, ten days ago."

"Escaped?" Jude asked, the hairs on her neck prickled.

Lucy nodded, a gleam in her eye.

"An orderly helped her. And they killed him for it."

Jude held up a hand before Hattie started in with ten thousand questions.

"Tell me something about our mom?" Jude said.

"Don't believe me? I'm not surprised. Nobody else did, either."

"I believe you," Hattie breathed, reaching for the woman's hands across the table.

Hattie held tight to the woman's worn hands as if she might magically turn into their mother.

"You are a spitting image of your mama," she told her, offering another gap-toothed smile. "She wore a necklace." Lucy tapped on her chest. "They took it away when they admitted her, but I snuck it to her a few times. Her own mama gave it to her."

Jude knew the necklace well, a heart shaped gold locket engraved with a rose. Her mother never opened the locket. Several times she had told Jude she kept a flower petal from her childhood home in the locket and feared if she opened it the dried bits would disappear forever.

"What did it look like?" Jude asked, not ready to trust the woman before them.

"It was gold, a little heart locket. A rose or some other flower was carved into the surface though I think your mama had rubbed on that necklace so much the image was about gone."

Jude sighed, unable to deny the woman's description.

"Satisfied?" she asked, narrowing her eyes at Jude.

Jude nodded, drinking her coffee and regarding the woman thoughtfully.

She realized she'd make a terrible reporter. She was too suspicious of people. With good reason considering again that Damien had not called. And why did she care? Perhaps that was the most frustrating realization of all - that he had hurt her.

"Fuck him," she grumbled, and Lucy widened her eyes in surprise. Hattie spurted tea onto the table.

"Jude!" she exclaimed.

"Sorry, my thoughts carried me away," she apologized. "Please, tell us what happened to our mom."

Lucy leaned back and rested her hands on the table, satisfied.

"Dr. Kaiser is what happened to your mother. A mean, sick man with a fascination for certain kinds of patients."

"He's a doctor at the asylum?"

Lucy nodded.

"He took a special interest in your mom, which isn't good. He hurt her, tortured her. Your mama wasn't kooky. Some of em' in there are, that's to be sure, but not your mama. She's special. You know what she told me? She told me my firstborn, a still-born mind you, visits me all the time."

Jude pursed her lips. Not another ghost story.

"How could she have contact with a baby that never learned to talk?" Jude asked, reverting to her earlier skepticism.

Lucy shook her head sadly.

"I feel sorry for you. You've got no faith. Not even in your own mama."

Jude glowered at her and fought the urge to stand up and leave the diner. How dare the woman pass judgment on her for not believing in such silly nonsense?

"She told me his name, Phillip. How could she know that? I never told another soul. I chose the name Phillip and then he was born dead and I kept the name a secret, I couldn't bear to share it with anyone in the whole world. Not even my husband. Your mama knew his name. He lives. He didn't get to live as my baby, but he lives."

Jude dropped her hands in her lap and focused on channelling her frustration into her fists. She squeezed them together as hard as she could.

"I feel him," Hattie whispered, leaning over the table. "Phillip. He was born early. Seven weeks premature."

Lucy looked at her in surprise, her mouth falling open.

"You have it too? The gift?"

Hattie nodded, her eyes filling with tears.

"Oh Jesus Christ!" Jude exclaimed. "Listen if you guys want to talk mumbo jumbo you can do it after we get the facts. Where is our mom?"

Lucy sighed and squeezed Hattie's hands as if apologizing for Jude's outburst, which only made Jude angrier.

She reminded herself again not to take Hattie when investigating their mother's whereabouts. She only complicated things.

"Kent helped her escape. He was an orderly at the asylum. He took extra care of your mama, looked out for her. The night she disappeared, he wound up dead."

A horrible pressure seemed to invade Jude's skull, and she closed her eyes, pressing her fingers hard into her temples.

"An orderly died and my mom disappeared. What makes you think she escaped? Maybe she died too?"

Lucy shook her head. "Everyone was whispering about it. A few of the patients saw Kent escort your mother out of Hall Five in the middle of the night. He returned a short while later alone. The next morning another orderly found him hanged in Sophia's bedroom."

Hattie let out a strangled gasp and clutched her throat.

Jude ignored her.

"Did he kill himself? Or do they think someone killed him?"

"They told the patients it was an accident. Course Lord knows how somebody can strangle their own selves with a bed sheet while making up a bed. They glossed it over real nice. Not to mention the orderlies don't make the beds."

"What happened to Mama?" Hattie asked, pulling on her hair.

"Well," Lucy leaned in conspiratorially. "One of the orderlies was having a smoke outside and saw a woman in men's clothes with long blond hair running through the woods on the morning your mama disappeared. She got into a little red car and drove off. Another orderly said the car belonged to Barbie, Kent's girlfriend who lives over in Buckley."

"Has anyone spoken with Barbie?" Jude asked.

Lucy shrugged.

"Don't know. They released me from my position a few days after it all went down. I'm out of the loop now."

Jude took a deep breath, trying not to allow hope to overwhelm her. Until that moment, she had expected to find out her mother had died in the asylum. When Lucy began her story, she thought perhaps it would all be a big misunderstanding, their mother had died ten years ago and the last few days had been a fantasy.

"How can we find her?" Jude asked, wrapping her hands around her cup to steady them.

Hattie was fidgeting beside her, shifting back and forth in her seat, braiding her fingers again and again through her hair.

"She's alive," Hattie murmured. "I knew she was. I knew..."

Lucy beamed.

"She is."

"Why didn't she ever write to us?" Jude asked. "How could she have been alive for ten years and we never heard anything from her?"

Lucy frowned.

"I don't know nothin' about that," Lucy admitted. "But the nurses opened and read all the mail. A downright injustice to some of the patients. Your ma talked about you kids to me and a select few others, but no one ever visited. Odd, it was odd. Why didn't you ever visit?"

"We thought she was dead," Hattie blurted before Jude could cut her off.

Lucy frowned, studying each of their faces.

"Why in heaven would you think that?"

Jude sighed, finishing her coffee.

"It's a long story and we have to get going. Can you help us find Kent's girlfriend?"

"Name of Barbie or Barbara, real curly black hair, lives in Buckley. I can't give you no more than that but ask around. You'll find her."

After Jude paid, they left Lucy hovering at the counter asking the waitress for more coffee.

Hattie practically skipped to the car but grew quiet once inside.

"You okay?" Jude asked.

Hattie turned and offered a small smile.

"I'm worried about Mama. If someone killed that Kent man, maybe they found out where Mama went and...."

Jude feared the same thing but had not intended to say it out loud to her sensitive sister.

It was going on ten at night - too late to start picking around Buckley looking for Barbie. They'd have to wait.

"Maybe I should talk to Gram Ruth," Hattie started.

Jude squeezed the wheel and bit back the stream of profanity that bubbled forth every time she thought of their grandmother. It had become increasingly clear that the woman had participated in faking their mother's death and hiding her whereabouts in an asylum.

"Something went wrong," Jude muttered.

"With Mama? You think she's hurt?" Hattie asked, anxious.

"No, not now, back then, ten years ago. I remember thinking Dad was acting funny. He wasn't in mourning. I was too wrapped up in my own feelings to realize it, but he was busy. He was packing stuff. I walked in once when he was packing up the house, humming a song he and mom used to dance to. I was crying, and he gave me a hug. He said something too, and I forgot it all these years. He said, "It will all be better very soon." I figured he meant grief fades with time, but now I know... that's not what he meant. They had a plan. He and mom had a plan."

"But what plan could include Mama in a mental institution. Daddy would never-"

Jude nodded. "I know. He would have taken us and run before he let that happen. He would have done something crazy like..."

"Fake her death," Hattie finished.

CHAPTER 19

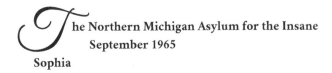he Northern Michigan Asylum for the Insane
September 1965
Sophia

BLINDFOLDED, her arms stuck to her sides by a tightly wound sheet, Sophia walked through the forest. Twigs snapped under her feet and the freshly fallen leaves of early autumn crunched and swished around her bare ankles.

Alice had covered her face, but the gap beneath her right eye showed a sliver of their path. They moved in and out of trees, onto a grassy hill matted from Kaiser who stomped ahead. Night had come, and the half-moon offered snatches of light when the clouds parted.

Despite the wool coat she wore over her nightdress, Sophia shivered - as much from the crisp air as the fear that began with a trembling deep in her belly and radiated out to her fingers and toes.

Was Dr. Kaiser going to killer her? Or had he discovered some new experiment that he must perform in the darkness of the forest?

"This part is steep, Alice," Kaiser said quietly. "Guide her."

Alice's strong hands grasped Sophia on either side, pinching her arms into her ribs.

"Sophia..."

She heard her name whispered across the forest, and she bucked forward, eyes widening.

"Ouch!" Alice bellowed as Sophia stepped on her foot.

Sophia strained to hear the voice, but Kaiser grabbed her roughly and dragged her down a steep embankment.

Alice huffed behind them as she hurried to keep up.

"What is this place?" Alice murmured, a tremor in her voice. The hardened nurse was not one to show fear, or ask questions, and Kaiser only shushed her.

Sophia gazed at a nest of huge trees twisting together. They seemed to grow across the ground rather than into the sky.

She thought of her mother. When Sophia had nightmares as a girl her mother told her the fear lived in her mind, it would only get bigger if she let it. For years Sophia had clung to those words, to the power within her to dispel the monsters lurking, but now the fear gripped her and held her with an untouchable force. She shook violently in Kaiser's hands.

The trees no longer looked like trees, but huge bone-white skeletons clawing at the ground. They were patients who had died in the asylum, painful violent, unjust deaths. They were eternally trapped there raking at the earth for escape.

"Alice, help me here," Kaiser growled practically dragging Sophia as she dug her feet into the dirt floor.

Sophia's heart thudded in her chest and cold sweat poured down her face. The blindfold had mostly slipped away, but Sophia saw only black shadows darting in and out of the skeletal trees. They slithered and groaned, pain and rage bubbling up and out of their long dead mouths.

"No... no... no," Sophia muttered shaking her head, trying to close her eyes but unable to jerk her gaze from the gathering phantoms.

"In here," Kaiser barked, shoving Sophia hard from behind.

She stumbled forward, suddenly out of the forest, into a damp tunnel lit with kerosene torches. The firelight flickered and Sophia closed her eyes against the shadows cast by the flame.

"What on earth was that about?" Alice grumbled, again placing her hands on Sophia and urging her forward. Sophia felt the trembling in Alice's hands and knew she too had sensed something amiss in that odd hollow of trees.

They followed Kaiser down a winding tunnel similar to the transport tunnels beneath the asylum. Instead of arriving at a door, the tunnel opened into a large circular room with rows of stone benches surrounding a raised wooden platform. On the platform stood a hospital bed made up with a clean white sheet. The objects next to the bed were unfamiliar to Sophia - a leather mask that looked like a dog muzzle and a metal tray of sharp instruments.

"No one is here?" Alice asked. Her hands had stopped shaking, but her eyes darted suspiciously around the room.

"I am presenting this evening," Kaiser told her curtly. He stepped close to Sophia, and she felt a prick in her neck. He slipped the syringe into the pocket of his coat. "Unwrap the patient and place her on the bed. There are straps to secure her."

Kaiser opened a leather satchel and walked along the wooden benches placing a sheet of paper every few feet.

Sophia wanted to resist Alice or beg for answers, but her eyelids drooped and her legs collapsed beneath her as the nurse guided her onto the platform. She slumped onto the bed unable to roll sideways as Alice unwound the sheet from her torso. Her arms burned with a thousand pinpricks when they were freed, and Sophia used the last of her energy to wiggle her fingers welcoming blood flow back to the tingling tips.

She stared at the slimy bricks lining the ceiling. The chilled room grew ice cold, and she shivered. Her lips lay heavy on her face and her tongue rested like an anchor on the floor of her mouth.

"Sophia..." again that whisper, but different this time. It sounded like a hundred voices, hurt, angry, vengeful.

A face flashed close to her own - pale and gaunt in the firelight. The woman had died young. Stringy black hair clung to the mottled skin of her scalp, and tiny red spiderwebs filled the whites of her eyes. A single spot of blood seeped from the corner of her lips, and her mouth seemed to fold in as if someone had removed her teeth. The woman reached for her, grabbed Sophia's neck and Sophia perceived an instant of the woman's terror, years before when she had died in that same room. The vision vanished, and Sophia's eyelids grew heavier, impossibly heavy.

She welcomed the darkness.

WHEN SOPHIA WOKE, voices filled the room. She blinked through gritty eyes into blinding lights. They had assembled more lamps around the bed. Dr. Kaiser stood near her head. Sophia turned and looked for the men she heard speaking, but they had moved the kerosene lamps to the platform. They lay in shadow and she in light.

Her thoughts swam in a pond of sludge. They traveled slowly, lethargically and barely made it to consciousness before slipping back beneath the surface. She tried to remember where she was, how she'd gotten there, but could not reach deep enough into that dank water to retrieve the memory.

Dr. Kaiser held up a hand and the group of men fell silent.

"This evening I am presenting Patient Number seven-twenty-two, Sophia Gray. I've had her in my care for nine years and eight months."

Sophia listened to murmurs among the men. The word medium drifted to her.

"Many of you have requested that I bring her to our meetings over the years and I admit, I've been reluctant. Her mind is strong and has often been resistant to my efforts to wipe her memories after our more creative experiments. However, last month, Dr. Fritz wrote me about his experiments with LSD."

The group of men whispered amongst themselves at this declaration.

"Since we are always in service to studying that which regular society refuses to look upon, I felt it was my duty to succumb at last and bring Ms. Gray so our collective minds might determine with whom she is communicating."

Another man stepped onto the platform. He was short and thin with beady green eyes and a speckling of hair over his upper lip. He floated in his over-sized doctor's coat - the head of a man stuffed onto the body of a small boy. She turned her head and noticed Alice hovering just beyond the platform - her mouth set in a grim line.

The man rested his small boy's hands on the table beside her. Sophia had no use of her arms and legs, strapped to the table, she turned her head away, but Alice stepped up and clamped her strong hands on either side of Sophia's skull. Kaiser forced open her mouth.

He leaned close.

"If you bite me, I'll cut out your tongue and claim you chewed it

131

off," Kaiser hissed, staring hard into her eyes. She blinked, refusing to nod, but knowing better than to bite him.

He slipped something into her mouth. She tasted nothing. No pill dissolved on her tongue.

She closed her eyes and tried not to imagine what he had given her. The voices continued to murmur, the men talking of other things. After a short while their voices transformed into a wave of sound floating up, washing over her, and slipping out to sea. When she opened her eyes, the ceiling yawned into a chasm of shadows. The shadows darted and swam, took shape and vanished. Faces glared at her from the disintegrating forms, angry faces, sad, anguish-filled. Some of them laughed, high insane cackles while others screamed as if someone had pressed a hot poker into their flesh.

Sophia blinked and shook her head from side to side.

"No, no, no, no," she murmured pulling at her restraints, needing to clamp her hands over her ears and silence the cries of the dead. The voices of the men had all but faded. She had forgotten them until Dr. Kaiser loomed above her huge, as tall as the ceiling, with those pale blue eyes which seemed to stretch into infinity. She followed his eyes down and down past the flesh of his body into the blackness of his soul, a soul of torment and terror.

"What do you see, Sophia? Tell us," he whispered, licking his lips, his eyes growing large and small in the sallow skin of his face.

A woman appeared behind him, the skin hanging slack from her skeleton. Her jowls hung, and she chomped rotted teeth at Sophia as she tried to claw at the doctor's back.

"Lilian Hyde," Sophia cried out when the woman's name streamed through her mind. "Murdered by her doctor."

Sophia watched Lillian move away from Kaiser into the crowd of men. Sophia could see the doctors now, they glimmered and changed shape, shrunk tiny and grew tall. Their faces were like wax candles dripping to the floor. Lillian, dead now a decade at least, stopped behind a short doctor with a pointed black mustache and a bowler hat perched on his head. His eyes narrowed toward Sophia. His body trembled, an aura of black surrounded him, and Sophia smelled the sweat of his fear fanning out.

"You!" Sophia hissed at the man, looking into his eyes. "Paul Strine, son of Jack and Carol Stine, husband of the deceased Helena Strine, father of one aborted child, doctor of psychiatry at the Eastern Michigan Asylum for the Insane. You strangled her," Sophia gasped, trying to catch the words as they floated in light waves across her vision, she watched them, heard them, knew them. "You strangled her because she threatened to tell. Her husband was on to you, Paul. Lillian told him about your sick experiments."

Paul stood, and Lillian's corpse clawed and rolled at him. She moved through him and around him, shrieking, wild, a demon more than a spirit, but only Sophia had power in this room, the dead were only wisps of energy drifting by.

"Lies," he growled, pointing at Sophia with a shaky hand, so shaky it weaved and bobbed.

The man beside Paul, touched his coat and Paul jumped in the air.

"Be still, man," the other doctor chided. "You're making a spectacle of yourself."

Paul dropped his hand, he looked around the room as if remembering where he was. These men were not the law, they were his counterparts, they too experimented, murdered their patients in their quest for what-? Sophia saw images and words jumbled as she put the question into the void of spirits.

"Power, control, to prove that death is the end, to prove life after death, for the sake of science, to see my child again, to rule the world...." The men's motivations poured over her, and she muttered them out loud. The spherical room sent her words echoing and reverberating. Some men listened, others still watched Paul, and it was not an accusation in their eyes, but fear - fear she would call out the blood on their hands.

Kaiser circled her like a lion toying with his prey, his hands clasped and unclasped, his eyes gleaming with ferocity. His body appeared to grow huge and black filling the entire space. Another figure stepped near him, a young man with a red beard and sad blue eyes. He did not look decayed as the last spirit had. The word *fresh* rose to Sophia's mind.

"Fresh," she whispered. "Andrew Rogan..."

Immediately another doctor in the crowd seemed to shrink away from the name.

"Age seventeen, Andrew saw things, the future. You," she spat the word and looked at the cowering doctor who likely stood well over six feet tall, his square face red and blotchy in the firelight. "You killed him with insulin, more and more and more. How much can he take? Will he still see what's to come? No, no. Just this morning," Sophia continued. "Just this morning Dr. Edward Coleman gave one final injection."

"Enough," the man, Edward Coleman, announced, standing and yes he was tall, so very tall, and his patient, his dead patient only stood looking at him, past him, through him with those sad blue eyes. "I too am curious about this patient's visions and clearly she... knows things. But I suggest a more controlled therapy."

"This is a break-through," another doctor chimed in. "She's speaking names. She's communing with the other side!"

"I agree," Kaiser said, putting a hand on Sophia that made her convulse. His skin against hers felt like a thousand pricks from a needle. Her eyes rolled back, and she realized the more she spoke the longer it would go on. That was why they'd brought her here, like a circus monkey she'd performed and now they wanted more.

She pushed her teeth together and clenched her eyes shut and silently begged for the dead to depart.

"How long does the LSD last?"

Sophia had been listening to the voices for hours, or perhaps lifetimes, time ceased to make sense. She had not opened her eyes and remained still, traveling the corridors of her mind as the drug carried her into dimensions of thought previously unexplored.

"Hours, anywhere from four to twenty-four, according to Dr. Fritz," Kaiser said.

Sophia sensed them standing over her, the energies of their bodies rumbling like dark cold waves. She shivered, and a burst of colored light filled her eyes. The words twenty-four hours made her mouth dry and sticky and her mind panicky. She wanted to scream, open her mouth and scream and scream. The thought almost made her laugh, and she knew the laugh would be high and hysterical, signs of the mad person they believed she was.

"Do you think she's unconscious?" the same man asked, but his voice sounded doubtful.

Kaiser pressed a finger on her cheek and used another to wrench open her eyelid.

Sophia allowed her eyes to roll up, not sure how else to simulate sleep. He released the tender flesh, and she forced her eyelids not to flutter.

"Or in some hallucination. I read about patients who spent their entire experiences in a kind of catatonia, but it was rare."

"Was she speaking true things?" the doctor whispered.

"Yes," Kaiser said, and Sophia heard pride in his voice. "She sees the dead. It's miraculous, isn't it?"

The other doctor was silent and Sophia had to focus to keep the thread of their conversation. Strange sights tried to pull her away, a giant fat snail sitting in the corner of her vision beckoned to her.

"Yes, but also dangerous... How could she know the names? It's one thing to observe a telepathic patient or a seer, but a medium who receives the stories and names of the dead? I must admit, I hardly believed you when you wrote the group. I thought she must be pulling your chain and yet..."

"It's real," Kaiser whispered. His hands wandered to Sophia's wrist, he stroked his thumb back and forth along her pulse as if ensuring himself that his prize pig was still alive. "The implications," Kaiser continued, "can you imagine the power such a person could have in the world?"

"Except she's not in the world because she's insane. Who would ever believe her?"

"That's why it is so important that she have our guidance. I'm less interested in offering her gift than in obtaining the information contained there-in. If we proved..."

Kaiser had not trailed off, but Sophia had slipped down a long shimmering hallway of blue light. It seemed to spin circles around her and she wanted to press her hands into the walls, but they had no substance. She walked and walked, her legs never tiring, her body as buoyant as the sparkling lights that danced in her vision. The tunnel ended into a bright white nothing, but there suspended in the center was a small table with two chairs. In one chair sat Jack.

Sophia wanted to collapse, but of their own will her legs carried her forward. He smiled up at her and patted the other chair. She sat, trying to reach for him, but never grasping more than air. He was so close and yet she could not touch him.

CHAPTER 20

*S*eptember 1965
Jude

JUDE PULLED the car down a dusty driveway that ended at a tall farm-house. It was old, but a fresh coat of white paint and a porch arranged with pots of flowers, gave the home an air of cared-for that the rest of the desolate road lacked. An old swing-set stood to one side, and Jude saw a baby doll with only a single arm swaying in the baby swing that hung from the rusted frame. It gave her the creeps, and she wished she'd taken Clayton up on his offer to join her.

Grabbing a notebook and slinging her camera around her neck, she walked to the front door. She peeked through a screen into a long, dark hallway listening for voices, but heard only the hollow tick of a grand-father clock. She knocked hard, and the screen jostled in its frame.

The unseasonably humid September day made the experience rather disjointed and dreamy. If she stood for much longer, she'd grow dizzy and swoon, a behavior she'd often observed in Hattie over the years, but rarely experienced herself.

"Is anyone home?" she called into the darkness, knocking a second time.

More silence.

She turned to leave, and saw a man moving out of a thicket of corn rows, a young girl clung to his hand bouncing up and down excitedly. "A visitor, Mr. Dale! Look, look!" the little girl practically screamed as she pointed at Jude and tried to break from the man's grip.

He didn't speed up at the sight of her, and Jude reached into her jeans pocket touching the little switchblade she'd tucked there. He was harmless surely, but she had learned to be cautious of strange men, especially when meeting them at isolated country houses.

"Can I help ya?" he asked. His eyes darting to the camera around her neck and then to her little car parked in the driveway. He frowned as if making an assessment.

"I hope so," she said offering a smile and her hand as she walked down the stairs to greet him. "My name's Jude and I work for the Wexford County Gazette. We've been investigating cold cases. I came across a newspaper article about Rosemary Bell. I wondered if you knew her?"

The moment he heard Rosemary's name his face darkened.

"Aunt Rosemary died!" the little girl squawked. Her mousy brown hair was pulled into a ponytail and her clothes were splattered with mud.

"Sarah," the man told her. "Go play on your swing set."

He gave her a little push, and she ran off to the swings snatching the one-armed doll and tossing her high in the air.

"She's sweet," Jude lied. Not that Sarah wasn't sweet. Jude didn't have a soft spot for children, especially the loud, mud-smeared kind like Sarah.

"She's a handful and belongs to her mama, not me. Name's Dale," the man told her, offering her a rough handshake.

He gestured towards the aged wicker furniture that faced out at the dusty driveway. "Rosemary was my sister," he said, settling into a chair.

He wore jeans and a polo t-shirt that stuck to his chest and back in little pockets of sweat. He was mostly bald, and gray in the other areas. Jude pegged him at fifty but aged beyond his years. He rested his hands on a belly that had once likely been flat and now revealed a love of cheap beer and ball games.

"Rosemary was murdered?" Jude asked. She wasn't a reporter and didn't know how to go about easing into her questions.

137

He nodded and wiped a hand along his sweaty brow. Jude noticed he wore a brown leather glove on his left hand despite the warm day.

"Can I get you something? I need a drink if we're going to talk about this."

"Umm sure, I'll have what you're having," she offered, figuring the more accommodating she was the more open he'd be.

He stood and walked into the house returning a few minutes later with three cans of beer. He slammed the first in two huge gulps not bothering to sit back down. When he opened the second, he returned to his seat. Jude took a sip of her own and tried to contain her grimace. She had stopped drinking beer after her teenage years, and had never much cared for the taste.

"Nobody's asked about Rosemary in ten years, I'd say," he told Jude, flicking the tab on his beer can. He gazed out at the little girl who'd returned her doll to the swing and was pushing her high into the blue sky. "We grew up here, me, Rosemary and my little brother, Kurt. My mom and dad too. Dad's been dead going on twenty years and my mom moved into a home last February. Real nice place, too. Not one of those kind ya hear about on TV where people are layin' in their piss all day."

Jude nodded.

"Both my parents are dead," she offered. Clayton's voice popped into her head: "Don't share any personal information. If you share nothing, you can't get caught in a lie." She bit her lip and didn't say more.

Dale nodded, but Jude doubted he heard her. He seemed to be lost in his memories.

"I was seventeen when Rosemary died. They found her in Earl's cabin out in the woods, about five miles yonder." He pointed indistinctly towards the cornfield that edged their property. "Murdered, stabbed a dozen times." His tone held a hardness that Jude found disconcerting. She pretended to take another sip of beer, but suddenly didn't want to be even vaguely incapacitated.

Jude glanced toward the empty country road and wished a car would go by.

"Did they ever find her killer?"

Dale nodded and took another long drink, crushing the can in his large hand and letting it fall to the porch. The clatter made Jude jump despite watching its passage.

"Girl by the name of Sophia Gray. A strange one who lived on the property that bordered those woods. Only thirteen years old."

"A thirteen-year-old stabbed your sister?" Jude asked, trying to keep her voice neutral, curious, but not invested. "That seems odd, right? I mean most murders are committed by men..."

Dale set his jaw and something in his eyes told Jude he was holding back.

"You know something I don't?" he asked, eyes boring into her.

The hairs on Jude's neck stood on end and she shook her head, slipping her hand back into her pocket to touch the little blade.

"Knife was in her barn. She said she found the body, but how'd the knife get in her barn? Her footprints were all over and her mama cleaned her up, but she had blood on her all right. They found her bloody smock in the wash bin."

Jude grimaced, imagining her mother running home, terrified, covered in the blood of her murdered friend.

"So, they tried and convicted her then?"

Dale shook his head.

"She took off, ran away. That just made her look more guilty. But you can't run away from a crime like that, it follows you like a mad dog, even if ya shoot it, it gets right up and keeps comin'."

Jude followed the line of Dale's eye to the child who kicked higher and higher on the swing, her hair whooshing forward and covering her face each time she went back. Jude wondered if he saw his own sister there, swinging, smiling.

"My mama found that girl, believe it or not. All the way up in Cadillac, over two hours drivin' from here. My Aunt Katherine lives out that way and my ma went for a visit. She was pickin' up a few things at the grocery and that Sophia Gray walked right in front of her."

Jude slumped back in her chair with a sigh, understanding how Sophia's past finally came back to claim her.

"So that's what happened," Jude sighed.

Dale glanced at her funny, and Jude tried to return her expression to one of indifference though she assumed the beer was reducing his ability to notice one way or another.

"Yeah. She wrote down the lady's license plate and they tracked her back to a big ole fancy house. My ma figured she'd try to run again, but the woman who'd been harboring her gave her up, said she'd been livin in fear her whole life. Thought Sophia had likely murdered again but couldn't prove it."

Jude frowned.

"The woman that hid Sophia from the police as a girl turned her in?"

"Yep." Dale scratched at his chin, examining his fingers afterward. "Guess the rich lady's dead husband took the girl in without askin'. The woman only found out later she was a little murderer. She wanted to give her up, but things got all tangled. The girl, Sophia, went into the asylum and my ma could rest knowin' that Rosemary's killer was punished."

Jude realized she'd begun to squeeze her can. She loosened her grip before she sprayed both of them with beer. Gram Ruth had turned her mother in. She'd given her up.

"I'm really intrigued by this, Dale. I appreciate your sitting with me. What happened to Sophia's family?"

~

DAMIEN

DAMIEN STOOD in the cave of trees and watched her. Hattie's man-sized sweater had fallen down, revealing one pale shoulder. Tendrils of honey colored hair blew lazily in the wind having escaped from the sloppy ponytail at her neck. The canvas before her depicted the towering oak tree in the center of the clearing, but he thought he saw faces in the whorls of bark and the chaos of leaves.

Hattie's slender arm wove back and forth, brush in hand, streaks of green revealing deeper shades to the forest beyond the tree. She paused, put the brush unwittingly against her temple where it left a streak of green before returning to the canvas. Damien smiled and stepped from the trees.

"Hattie," he called.

Her shoulders grew rigid and the supple flow of her arms became stiff. She craned around in her chair, eyes wide at the sight of him.

"Hi," she said, looking at him, but also beyond him as if she had been in another dimension as she painted and not fully stepped back into their own.

He waved, and hurried across the expansive yard, feeling awkward. The space was wider than he realized, and his initial trot lost its momentum and turned into a long gait. He realized, not for the first time, that something about Hattie turned him into a bumbling idiot.

She didn't stand, but smiled up at him, a palette of paints nested in her lap.

"Hey," he offered her a little pat on the shoulder, self-conscious in his formal slacks and tie. He tugged on the tie. "I was at a department meeting just before this."

Hattie didn't say anything. She was not a woman of many words and as usual he tried to fill the emptiness with his own.

"Beautiful painting. I didn't mean to interrupt you. I stopped by the church and Pastor Greg said I'd find you out here."

"My mama was a painter," she told him, shifting back to her canvas and smudging a branch with her finger.

He nodded, rocking on his heels and fought the urge to lean forward and wipe the smear of green paint from her temple.

"A lot of our patients paint. Not to say there's a connection," he added quickly. "I mean some doctors have surmised a possible link, but I think the insane merely need an outlet. In fact, more creativity is encouraged. Idle hands are the devil's plaything after all."

He could not stop talking. The only consolation was that Hattie seemed only to be half-listening as she studied the painting before her.

"Do you sell your paintings?" he asked.

Hattie frowned and shook her head.

"Is that the usual thing to do?" she asked, again leaning forward to smudge an edge of the sky. The simple movement altered the painting. The sky now had a dark shadow as if a storm were coming.

He shrugged and adjusted his tie again, pulling it loose and balling it in his fist.

"I don't know, maybe. I mean there are people who sell them, and you're very talented. I'm sure an art dealer in town would happily display them for you. I have a friend in Chicago who owns a gallery. I could speak with her..." but he trailed off when Hattie stood and set her paints on the chair.

"No, thank you," she told him. More of her hair had pulled free of her ponytail. Some caught in the smudge of green paint, but she didn't seem to notice.

"Your detail is amazing," he said, leaning toward the painting. The ridges and curves of the trunk were identical to the tree in front him. He felt like he looked at a photograph, but again with the added sense that faces peered out from the within the bark, trapped there, screaming.

He shivered and swallowed the lump in his throat.

"Are there faces in your painting, Hattie?"

She frowned, and bit her lip, nodding.

"I see things, sometimes. They're people, but they're... more like spirits," she whispered.

"Shall we walk and talk?" he asked, offering her his arm.

She nodded, not taking his arm, but wandering toward the trees.

～

Jude

"GRIMMEL GRAY, at your service, young lady. Shopping for a new television, are ya? This Westinghouse right here is full color and insta-on TV, meanin' you don't have to wait." The man rested a beefy hand on a large television sitting on the ground, balloons drifting above it.

Jude stared at him, dumbfounded. He was a spitting image of her twin brother, Peter. If she'd doubted the story of her mother's life before, she was quickly abandoning her skepticism.

"I'm not looking for a TV," she said, watching his face fall. "I'm looking for you."

He rested his hand on his chest as if to say 'who me?'

"Okay, well that's a slight more interesting. Are you one of Sophia's friends?"

Jude's eyebrows shot to her hairline at the mention of her mother's name.

"Sophia?" she breathed.

"My daughter," he explained. "Guess not. She's at college over in

Grand Rapids. I thought maybe you two chummed around. You seem about her age."

Jude realized Grimmel had named his daughter after his sister. She felt off balance standing in the store staring at him. She pulled a pack of cigarettes from her back pocket and shook one out.

"Mind?" she asked, though by the way his eyes lit up, he didn't mind.

"Not at all. Can I bum one? Wife never lets me buy em' anymore." He grinned sheepishly and again she was staring at her twin brother. The only thing missing was Peter's chipped incisor and the scar over his right eyebrow from an accident on his bike.

"Why are you looking for me then?" He asked releasing a long satisfying exhalation of smoke.

Jude pulled her notebook from her bag and held it up as if in explanation.

"I'm a reporter checking into an old case." The moment he heard the words, Grimmel's demeanor changed. He stiffened and took an unconscious step back.

"It's about-"

"I know what it's about," he said, glancing around the store as if he feared people might overhear.

"I just wanted to ask…"

But he stepped close to her and held up his hand. His eyes looked troubled, and Jude couldn't tell if he was angry or merely sad.

"I can't talk about this here. Meet me in twenty minutes at the cemetery out by Barnes Road."

"The cemetery?" she grimaced, shaking her head.

"It's private," he told her, rolling his eyes as if exasperated at her immaturity - another signature Peter move.

"Okay," she sighed, reluctant, but afraid he wouldn't talk to her otherwise. "How do I get there?"

CHAPTER 21

 eptember 1965
Hattie

"You can talk to me. I am training to be a psychotherapist, you know. I'll soon have a degree in a frame and everything," Damien told her, sitting on a park bench and patting the seat beside him.

Hattie sat, clasping her hands together. She looked at the light as it danced off the gold bracelet Gram Ruth had given her for her sixteenth birthday. A tiny gold heart seemed to shimmer and almost melt as she tilted it from side to side. She thought of Lucy's revelations about their mama. Jude had insisted she was looking into it and in the meantime, Hattie keep her mouth shut.

"Do they mean anything?" Damien asked touching Hattie's wrist. "The charms?"

She stared at his fingers trying to discern where her skin ended and his began. A cloud moved into the path of the sun and her momentary reverie slipped away.

She touched the heart.

"My Gram gave me the bracelet with this charm - a symbol of her love, she told me," Hattie responded, tugging at the gold heart and having a terrible impulse to rip it off the delicate gold chain. She fought the urge and pointed at a paintbrush. "Jude gave me this because I paint, and Peter bought me this one." She held up a little cat.

"Did you have a cat?" he asked.

Hattie smiled, remembering Felix, and shook her head.

"I did, but this one symbolized a dead cat."

Damien made a face and cocked an eyebrow.

"Care to tell me more?"

Hattie looked at him realizing she was hearing the same words his patient's heard when they sat in his office, perhaps reclining on a stiff sofa while he sat behind them taking notes, or scribbling pictures of the back of their heads.

"It's a long story," she said, and pointed at the last charm. It was a gold maple leaf. "My parents loved trees. We used to tap maple trees on our property though I only vaguely remember it. Jude and Peter have helped me fill in the blanks. This one's for them."

Damien had taken his hand away, but now he reached for her again, touching his finger to the leaf. Hattie looked at the knobby protrusions on his knuckles. His hands were so much larger than her own. Fine blonde hairs stood along the backs of his fingers. The sun had re-emerged, and she watched the light playing off those delicate hairs.

"Would you like to have dinner with me?" he asked.

She watched, mesmerized as his hand moved from the bracelet and took her own. It was soft, and warm, and strong, nearly swallowing her hand whole. She allowed her eyes to drift from their hands to his face. His gray eyes searched her.

"Do *you* want to?" she asked. Hattie had been told many times throughout her life she was beautiful, but it was always spoken by people who loved her: Gram, Camille, Jude and Peter. She had never kissed a boy, never even had a strong urge, but now she sat with a man and he looked at her in a way that felt good and terrifying.

He grinned and nodded.

"Okay, yes. I think I would like that," she murmured, a rush of warmth flooding her face. She took a deep breath and looked back toward the canopy of trees.

Jude

. . .

THE CEMETERY SAT on the edge of town, tucked behind an eight-foot stone wall crawling with ivy. Iron gates opened to the country road beyond. It seemed out of place with its towering oak trees and lush green grass.

Jude parked and walked among the headstones reading the names. After twenty-five minutes a red pickup pulled into the cemetery. Grimmel parked behind a towering row of evergreen trees.

He walked to Jude, looking over his shoulder.

"Why so skittish?" she asked.

He hooked his thumbs in his belt loops and squinted at her in the sunlight.

"If you're here why I think you're here, then you already know."

"Fair enough," she said. "Can you tell me about Sophia and Rosemary?"

He closed his eyes for a lingering moment as if the mere sound of their names physically hurt.

"Why are you looking into this, Jude? It's been thirty years for Christ's sake."

Jude nodded, contemplating her answer. A part of her wanted to spill the truth, tell Grimmel everything, and enlist him in the search for their mother. But at Jude's core she lacked the trust instinct. Grimmel was a stranger, her history was a web of lies, and she felt safer when she worked alone. That was why she hadn't told Hattie she was going to Mason - her mother's home town. Hattie opened up to people, she let things slip without thought of how that information might be used against her.

Jude shrugged playing only mildly interested.

"My editor heard about it from a friend of a friend - that kind of thing. He sent me down here to see what I could find out."

"So, there may be no story?" Grimmel asked, scanning the stone wall like someone might climb over it at any moment.

"If there's no story, there's no story," she said flipping open her notebook to a blank page.

Grimmel nodded.

"Sophia didn't do it. Let me just start with that. She was thirteen years old. How Rosemary's mother could have blamed her-" He threw up his hands, his face growing red. "They gathered at our house like it was a witch hunt. I swear they would have dragged her through the streets. When the Sheriff found the knife, well…"

"Whoa, whoa, slow down," Jude stopped him. "Start at the beginning."

Grimmel pushed his hands through his reddish hair leaving it sticking up.

"Sophia was playing in the woods. It was August. The sheriff had stopped by that morning looking for Rosemary Bell, a little girl who lived a few miles away. She and Sophia weren't real close, but they chummed around now and then. Rosemary hadn't come home the night before. Anyway, Sophia was out playin' in the woods and saw Rosemary." He stopped abruptly, and Jude spun around thinking someone had entered the cemetery, but they were alone.

"I mean, she found her in the cabin. Sophia was playing in the woods and opened the cabin door and saw Rosemary's body."

Jude noted his hesitation, but let it go.

"Rosemary was under a blanket and Sophia pulled it off. I guess she panicked. She picked up the knife laying there and ran back to the house. She told us what happened, and Mom called the sheriff. He came out right away."

"Sophia picked up the knife?" Jude asked, frowning. Thirty years earlier crime investigation was barely a thing. And they could hardly blame a thirteen-year-old girl who found her friend murdered for corrupting the scene.

"Yeah, it was a bad move, but she panicked. That night Rosemary's family and some other townsfolk showed up at our door. They wanted to question Sophia themselves. That's when the Sheriff walked into the barn and came out with the knife. Our mother about fainted right on the spot."

"Where was Sophia?"

"Up in a tree in the woods. I told her to go because our big brother, Timothy asked me to. He could tell people were gettin' riled up. He didn't want her caught in the middle."

"Did she run away?"

Grimmel's eyes darted to the side and Jude realized he was about to tell her a lie.

"Yeah. She ran away. We never saw her again."

Jude bit her lip and stared at him, hard.

"You're telling me, you let your thirteen-year-old sister disappear into the same woods where another little girl was murdered? And you called her a runaway?"

"Hey now, wait just a minute. We would never have put Sophia in danger. It was Mama's idea and..." he stopped, closing his mouth hard.

Jude contemplated her next question.

"Grimmel, I don't believe for a second that Sophia hurt that little girl. And I also don't believe Sophia ran away. Let's talk off the record, okay? I swear it won't get out."

Grimmel frowned.

"I was never good at keeping secrets," he confessed. "My mom was so scared I'd spill the beans to my friends or a girlfriend. I never did though. Course now it's been thirty years, and in the end, they got her, didn't they?"

"Our conversation isn't leaving this cemetery, Grimmel. I need to know."

Grimmel sighed and rubbed his face, freshly shaved, but prickly and red looking. He had Peter's sensitive skin.

Never had she wanted so much to open up to a stranger. Grimmel was so much like her twin brother she felt it was him she was talking to.

"Did you help her run away?" Jude asked.

Grimmel fidgeted, pulling his truck keys from his pocket and then shoving them back in.

"You swear this ain't gettin' printed?"

"I swear." Jude put her hand over her heart.

"My mama helped her. Our daddy had died the fall before. Worst year of my life that was, for all of us, I guess. Anyway, my dad had a friend from childhood. Man had grown up to be real wealthy, a lawyer who had connections, never did know what they were, political maybe. My ma reached out to him. She called him up and told him what had happened. He offered to take Sophia, raise her up."

Jude frowned.

"Just like that? Your mom gave away your sister?"

"Hell no!" Grimmel practically shouted. "You didn't see the look in those people's eyes. They were fit to kill our little Sophia. At the very least she was gettin' blamed for that murder."

148

"But she was a juvenile. She would have been out in two years," Jude argued.

"I thought about that later on," he admitted. "We all did, but at the moment it felt like life or death. And Rosemary's granddaddy was a judge. Ma was convinced they'd find a way to get her locked up forever. You see, Sophia..." He stopped as if only just realizing how much he'd already revealed.

"Please," Jude urged. "Tell me the rest."

"It's weird, you know?" He said cocking his head and looking at her. "You remind me of Sophia."

"I do?" Jude asked self-consciously touching her cheek. Hattie had always looked like their mother - long and willowy and waif thin. But her father too had commented more than once that Jude had her mother's smile.

"Yeah, it's strange," he murmured, shaking his head. "Somethin' in your..." He gestured at his own face but didn't elaborate. "She saw things. Sophia saw things that weren't there, that couldn't be there."

Jude thought of Hattie and her ghosts as Peter had often referred to them as if they were a gang.

"Ghosts?" Jude asked, though if she'd heard the way she uttered the word, she would have kicked herself. When had she ever believed such nonsense?

Grimmel nodded.

"That's the real truth. Sophia didn't find Rosemary in the cabin. She saw her walking in the woods, dead."

CHAPTER 22

*T*he Northern Michigan Asylum for the Insane
September 1965
Sophia

"Just breathe," Kent told Sophia, holding tight to her hand, grown clammy as they entered the tunnel.

"Someone died down here," she whispered, bracing her hand against the limestone wall.

The tunnel opened before them. A long, round corridor of brick illuminated by bare light-bulbs suspended overhead. The bulbs did little to cast out the darkness. Everywhere shadows lay. Steam pipes echoed and clanged, hissed with the energy passing through.

"It's okay, Sophia, you can do this."

Yes, she had to. Except the dead girl, a child, murdered, flitted in and out of her vision. A white, blood-soaked nightgown, bare feet caked with dirt, dark hair in tangles.

"Marybelle," she whispered. "Marybelle needs our help."

Kent tightened his grip and Sophia saw a flash of horror cloud his eyes. He blinked and pulled her forward.

"She's dead, Sophia. Long dead and we can't help her now."

Again the little girl, maybe eight or nine, appeared. She held out a hand, fingernails torn away. Sophia stumbled and fell, nearly took Kent with her, but he yanked hard and pulled her to her feet.

"There's not time. No time, Sophia," he grunted and overhead the lights flickered. He stopped and stared desperately around the tunnel. They had two choices, forwards or backwards, he pulled her along.

By now, someone would have noticed her absence. One of the orderlies, or Kaiser's nurse, Alice who frequently checked on her.

Kent, supposedly washing out the solitary confinement rooms would hopefully not be missed.

The lights flickered a second time.

"Run," Kent whispered, as if afraid the dead girl would hear him.

Sophia's bare feet slapped the grimy brick floor. Her hair pulled loose from her ponytail and her breasts bouncing tenderly beneath her thin nightgown. Her thighs burned after years of walking and sitting with little chance for strenuous activity. She slowed them both down, but Kent, powerful and frightened, surged forward.

"This way," he breathed and turned down a tunnel leading to their left.

He slowed as they came to a large gray metal door, and fumbled in his pocket for a set of keys, glancing behind them. He shoved the door open, and they stumbled into another tunnel, this one square. They hurried down it and up a short flight of concrete stairs.

"We made it," Kent murmured, shoving through another door.

The darkness of early morning greeted them.

Straining for breath, lungs burning from her short run, Sophia doubled over, hands on her knees, and coughed.

"We can't linger here," he whispered, gesturing to the buildings surrounding them, lights flickering in the windows.

Kent pulled Sophia away from the buildings. He grabbed a large canvas bag from behind a tree.

"Here, put these on."

She pulled on a pair of corduroy pants, and Kent helped her strip off her nightgown.

"Grab my shoulder," he said, as she struggled into heavy brown boots, not bothering with the laces.

A thick patterned sweater, followed by a camel colored wool coat, shut out the chilly morning air.

"Quickly, now," he told her, and they hurried across the dewy grounds. Behind her the hospital loomed huge and bright, windows ablaze as the morning rituals of bathing and breakfast commenced.

Further and further from the light, the oak and maple trees rose, menacing against the half-light of dawn's approach.

They stopped at the edge of the woods, and Kent pulled Sophia into his arms, crushing her in a hug.

"You've changed my life forever, Sophia," he told her. "And I can never thank you enough."

"I would say we're even," Sophia told him, muffled with her face pressed into his shoulder.

"No, not even close, but we have to part here, for now. There's a path, it's not very clear, but the sun will be up soon. The deer use it mostly. I've been leaving food along the way, for them, and I've tied some cloth in the trees. It will take you clear through the forest, there's a big hill and you'll follow the base of it. Don't go up or you'll get lost. You'll see a footpath that leads to the road. My friend Barbie is waiting for you. She drives a black Pontiac."

"I'll see you soon," he promised and kissed her on the forehead. Sophia watched him hurry back toward the hospital, his breath crystallizing in the early morning air. An emptiness gaped within her as he disappeared from her view.

She had the unnerving sense she would never see him again.

SOPHIA WATCHED the sunset on her third day of freedom. It spread across the sky in frothy pink and orange waves, cascading over and through the trees, illuminating the yard in a rainbow of color. She longed for her paints for the first time in years. In the asylum, a little table contained a child's watercolor palette and sheets of white paper. Sophia never touched them. Sometimes when she looked at them it made her sick to her stomach.

Now she longed to capture the sunset. Searching through the cabin, she found a yellowing notebook and dull colored pencils. She pulled a chair onto the porch and sat, propping a wooden crate in her lap as her easel.

As she drew, she thought of Kent. Barbie told her he would arrive the evening after her escape, but he never appeared. He had stocked the cabin with food, matches, a few pairs of clothes, some freshly laundered towels and a bar of soap. She took her first solo shower in ten years, delighted in the warm water, but also terrified. The shower blotted out other sounds, the creak of a door, footsteps in the hallway.

At night she slept fitfully, dreaming of Dr. Kaiser, and waking sure he leered over her in the darkness. After restless hours her first night in the cottage, she turned on a lamp and slept with a kitchen knife close by.

Something had happened to Kent. No, not something.

Dr. Kaiser had happened to Kent.

Nevertheless, she watched the rutted drive that led to the cabin hoping to see him walking in, his white orderly clothes replaced with a pair of jeans and a soft sweater. He was too young to have left the world and Sophia was responsible. He helped her escape and he'd paid with his life.

She drew for an hour, capturing a dozen versions of the sunset before retiring inside to eat a can of cold soup. Soup had been a staple at the asylum, sometimes so hot it scalded her tongue, and she wanted nothing that reminded her of that place.

When darkness fell, she locked the doors and windows and closed the heavy drapes. In the kitchen, she took out a butcher knife and went into the bedroom, barricading a chair beneath the doorknob.

Each night dread descended over her like a weighted blanket. Irrational fears that Dr. Kaiser and the others were surrounding her cabin. Maybe they would not try to take her at all. Instead they would burn it to the ground ensuring she took their secrets to the grave.

She lay curled on the bed with a book propped open, but couldn't concentrate on the words. When she heard an engine break the silence, she shot out of bed. Blowing out the kerosene lamp, she peeled back the curtain and peeked out. In the darkness she could barely make out the silhouette of a car, but when the door opened the interior light turned on and she saw Barbie, the woman who had driven her to the cabin three days before.

Sophia removed the chair and hurried to unlock the front door. When she opened it, Barbie stood on the porch, red eyed, with a wad of tissue clutched in her hand.

"They killed him," she wailed rushing into Sophia. Barbie sobbed into her shoulder. "They murdered him. I know they did. It happened only hours after he helped you. Got tangled in the bedsheets. Horse-shit! What do they think we are, morons?"

Sophia didn't have to ask who Barbie spoke of. She pulled back and drew the crying woman into the cabin, closing and locking the door behind her.

She bit back the words 'are you sure no one followed you?'

Barbie slumped onto a floral-patterned chair with springs nearly bursting through. Her blouse was soaked with tears and her bell-bottom jeans had wet grass stuck to their hem.

Looking at the young woman, Sophia thought of her own daughters. Jude was probably a few years older than Barbie, Hattie younger.

"It's my fault," Sophia whispered, sitting on the couch, pushing her fingers hard into the worn fabric. She felt an irrational desire to tear into the cushion and send feathers exploding into the room.

Barbie shook her head.

"It's not your fault," she hissed. "It's their fault. They're killers, tormentors. Kent told me they were doing unspeakable things to you. He couldn't turn a blind eye."

Sophia nodded and then shook her head.

She touched a hand to her face remembering that dark room hidden in the woods.

"It wasn't worth it. He should have left me there. Oh, poor Kent." Sophia felt a heaviness she often experienced in the hospital descending over her. Sometimes days would pass, and she would lie in her bed staring at the ceiling, unable to remember the day, the year, her own last name. Kent was the only one who could pull her out. Other nurses tried in harsh ways with cold baths, but Kent did kind things. He brought her homemade oatmeal cookies, her favorite, or sang her the lullabies she had confided to him she used to sing to her children. He never pushed her to snap out of it because he knew Sophia was being experimented on, researched, tortured.

"Have you told anyone?" Sophia asked, swimming up from the depths of her own despair, refusing to slip away while Barbie sat before her in tears.

Barbie looked up and laughed, a short harsh sound.

"They're blaming you, Sophia. A criminal history, they said. The police looked at me like I needed to be admitted too. Doctor Kaiser already reached out. He told them there was an escaped and dangerous patient on the loose. They're hunting you."

As the words left her lips another sound reached them. A car coming up the dirt two-track that led to the little cabin.

"Does anyone else know I'm here?"

Barbie stood, eyes wide.

"You have to run, Sophia. If they get you back into the hospital," she didn't finish the sentence. The engine grew louder. It sounded like more than one car.

Barbie pushed Sophia into a back bedroom and jerked open the window. She reached beneath the bed and grabbed a green duffel bag.

"It's an emergency bag. Kent was always prepared," she whispered.

Sophia climbed out the window and Barbie handed her the bag.

"Straight through," Barbie told her pointing at the woods. "You'll reach a lake and follow it east. On the other side, you'll come to a country road."

Outside car doors slammed and voices rose in the night. Sophia didn't wait to hear more, she slipped the bag over her shoulder and ran.

CHAPTER 23

 eptember 1965
Jude

JUDE ARRIVED at Hattie's apartment unannounced, and Hattie opened the door with sleepy eyes and tousled hair. She wore a frilly pink nightgown that Gram Ruth bought her when she was ten that somehow still fit.

Jude sighed.

"Hattie you realize you're nineteen, right? And have your own apartment? It might be time to buy some new threads."

Hattie wrinkled her baby-smooth forehead and looked down, backing into the apartment to let Jude in. Hattie rarely took her snide comments, or advice for that matter, seriously if she heard them at all.

Jude sputtered at the state of the apartment. One corner of the small living room was coated in newspaper and splattered with paint. Hattie's easel leaned against the wall.

The kitchen counter and table held bowls of paint water, dirty dishes, and a jumble of Hattie's stuff she'd likely started to unpack and then forgot about midway through.

Jude marveled at Hattie's desperation to control her chaos. Hattie was not an organized person by nature, but their grandmother had spent years reinforcing that *cleanliness was next to godliness*, which

Hattie seemed to take literally in her endless quest to keep her disorganization in check, and wake up on time for Sunday services.

Jude picked up a coffee mug and sniffed.

"Tomato soup?"

Hattie shrugged and plopped into a kitchen chair, yawning.

Jude set about making coffee, a challenge since most of the kitchen boxes were sealed in the corner.

"Where's your percolator?" Jude asked, pawing through a box crammed with baking sheets and hand-knit kitchen rags. "Please do not tell me you've been living here for a month and haven't unpacked your percolator?"

Hattie watched Jude and blinked several times as if still caught in the world of dreaming. Her eyes popped opened, and she looked up.

"It's in that box." She pointed to a box splotched with blue paint. "I remember Camille said she was putting it in the blue box." Hattie laughed and shook her head. Jude did not understand why it was funny, but ripped the box open and hauled out a can of coffee, the percolator, and a box of sugar.

"Why are you so tired today?" Jude asked after she'd delivered Hattie a coffee with more milk and sugar than caffeine and poured her own piping hot and black. "Painting last night?"

Hattie nodded.

"I couldn't sleep. I kept hearing... things."

"Your ghosts?" Jude asked careful to keep the teasing edge from her voice. Despite Jude and Peter's years of ribbing Hattie over the voices and visions, Jude no longer found the idea funny. If their mother experienced the same thing, maybe the stories weren't stories at all.

Hattie stared into her coffee but didn't speak. After several minutes Jude pulled out her notebook.

"I've been looking into mom's past," Jude announced. "Yesterday I drove down to Mason, the town where Mom grew up. I met our uncle Grimmel."

"Our uncle?" Hattie looked up, confused.

"Yes. Mom had two brothers, Grimmel and Tim. Grimmel still lives in Mason. He's a TV salesman."

Hattie stared at Jude, unblinking.

"Mama had brothers?"

"That's what I said, yes. And yesterday I met Grimmel."

"Why didn't you call me?" Hattie sounded hurt. "I would have gone with you."

Jude had come prepared for the question.

"Because I wasn't sure what I'd find, Hattie. Simple as that. Mom's family might have been long gone, or dead. I didn't want to get your hopes up."

Hattie picked up a cup of dirty paint water and lifted it to her lips.

"Hattie, you're about to drink paint."

Hattie looked at the cup, grimaced and set it back on the table. She shrugged and picked up her coffee.

"Does he know where Mama is? Can I meet him too?"

"He doesn't know where she is, and he doesn't know who we are yet either. I posed as a reporter, but yes, soon. I've got a few more things to do and then we'll go visit him together."

JUDE PARKED at the address Clayton had found. She walked up the driveway pausing when she spotted the woman with wild black hair standing in her garden.

"Barbie?" Jude said

The woman pulled tomatoes off a vine and jumped a foot in the air at the sound of Jude's voice. She dropped the tomato, and it splattered on her tennis shoes.

Jude flinched and held up her hands.

"Sorry. I didn't mean to startle you."

Barbie didn't speak, but stared at Jude suspiciously, looking her up and down as if she might carry a weapon.

"My name's Jude. I..." the words "work for the Wexford County Gazette died on her lips. This woman had rescued her mother from the asylum. She would not lie to her.

"I'm trying to find my mother," she started again. "Sophia Gray."

It felt strange to call her mother by her true name when she'd only ever known her as Mom or Anne.

Barbie narrowed her eyes but didn't move from the garden as if the wall of tomato plants would protect her.

"My sister and I have been searching for her. I just found out she was in the asylum. We thought she had died." Jude searched for any recognition in the woman's face. Could she have the wrong Barbie?

Jude stepped closer and reached into her back pocket pulling out the faded Polaroid she'd found in Gram Ruth's barn. Jude and Peter stood with their parents. Sophia, or Anne, hugely pregnant with Hattie, held Jude's hand. The four of them posed in front of Gram's house, their arms intertwined.

Barbie didn't take the picture, but she stared at it for several seconds looking between the small girl in the photo and Jude as if trying to discern a lie in the image.

Barbie looked about Jude's age or younger. Her thick black curls were piled on top of her head and she wore a dirty white apron over her clothes.

Biting her lip, Barbie wiped her hands on her apron and glanced toward the sky as if searching for a sign of what she should do.

"Please," Jude said. "I've thought she was dead for ten years."

Barbie sighed and stepped from the garden.

"Come inside," she said, leading Jude back to the little cape cod that badly needed a coat of paint.

Despite the rundown exterior, the interior of Barbie's home looked bright and clean. Sunflowers burst from a vase on the kitchen counter.

"Can I get you a glass of tea, or something stronger?" Barbie asked tilting her head toward a half-empty bottle of gin near the sink

"Tea's fine," Jude told her though she would have preferred the gin. Too much wine the night before had left her fuzzy with a dull headache that morning, and the fog of hangover still lingered.

Barbie poured Jude a tea and herself a short tumbler of gin and water with a squeeze of lime. She sat down at her table and folded her hands in front of her, clasping her fingers together and staring at them before looking at Jude.

"I helped her escape. Well, mostly my friend Kent helped her escape."

"Your boyfriend?" Jude asked remembering what Lucy had told her.

Barbie offered a half smile and rolled her eyes.

"We called each other that, but it was a ruse. Kent is gay. Was. Kent was gay." Barbie took her glass and swished the ice around before taking a long drink.

"He lived here with me except when he was working in the asylum, and then he came home on days off. We've lived together since we graduated from high school. Everyone assumed we were together, and it was safer for him if we didn't correct them. I didn't care either way. I date here and there, but commitment's never been my thing. Kent made all that easier. My whole life, in fact." Her lower lip quivered, and she stopped it between her teeth.

"I'm sorry about Kent," Jude said, noticing for the first time the men's flannel shirt hanging over a chair. Other remnants of him trickled through the kitchen too - a pair of worn loafers by the back door, a baseball cap hanging from the coat rack.

Barbie sniffed and shook her head.

"I was there the day Kent's mom died. We were ten years old. Kent told me his mom was bringing us Popsicles and then we could walk across town to Georgette Hanson's pool. It was one of those scorching summer days in August when you start to look forward to falling leaves and hot cocoa."

Jude listened, not sure what Barbie's story had to do with her own mother, but understanding when the damn broke, you let it flow - eventually all the water would run by.

"A policeman drove up Kent's driveway. We were sitting in the grass braiding dandelions stems. Even when we were little Kent liked… girl things. He loved flowers and dancing and brushing my hair. I didn't understand gay and straight then, but I felt more comfortable with Kent than I ever did with the girls I went to school with. The policeman got out and walked up to the door. When Kent's dad answered, he took his hat off and held it over his chest, and I knew what that meant. I'd heard my Nani Elda tell the story of my uncle Freddy's death in the second war. Kent didn't seem to understand. He ran over and asked the policeman to take us for a ride. His dad slapped him right across the face."

Barbie touched her own cheek and winced.

"It was so terrible. His dad didn't cry, but sort of rocked on his feet until the policeman took him inside. Kent followed them in, and I waited for an hour in the yard, sweating, scared, but I had to wait. I knew I had to wait."

Jude wrapped her hands around the glass of tea; the cold perspiration coated her fingers and palms. She thought of the day she learned her own mother had died. Gram Ruth's harsh angry words and then emptiness, as if for a few moments the entire world stopped revolving. The memory hung suspended in Jude's mind. She felt as if she looked at it glinting off the blade of a pendulum swinging back and forth, back and forth.

"When Kent came out he was crying and red in his face. He laid in the grass and wailed. It was his fault, he said. He demanded those fucking Popsicles and now his mother was dead."

Barbie finished her glass and rose for another. This time when she held up the bottle, Jude nodded.

"Just a pinch."

Barbie poured her a glass and returned.

"That experience bound us. Kent never got over it. The guilt tortured him. Until," she paused and took a drink, "he met your mother."

Jude frowned, swallowing her own gin and sinking deeper into her hard-backed chair as the blaze lit her stomach.

"My mother?"

Barbie nodded. "He heard about your mom around the ward, Sophia the Seer - a few of the orderlies called her though that name didn't quite fit, he said. People claimed she spoke to the dead. He didn't exactly believe it, but when he first told me about her, he had that dreamy look in his eyes. He would never bring it up though because he was terrified that his mother was angry with him. But then one day when he took Sophia's pills to her room, she told him that his mother didn't blame him."

"And he believed her?"

Barbie smiled. "She told him much more than that, secret things that existed between him and his mom. He never doubted for a moment that your mother saw and spoke with his. He acted different after that day, Jude. His whole life became lighter."

Jude didn't know how to respond. The stories of her mother's mediumship brought her to the edge of life's mysteries. Mysteries she'd spent a lifetime denying. Jude lived in a rational, practical world. She didn't want to believe in ghosts - let alone her mother's ability to see them.

"Your mom, Sophia, didn't belong in the asylum. Kent didn't know everything, but one particular doctor had taken control of her care when she was first admitted. The doctor did experiments on her."

"Experiments?" Jude said the word, and it seemed to grow huge and ugly and wash the whole room in darkness.

Barbie nodded. "Kent snuck her out in the early morning when it was still dark. I waited in my car on the other side of the woods. He had laid a trail with bits of cloth so she could find her way. I took her to a cabin that Kent owned a few miles outside Traverse City."

"When? When did all this happen?"

"Twelve days ago."

Jude clutched the edge of the table. Lucy had been telling them the truth. Her mother had escaped. She lived!

"So, she is alive?"

"Yes. And the morning Kent freed her, he died in the hospital."

"And you think someone murdered him?"

"I know they did. The hospital is calling it an accident while implying that your mother did it." Barbie shook her head bitterly.

"Where is she now? Still at the cabin?"

Barbie's face fell and Jude waited for the blow.

"I went to see her two days after the escape. I told her about Kent, but she'd already sensed it. Dr. Kaiser must have followed me. He showed up with a group of police searching for her. I helped her out a window, and she ran for the woods. That's the last I've seen her."

CHAPTER 24

eptember 1965
Hattie

HATTIE STOOD before her full-length mirror. She'd started in a simple white dress with yellow flowers Gram Ruth bought her from a boutique years before. Hattie had never worn it. It looked too much like the frilly baby dresses Gram forced her into in the years after her mother died.

"She didn't die," Hattie reminded herself out loud. "They stole her."

She shrugged it off and left it in a pool on the floor, putting on a dress Jude had given her, a hand-me-down.

The orange mini dress fell well above Hattie's knees. Sleeveless with a white collar, her long pale arms seemed octopus-like jutting from the brightly colored fabric. It was all wrong on her, likely a perfect fit on Jude, but Hattie pulled down the hem with no luck and set about braiding her long blonde hair.

Hattie had seen Jude wear the dress with high boots or stylish heels, but Hattie owned only a pair of nude high heels that Gram Ruth had bought her, and the scuffed white flats Hattie wore whenever she wasn't barefoot. She slipped on the heels and walked the length of her apartment feeling gangly and awkward.

"Better not," she huffed, kicking off the heels and sliding into her well-worn flats. Hattie admired all things of beauty, but fashion had never made its way into her consciousness. Over the years she had tried a handful of times to mimic Jude's sleek way of dressing, but shopping exhausted her, making clothes seemed impossible, and she didn't much care how she looked.

Damien had offered to pick her up at her apartment, but Hattie had declined. Romeo's Italian Eatery was walking distance and Hattie needed to calm her churning emotions. She had never been on a date before. She wasn't entirely sure it was a date though something in Damien's demeanor had told her it was. Jude would have known right away and laughed at Hattie's obliviousness.

"But I'm not Jude," Hattie whispered tears pricking the back of her eyes, which reminded her she hadn't put on any makeup. Jude had given her a makeup set, but the small compacts still sat in their original packaging, unopened.

Hattie missed her mama terribly and slumped onto her sofa, leaning her head against the floral fabric. Mama would have helped Hattie prepare for her first date, for her whole life, but they were interrupted. Sometimes Hattie felt interrupted as a person as if she was just developing when a cog got stuck in the wheel and the machine spit her out unfinished. She glanced at her easel in the corner, paints spread across the floor, and wanted desperately to take off the orange dress, put on her nightshirt and paint until midnight.

Jude would never miss a date. She'd rearrange her entire schedule to meet a man she liked.

"I can do this," Hattie whispered, glancing at the yellow telephone sitting on her side table. She could call Jude, ask her what to wear, how to do her makeup. Or call Gram Ruth, but that idea formed a knot in her stomach.

She had spoken with Gram Ruth several times since discovering the newspaper clipping. Gram would have been suspicious otherwise and outright angry.

Gram had always been involved in Hattie's life, bought her clothes, braided her hair, insisted that Hattie keep her girlhood room exactly the same until her sixteenth birthday when she was allowed to put on a paisley bedspread that Camille sewed for her. They packed her dollhouse and toys into the barn, and Hattie brought in books and paints though Gram Ruth did not allow painting on the carpet so they sat untouched on her desk.

Her real painting happened in the barn. Hattie had cleaned out one of the old stables and created a makeshift artist's studio. Sometimes she fell asleep on a pile of moth eaten horse blankets, memories of riding horses that never existed flitting through her dreams.

The phone rang, and Hattie jumped, startled. She stared at it for a moment as if the sound were alien and the person on the other end brought premonitions of doom. Three rings later, she picked it up.

"Hello?" she said, hoping it wasn't Gram who chastised her if she didn't answer the phone: *Hattie Porter Speaking.*

"Hattie? Hi, it's Damien. I'm at the restaurant and just wanted to check on you."

Hattie glanced at the clock hanging over her little Formica table and realized it was almost six-thirty pm. She was already fifteen minutes late.

"Oh, oh no. I'm sorry. I'm leaving right now."

"Would you like me to pick you up?" he asked. He didn't sound annoyed, and Hattie considered his offer, but no, she wasn't ready to share her home yet.

"No, umm thank you though. I'll be there in five minutes."

She hung up the phone and rushed from the apartment forgetting all about make-up and mothers.

DAMIEN SAT in a little half-moon booth lit by a tiffany lamp suspended overhead. He'd ordered a bottle of wine, which Hattie sipped nervously as he talked.

"My parents spend their winters in Florida, snow-birds as they're called these days," he laughed, and Hattie noticed a dimple at the edge of his full lips. "My brother's an Anthropology professor at the University of Michigan. He and my father love to have these long philosophical debates about religion versus evolution. I tend to side with my mom and stay out of it. The truth is they're both dogmatic men, they believe in black and white truths. I'm just not that way. There are shades of gray, in fact, all the world exists in shades of gray. I've yet to find a universal truth where its exact opposite doesn't have a sliver of truth as well."

Hattie considered his words. She too could not say where her beliefs laid. Did she think God created man? Sort of, except in her mind God was not a man, but love, a love so huge it gave life to all things including the spark that started man.

"I hope that doesn't bother you," Damien continued. "I know you attend church so…"

Hattie shook her head.

"I go to church because I feel connected there. It's one of the few places I can sit and focus without thinking I might float away," she admitted, blushing as if he might laugh.

"I appreciate that. I grew up going to church every Sunday, my father insisted on it. On my own, I'm less dedicated, but I have grown fond of Pastor Greg and I know what you mean. Last year I traveled to London with my mother and visited the Westminster Abbey. Something about it was so rooted, like it grew out of the earth. I walked in and felt held." He cupped his palm and Hattie imagined curling into a teeny little ball and falling asleep there in the creases of his flesh. She thought she might paint that image later.

"I've never been out of Michigan," she admitted. "London is so far away."

He smiled and reached across the table touching her wrist.

"Maybe someday we'll go there together."

Jude

JUDE WALKED into the squat brick building that served as the Mason police station.

Her heels clacked against the green linoleum that reminded her of the color that danced behind her eyes after too much drinking. She blinked at the four small desks arranged haphazard around the room, all stacked waist high with papers. She paused at the reception desk.

"Hi. I'm Jude Porter, with the Wexford County Gazette, and I was hoping to speak with Sheriff Hal Jones." Jude said offering the press I.D. that Clayton had given her.

She barely glanced at the card, or at Jude. Apparently, the advertisement in her magazine about *Husband Pleasing Coffee* was more interesting than her job.

"Retired more than a decade ago," the woman, Lori according to her name tag, replied, still not looking up.

"Okay, well I would like to speak with a detective then. Please?" Jude tried to keep her voice even but knew her irritation seeped through. Seriously how many people came into the office in a day? And the woman couldn't be bothered with eye contact.

Lori looked up from her page and stared at Jude with a bored expression. She was perhaps considering how to do her job without standing from her desk.

"Detective Bell may be available," she said tapping her pencil on her teeth and again looking at her magazine.

"Bell?" Jude asked not missing the connection to Rosemary.

"Yes, Kurt Bell. He ran for a sandwich across the way but should be... oh there is he now."

The glass door opened and brought with it a gust of hot wind. Kurt Bell held a paper sack in one hand and beat-up novel in the other. When he saw both women staring at him, he stopped.

"Somethin' happen?" he asked, looking at Lori.

"The press," Lori said in that distasteful way that Clayton had often described to Jude.

Detective Bell smirked. He had ten years on Jude, his tanned face showing the early lines of middle-age. He wore a white shirt that needed a wash over black slacks, and still maintained a full head of black hair, shot with only a few grays. Overall Jude found him handsome in a sloppy sort of way.

"Must be low on the totem pole if you're lookin' for a story around these parts," he said letting the door swing closed. "Follow me."

Jude trailed behind him, feeling the eyes of the other men in the room. She had worn a black pencil skirt and a red blouse which seemed out of place in the dingy office.

"Have a seat," he told her, swiping a stack of papers from the single chair next to his desk. She sat down and surveyed his work space - a disaster of half-full coffee cups, M&M wrappers and paperwork scrawled with illegible notes.

"Quite a fancy place you have here," she mumbled, wiping a coffee stain from a corner of the desk where she sat her notepad.

Detective Bell opened his paper bag and pulled out a hefty sandwich near to exploding with roast beef and cheese. Before taking a massive bite, he spoke.

"What can I do for ya, Miss...?"

"Porter," Jude said, not bothering to extend her hand since his were full with his lunch. "I'm looking into an old case and strangely you share the girl's last name. I hope I'm not treading on something personal here...."

Bell chewed and regarded her.

Jude shifted in her chair and pulled her skirt a little lower wishing she'd opted for slacks.

"Rosemary," he said after he swallowed. "What does the Wexford County Gazette want with a murder that happened over thirty years ago?"

Jude took out her cigarettes packing them against her palm and pulling one out.

"May I?"

"Sure."

"My editor is doing a series on cold cases," she lied. "Rosemary's name came up and I'm the lucky reporter on the case."

"It's not a cold case," he told her, setting his sandwich on the flattened paper bag. "They caught the woman who did it and sent her to a mental institution."

"Is there a relation? I only ask because this is a small town..."

"Rosemary was my sister. I was only five when it happened so..." he shrugged.

"The woman accused of her murder. What kind of proof was there that she did it?"

Bell leaned back in his chair, folding his hands across his flat stomach.

"Bloody knife in her barn, her bloody footsteps all over the scene, her fingerprints at the scene. Can't get much more evidence than that."

"But she was a child, right? The accused girl?"

"The person who committed the murder was a child by law, yes, she was thirteen, but as a journalist, I'm sure you're aware that teenagers can be pretty nasty, especially sick ones." He twirled his fingers near his head. "She was insane."

"That was known around town? Before the murder?"

"I was only five, as I mentioned, so I can't say that, but there were rumors about her, sure."

"I was told that she and the murdered girl were friends. What motive could she possibly have?"

Detective Bell narrowed his eyes at her and unfolded his hands.

"I sense, Miss Porter, that you're not looking for the facts here, but following some misguided belief in the woman's innocence. If that's the case then I can't help you."

Jude sat up straighter, glaring at Detective Bell.

"Criminal cases are public information. I have every right to request all the documents and find out for myself. And you are required as an agent of the law to investigate a murder and ensure you catch the actual killer, not pin it on some teenage girl because she's an easy out for the police and the community. I have every intention of investigating this murder myself, and I fully intend to print my findings. If you're wrong, I guess we'll know soon enough."

She stood and stomped to the front desk where Lori had switched to a cookbook. She was copying a recipe for pot roast.

"I need to request all the documents for the case concerning Rosemary Bell."

Lori looked up at her, surprised, likely taken aback by Jude's aggressive tone and perhaps also the name of the detective's older sister.

Jude glanced back at Detective Bell's desk. He sat watching her, his sandwich untouched.

CHAPTER 25

*S*eptember 1965
Jude

JUDE KNOCKED on the door and nodded toward the car where Hattie sat with her face turned away from the window. It was a dramatic gesture, sure, but Jude wanted Grimmel's help and figured this was the best way to get it.

A short middle-aged woman with black hair and dark eyes opened the door. She wore an apron over a knee-length floral house coat. Her apron was splattered with red sauce, likely spaghetti, but reminded Jude of blood.

"Hi," Jude said, holding out her hand. "My name's Jude. I'm a reporter and spoke with your husband, Grimmel, a few days ago. I wondered if he was home?"

The woman smiled and nodded, taking Jude's hand and shaking it warmly.

"Sure is. Finally got him to take down Sophia's swing set out back. It only took me eight years." She laughed and opened the door wide. "Sophia's in college now over at Grand Valley State University. She's a real bright girl. I could never have gone to college, but Sophia's real smart. Straight A's since she was this high." The woman held a hand up to her waist. "I'm Shirley. Should have started with that, maybe."

Jude smiled.

"I was wondering, Shirley, if Grimmel could come out here. I have a few papers in my car I wanted him to look over."

This was a lie, but since Jude intended to spill-all once Grimmel saw Hattie, she wasn't concerned.

"Oh, yeah sure. Let me do a quick stir on the spaghetti and I'll send him out."

She stepped back into the house leaving the door open a crack. Jude heard *I Love Lucy* on a television somewhere in the house.

Jude glanced at Hattie who looked back, and Jude spun her finger for Hattie to turn away from the window.

When Grimmel came out, the knees of his trousers were grass stained, and he looked red in the face.

"Well hello again, Jude. What can I do for ya?"

Jude smiled and took his hand. A look of surprise crossed his face, but he allowed her to lead him down the steps to her car.

"I have someone I'd like you to meet."

Jude knocked on the window and Hattie, without turning to face them, stepped from the passenger seat. When she turned, Grimmel's mouth fell open, and he pulled his hand from Jude's, taking a step back. He blinked several times and then looked at Jude.

"Are you...?" He let the question die. "You're her daughter. You're Sophia's daughter?"

Hattie smiled and nodded.

"So's Jude," she told him.

He took another step back and looked at Jude, his eyes lingering on her mouth and Jude knew he was making that unconscious connection between Jude's smile and his sister's.

"You're both her daughters?" he breathed, nodding his head.

"I also have a twin brother," Jude told him, grinning. "He's the spitting image of you."

Jude took a picture from her wallet and held it to Grimmel. It was a portrait that Gram Ruth had commissioned. Peter wore his army uniform, his hat slightly askew and a tiny smile playing on his lips. They had taken it three weeks before he went to Vietnam.

Grimmel stared at the photo for a long time.

"You girls better come inside," he said at last, holding the photo as he led them into the house.

~

GRIMMEL BROUGHT out a cardboard box and set it on the table.

"More coffee, Jude? Lemonade, Hattie?" Shirley asked them, bustling around the kitchen. "It's so nice to have kids in the house again."

Grimmel offered them a wry smile.

"She can't tell up from down since Sophia left," he told them. He opened the box which sagged on one side. A layer of dust coated the top.

Hattie drank her lemonade and gazed around the kitchen. Jude stood and moved next to Grimmel peering into the box.

"All the newspaper clippings are in here, and a few family keep-sakes." He held up a pair of worn baby shoes that were likely once white. "These were Tim's, then mine, and lastly Sophia's. We were a family of hand-me-downs."

"Aren't they precious?" Shirley asked, holding her wooden spoon far away so as not to drip red sauce near the box.

Jude handed them to Hattie who stared at them as if they might come to life.

"She wore these," Hattie murmured.

"This too," Grimmel said, pulling out a tarnished barrette adorned with a little gold butterfly. "Only when our mama made her. I'm not even sure why I saved it. Sophia would laugh at me. She could be a sentimental little fool, but she would have thrown this away just to ensure it never ended up in her hair again."

Hattie took the barrette gingerly and smoothed her fingers over the clip. She held it to the light streaming through the window and tilted it back and forth.

"I tucked most of the clippings in this old bible to preserve them. Guess I was trying to put Sophia's fate in God's hands. Not sure he was listening though. When they found her all those years later, I felt like somebody had stabbed me in the guts. Same time, I was so happy I knew where she was and that she was okay. I went up to that asylum five or six times and they never let me see her, not once!" His voice grew louder as he remembered, and Shirley put a hand on his shoulder.

"It was terrible, truly," she agreed. "Pushed poor Tim right over the edge."

"Do you mind if I ask what happened to Tim?" Jude said, sitting down and opening the bible, a sheaf of newspaper pages tucked inside.

Grimmel frowned, glancing at Hattie as if he reluctant to share bad news in front of her.

"It's okay," she told him softly. "I'm not as fragile as I look."

Jude looked at her surprised. It was unlike Hattie to even notice that someone was tiptoeing around her, let alone acknowledge it. It wasn't the first time in the previous few days that Jude had noticed a change in Hattie. She hadn't pinpointed it yet, but something had transformed in her little sister's demeanor, a new awareness.

"He got into the drink. Not long after Sophia left," Grimmel said. "It was real hard for our family after Rosemary's murder. People talked, Mama couldn't sell our vegetables in town and Tim had to drive her two counties away to a different market. He'd been runnin' the tractor on our farm and on Chapman's farm next door - they let him go. He'd been seein' a girl in town who broke things off lickity split."

Shirley took Grimmel's hand and held it tight.

"Once the drink got hold of him, he didn't care no more. About five years after Sophia left, he moved up north. Then he started shiftin around a lot. He'd come back and crash with Mama for a month and then off he'd go again. He wasn't a mean drunk. In fact, he was real nice, cried a lot. Thirty years to the day after Rosemary's murder he put a gun in his mouth."

Jude cringed, and Hattie let out a little gasp.

"I am so sorry," Jude whispered.

Grimmel nodded, kissing his wife's hand, and gently pushing her back towards the stove.

"I'm okay, honey. You can finish up. I don't want to take responsibility if your heavenly pasta sauce gets burned."

Shirley smiled and kissed his cheek.

"Did he have black hair?" Hattie asked, cocking her head at Grimmel. "And a funny little cowlick that sticks up no matter how often he spits and presses it down?"

Grimmel stared at her, blinking several times.

"And a scar in the center of his left eyebrow?" Hattie touched her own eyebrow with her fingertips.

"I stepped on a rake when I was six and it clocked him right in the face. That cut bled for two days, I swear," Grimmel whispered, watching Hattie not with fear, but a curious awe.

Shirley too had turned from the stove to gaze at Jude's little sister.

"I see him sometimes," Hattie told them. "He's never spoken to me, though."

Jude glanced between Grimmel and Hattie - again wondering what excuses or apologies she should make, but Grimmel did not look skeptical.

"Your mama had that gift, Hattie. My daddy always believed her. When I was a boy, her stories scared me, so I listened to Tim and my ma who called it nonsense. Only later we all realized it was true, after Rosemary, it's hard to question somethin' like that."

"I think I've always known Mama was alive because I've never seen her, not even a hint of her. She would have come to me, I begged for her a thousand times and she would have come," Hattie said.

Jude in an uncharacteristic show of affection scooted her chair closer to Hattie and wrapped her in a hug.

"Thanks, Jude," Hattie said, nuzzling her face into Jude's shoulder. "You smell like cinnamon."

"It's my gum," Jude told her.

"I wanted another daughter," Shirley told them wistfully. "Sisters. I have three."

Grimmel hugged his wife, taking her spoon and trying to lick it. She snatched it away.

"We have guests, no licking the spoon."

He grinned and shook his head.

"Sophia kept us plenty busy," he told them. "But we did hope for one more. Not God's plan for us, but that's okay."

"Of course, now that you girls are here..." Shirley said, her back to them as she stirred the pot of sauce.

"They're both over eighteen, Shirley. We can't adopt them," Grimmel told her, rolling his eyes at the girls who both laughed.

"Not legally, but we'd love to visit, often," Jude said and oddly she meant it. Never one to get too close - she felt comfortable with Grimmel and Shirley in a way she had never experienced at Gram Ruth's. It was so much like her own childhood she wanted to curl up on their couch and never leave. She saw a similar look of ease on Hattie's face.

"What happened to the Sheriff who worked Rosemary's murder? Is he still in town?" Jude asked, popping the bubble of nostalgia that seemed to form in the room. "Hal Jones?"

Grimmel frowned. "Sceezy old bastard. He never even considered another killer. Case closed, just like that." Grimmel clapped his hands together startling all three of them.

"Honey," Shirley told him, "let's not get your blood pressure on the move."

He nodded and let out a big breath.

"Doc says I need to stop gettin' stressed. Slaps me with a blood pressure cuff every time I go in there and it's always bad news. Our daddy died of a heart attack. Your mama ever tell you girls that?"

Jude shook her head.

"She didn't talk much about her family. A few times she told us stories, but always in this abstract way. She had brothers, but never offered your names," Jude explained.

"And did you find that strange?" Shirley asked, setting place mats on the table.

"I can help," Hattie offered, taking a stack of plates Shirley had put on the counter and dispersing one to each mat.

"Yeah," Jude admitted. "I kept a notebook when I was younger and wrote all kinds of quirky things like that in it. I liked to believe I was a detective."

"Makes sense you'd become a journalist then," Grimmel said, smiling.

"Oh," Jude paused realizing she had not told them the truth. "Technically I'm not a journalist, not the writing kind anyway. I'm a photo journalist and a photographer. I work with the newspaper, but only freelance. I told the journalist story to explain why I was looking into Rosemary's murder."

"Smart girl," Grimmel said. "If you'd have come back here saying you were Sophia's daughter people would have clammed right up - 'cept me of course."

"That sounds very interesting, photo journalism," Shirley commented, setting the spaghetti in the center of the table on a hot pad. "How did you get into that?"

Jude briefly explained her experience of viewing another world behind the camera and then cut off her story wanting to ask Grimmel a question.

"Grimmel, our mother escaped from the asylum almost two weeks ago," she said.

His eyes widened.

"She escaped?"

"Yes, and they're looking for her. They may even try to blame her for another murder though they're calling it an accident, so I doubt they will charge her for it."

Hattie twisted an endless spaghetti noodle around her fork but left it uneaten on her plate.

"Good grief! Where is she?" Grimmel stood as if they'd pile in the car and go to her that minute.

"That's what I wanted to ask you. Do you have any idea where she would go? Did you ever have any family around Traverse City, someone she might go to for help?"

He shook his head, sitting back down.

"She's lost?"

"The woman who helped her escape last saw her five days ago running into the woods. She didn't have a vehicle, money, identification."

Grimmel sighed and looked at his wife, who squeezed his hand.

"Our childhood home, but we're three hours from Traverse City and I don't know why she'd go there."

"I'd like to go the cabin," Hattie blurted looking back and forth between them.

"What cabin?" Jude asked, not following the sudden change of subject.

"Where Rosemary died."

Grimmel shook his head.

"I don't think that's a good idea, Hattie. It's a disturbing place considering what went on in there."

"I can find it on my own," Hattie cut in before he could finish.

Jude studied the determination in her younger sister's eyes. She was not a girl to make demands, and this was a demand.

"Why do you want to go there?" Jude asked.

"I can't explain it. I just need to, okay?"

Both Jude and Grimmel understood that Hattie felt compelled as part of the 'gift' Sophia had also possessed.

"I'd like to see your childhood home, and who knows, maybe she's there. I'm at a loss for where to start. Could you take us tomorrow afternoon?" Jude asked as if were settled.

Grimmel sighed, clearly losing the argument.

"Yeah. Meet me here around five. I'll leave the store early."

Hattie nodded eagerly, and Jude tried to trust the earnestness in her sister's face, but a slow uneasiness settled over her.

CHAPTER 26

September 1965
Damien

"Hi Katherine. How are the boys?" Damien asked the nurse who greeted him at the records office.

"Little heathens," she laughed, smoothing out her coiffed bun. Large, fashionable spectacles magnified her otherwise beady brown eyes, and she giggled though he hadn't said anything funny.

Damien knew women found him attractive. Many of the women in the hospitals and in his classes paid him special attention. They grew clumsy around him, dropping pens and notebooks, flipping their hair back and forth and blinking their long eyelashes as if performing a modern-day mating call.

He liked women, always had, but found their attraction dangerous in his profession, and preferred to work with male patients knowing they wouldn't color their stories to please him. He had read about Carl Jung and the far-reaching consequences of his affair with his patient, Sabina Spielrein. He admired the Swiss psychoanalyst and referred often to the man's theories in his work; however, he found the affair in poor conscience and strove to never have a similar experience himself.

Damien thought of Jude and Hattie and shook his head to banish their images. Ever since he'd agreed to Kaiser's request to meet the girls, he'd been spiraling further away from his good sense.

First a one-night stand with Jude, and now he courted Hattie like he wanted to marry her, which unfortunately he did. They weren't his patients, he reasoned. He was merely doing Dr. Kaiser a favor and he happened to fall for one of the girls - or was it both of them?

"Dr. Ross?"

Damien looked up. Katherine regarded him with a small, questioning smile. A few of the nurses called him doctor despite not having yet received his degree.

"Sorry. I've a lot on my mind."

"That's quite all right," she said, touching his arm. "If you ever need to talk-"

"No, thank you. I'm short on time if you could just grab those files for me."

"My pleasure," she told him covering her disappointment with a smile. "Which patient?"

Damien glanced behind him ensuring the doorway was empty.

"Sophia Gray," he said, looking toward his watch a second time.

"Oh, you'll have to ask Dr. Kaiser for those files," she told him, frowning. "He always keeps her files at his office. A lot of work that one. Course now that she's gone..."

"Do you know anything about that, Katherine? How she escaped?"

Katherine glanced over his shoulder, also checking for eavesdroppers and then took a step closer to him.

"Some of the nurses say she killed an orderly and got out with his key, maybe even wore his clothes."

Damien nodded, frowning.

"Any other rumors?"

"Well the patients are more kind. They claim the orderly helped her escape and the hospital killed him as punishment. They're not exactly right in the head, though are they?"

"Did you know her? Sophia?"

Katherine pursed her lips and shook her head.

"I work on the second floor and they relegated her to Hall Five. I saw her a handful of times, but the stories were enough to keep me away. She was quite a handful. Kaiser kept her in solitary most of the time. It wasn't safe to put her with other patients."

"Because she was violent?"

"Well she looked soft as a lamb to tell you the truth, but she told them things, weird spooky things that set the patients off."

"Like what?"

Katherine leaned in. Damien felt the warmth of her breath, it smelled like she'd been eating black licorice.

"About dead people. She told a patient on my floor that her dead son was with her husband now. The woman didn't even know her husband had died! She wailed for three days."

"Had her husband died?"

Katherine widened her eyes and nodded.

"Killed in a car crash that very morning."

Hattie

HATTIE TOUCHED EVERYTHING. Her mother had lived here as a child and she wanted the little energetic impressions left behind. Now and then she glimpsed her in her mind's eye running to the chicken coop with breakfast scraps or climbing the branches of the enormous oak tree behind the barn.

"Nobody's lived here in a few years," Grimmel told Hattie and Jude, kicking the post of a fence that had probably once corralled a horse. "A handful of people tried their hand at farming out here, but ever since people started buying their potatoes from Mexico, ain't no money in it. Not that we grew potatoes," he laughed, "but you get my point."

Hattie only half heard him. He and Jude had begun to talk about factory farming and the entire world getting poisoned. She drifted away, walking into an old barn, a splintered staircase led to the second floor. She walked up the stairs staring at the walls and the ceiling searching for signs of her mother.

Scratched into the surface of the floor, Hattie saw a tiny flower. She traced her finger over the image and knew her mother had created it. She wondered if she painted when she lived on the farm or if that came later in her life. A million questions danced through her mind - questions for Grimmel, questions for her mother, questions for Gram Ruth.

"Hattie?" Jude called from below.

"Coming," Hattie said making her way back down the stairs oblivious to the soft boards bowing beneath her.

"Your mama loved to hide up there," Grimmel told her. "She'd take a book and lie on an old horse blanket for hours and read. My mom would be calling for Sophia to do her chores and Sophia'd be tucked in the corner, her nose in a book."

"Sounds like Hattie," Jude said, cocking an eyebrow at her sister.

Grimmel led them toward the woods at the back of the property. Hattie trailed her hands over the tops of the tall grass. She bent and plucked a handful of milkweed, admiring the tiny purple flowers before allowing the wind to carry them away. Hattie imagined the forest in another month when the leaves began to turn. It would be a sea of gold and red, a beautiful painting.

As they moved from the tall grass into the forest, they grew quiet. Their footsteps were muffled by the dense foliage. The inner forest was dark, shaded by an enormous canopy of trees, and any path that used to exist had become overrun with goldenrod, nettles and ferns. Hattie would have liked to see rays of sun peeking through the darkness, but clouds prevented even that bit of light.

"Used to be a wide trail went in here from the far side." Grimmel pointed in the direction they were walking. "But old Earl passed on and he was the one who kept it up. My daddy told me you'd find him in here every summer hackin' away at the plants on his little road like they'd moved in just to spite him. He died when I was just a baby, so his cabin's never been more than an empty shack. Us kids played in it sometimes, but everyone liked to say Earl might show up with his walkin' cane to beat you out the door so that kept plenty of us away."

"I'm amazed they didn't destroy it after the girl's murder," Jude murmured.

"Couldn't," Grimmel told them. "This property belongs to some of Earl's family in Kentucky or Alabama, southern folks. After the death, one of 'em came up here and put No Trespassin' signs on a bunch of trees. The townies were afraid the new owners might have money, and they'd get in trouble with the law if they torched the place like they wanted to."

Hattie spotted an old, bullet riddled *No Trespassing* sign nailed to a tree.

Jude took out her camera and walked closer, taking several photographs.

They resumed their walking, and soon Hattie saw a squat hulking shape hunkered down in the forest ahead. The cabin reminded her of a sick animal sinking back and down, ready to attack if provoked. The roof, green with moss, had caved in the front right corner. If there'd been a door, it was gone - a black gaping hole in its place. Jude pulled up her camera and walked the perimeter taking photographs while Grimmel rambled on. Hattie had stopped listening.

A chill ran along her arms and traced her spine. She stepped to the doorway and placed a hand on the rotted wood frame. The interior of the cabin stank of mildew and mold and other dark decaying things that Hattie could imagine, but not name. Her legs shook as she stepped into the cabin. Terror coursed through her and she found it hard to breathe. In her mind, Grimmel and Jude had vanished, and she stood alone at the devil's door stepping into a fathomless mystery that would swallow her whole.

Images assailed her, some of her own imaginings, others from... where? *The girl in the yellow dress, ghouls in the shadows lapping blood from the floor, a hand reaching through the darkness to pull her inside, the glint of a knife rising and falling.*

She stepped into the cabin.

~

Jude

"HATTIE... HATTIE!" Jude said, louder the second time, shaking her sister who stood in the center of the cabin, her blue eyes wide and glassy like a doll's, her mouth hanging open.

"Is she all right?" Grimmel asked, taking one of Hattie's arms and pressing his finger against her wrist. "Her heart is racing."

"Hattie!" Jude yelled into her sister's face.

When she first entered the cabin with Grimmel, the sight of Hattie had given her a fright. She had only seen the strangely white silhouette of her sister and nearly dropped her camera, the precise reason she always left it hanging around her neck. Jude grasped Hattie by the upper arms and shook her.

"Wake up," she bellowed. Her sister's head snapped back and when she brought it forward she was blinking, her mouth closed.

She stared at Jude, dazed, and Jude felt guilty for shaking her so hard.

Hattie rubbed her hands over her arms where Jude saw red marks forming.

"Everything okay?" Grimmel asked. "You gave us a start, there."

Hattie looked at him blankly, offered a little nod, and shuffled from the cabin. Jude noticed she avoided touching anything as she left.

Jude shook her head, feeling an odd mixture of frustration and protectiveness for Hattie. Why did she always have to lapse into one her catatonic crazy states? And why couldn't Jude hold her temper when it happened? She shouldn't have shaken her so hard.

Jude sighed and opened her hands at Grimmel.

"Hattie has… episodes. That's the first I've seen in a while, but she sort of checks out," Jude explained.

Grimmel nodded.

"Believe it or not, your mama did something kinda like that. My ma called it daydreamin', but I could always tell it was more than that, like what Hattie was doin'. What does she say about the episodes after?"

Jude shrugged.

"A lot of times she can't remember them, not why it happened, not even coming out of it. I'll be surprised if she even remembers being in this cabin, which was her idea after all," Jude said mildly irritated.

"Anyway, this is it," Grimmel offered, waving a hand around the dark room. Jude's eyes had adjusted and the bits of gloomy light that filtered through the empty doorway and windows revealed a dirt floor strewn with leaves, a beer can or two and the remnants of a wooden chair someone had smashed.

"Seems like an awful place to die," Jude whispered, squatting down and holding her camera to her eye. She scanned the room through her lens, snapping pictures, but also taking in the other view. What had it been like for Rosemary Bell in the cabin? Had she followed someone she knew into a benign forest only to meet her death in that dingy little hovel? The walls were mottled with mold. Mushrooms grew prolifically in one corner, their fleshy white bodies perverse against the darkness surrounding them. They added an earthy rotted smell to an arrangement of odors that Jude couldn't discern.

"I've tried not to think of it," Grimmel admitted. "Makes me about sick, now that I have a daughter of my own. Doesn't justify how they went after poor Sophia, but I can tell you I'd be out for blood too if it was my little girl stabbed to death in this shit-hole."

Jude took a few more shots before following Grimmel out of the cabin. Hattie had walked a ways away, stopping near a tall maple tree she'd rested her palm against. She stared up into the maple leaves.

"Ready to go?" Jude called. Hattie turned and nodded.

Hattie trailed behind as they walked from the forest, and Jude almost apologized for squeezing her arms several times, but found she didn't have the words. Each time she envisioned her sister paralyzed in the cabin, she pushed up against her own irrational anger and coupling sense of fear.

Though she tried to squash the questions in her mind, she wondered what Hattie had seen in the darkness of the cabin.

CHAPTER 27

*S*eptember 1965
Hattie

HATTIE WOKE FEVERISH, her nightgown clinging to her body. She kicked off her comforter and stripped out of the nightie, letting it drop off the side of the bed. She rolled and stood, padding out of her bedroom naked, half-asleep, images racing through her brain.

Barely conscious, she set a white canvas on her easel and sat on the little leather stool Gram Ruth had given her. It was cool against her bare butt, but she hardly noticed. Leaning over, she pulled a palette of paints onto her knees, and swept the brush over the canvas, rhythmic, soothing; it quieted those images.

Soon she'd lapsed into a trance of sorts, a part of her realized she sat at the easel and painted, another part of her had not gotten out of bed at all.

Beyond the easel, watching silently from the corner, stood the girl in the yellow dress.

IN THE MORNING, Hattie woke naked in her bed, shivering. Strange, since she usually slept in a nightgown beneath a heap of blankets.

Drifting tiredly, she plodded into the kitchen and poured herself a glass of water, gulping it. Her mouth felt dry and tasted sour. She took another drink and swished it around, spitting in the sink. Gram would have hissed 'disgusting.' Not only did Gram detest spitting but would have considered spitting in one's sink tantamount to tracking horse poop through the parlor. Hattie giggled imagining Gram's face if she led one of Damien's horses across her pristine carpet.

She glanced into her sitting room and stared at the painting on her easel. It was dark, mostly blacks and browns, but as she walked closer, she saw the detail emerging. It was the cabin she had visited with Jude and Grimmel, but the angle was from the floor as if she were looking up. Silhouetted in the doorway stood a man, his features were blurry, but he held a knife clutched in one hand. His body blotted out most of the daylight, but she had painted his left arm clearly, it hung down at his side, fingers splayed except...

She drew closer to the painting. He had only three fingers, the pinkie and ring finger of his left hand were severed at the knuckle.

~

Jude

JUDE OPENED HER APARTMENT DOOR. Gram had been whining for an hour; he needed a walk, and though she was right in the middle of a photo piece, she gave in before he pissed all over her carpet.

"Jude," Hattie said breathlessly standing at the top of her stairwell. Her face was flushed, and her wispy blonde hair hung over her shoulders. She held her side like a cramp had taken hold.

"What are you doing here?" Jude asked, surprised. Hattie never visited her apartment. It was on the other side of town and Hattie hated to drive.

"I had a vision last night," Hattie breathed, still hunched over rubbing at her side.

"Did you drive here?" Jude asked, skeptical.

"I rode my bike."

Jude nodded, realizing why Hattie looked ready to take her last breath. Hattie loved to ride her bike but tended toward leisurely strolls in the country not mad races across town during morning traffic.

Gram whined and strained toward Hattie. He loved Hattie and insisted on abandoning Jude every time she was nearby.

"Traitor," Jude whispered, releasing his leash.

He ran at Hattie and she opened her arms, half falling to the floor as she hugged the dog vigorously who licked her face.

"Oh Grammy," Hattie said holding the dog around the neck and nuzzling her face against his furry cheek.

Jude remembered Hattie doing something similar with Gram Ruth's dead cat, Felix, and shuddered. Hattie's inkling for furry creatures extended to all animals - dead or alive.

"Here," Jude said tossing her the leash. "Clip her back on and we'll take a walk."

Gram half dragged Hattie off the concrete apartment steps and down the sidewalk. Jude had to jog to keep up.

"Hattie, you're supposed to walk her not the other way around."

Hattie just smiled and allowed the shaggy dog to stop at every tree, fire hydrant, and errant piece of garbage.

"Tell me about your dream," Jude said, pulling out a pack of cigarettes and propping one on her lip.

"Vision," Hattie corrected waving the smoke away as it drifted toward her. She wrinkled her nose but didn't complain.

"I thought about what that woman said, Lucy, about mom's gift," Hattie told her sneaking glances at Jude as if afraid she might make fun of her.

In the past, Jude would have, but lately... Well she wasn't ready to qualify it, but things had changed - that was for sure.

"I realized I could try to use it. The truth is I've been seeing Rosemary my whole life. And yesterday in the cabin, I felt her more strongly than ever."

Jude stopped, ashing her cigarette, and staring at Hattie.

"What does that mean you've been seeing her? Like you guys had tea parties together?"

Hattie frowned, pulling on Gram's leash as the dog tried to race into the street after a squirrel.

Jude sighed. "Okay, fine. I'm sorry. Lay it on me. Did you reach her?" Jude imagined Hattie dialing the operator on her rotary phone and asking to speak with the dead.

"She's always just been there. She's never spoken to me, but before I went to bed, I called out for her. I asked her to show me who killed her."

Jude took another drag and looked at her sister's earnest face.

"And?"

"She did."

Jude grimaced.

"Are you sure this wasn't a dream, I mean that cabin creeped me out."

"I understand the difference," Hattie insisted. "I painted it, and I painted a man."

"A man? Like a portrait?"

Hattie nodded, taking a stick that Gram brought to her and wiping the slobber on her pant leg before handing it back.

"You realize he carries it in his mouth, right?" Jude asked.

Hattie smiled and rubbed Gram's head.

Jude stubbed her cigarette out on the sidewalk and tossed it in the trash. They didn't speak for several minutes and Jude considered the cabin and how Hattie had seemed to... drift away.

"Let's go check it out."

～

Hattie

THEY ARRIVED at Hattie's apartment in Jude's car. Despite Hattie's maintaining that Gram could come with them, Jude left him at her apartment insisting the last thing she needed was a dog covered in blue paint jumping in her backseat.

Hattie had cleaned up since her last visit and though several surfaces revealed smears of various paint colors, she had washed the dishes and her paintbrushes were lined up and clean on a little table next to her easel.

"Gram Ruth would be proud," Jude smirked.

Hattie ignored her, leading Jude to a painting propped on the floor behind her couch. It faced away from the room and Jude wondered if Hattie preferred not to look at it.

Hattie lifted it onto the easel and Jude stared, a shiver running along her spine.

It depicted the cabin from the inside. In the doorway a man stood, mostly a silhouette due to the sun.

"What's that in his hand? A knife?" Jude asked leaning closer.

"Yes," Hattie said, reaching forward and touching the dark blade. When she pulled her fingers away a sooty gray paint remained.

Jude frowned.

"He's missing fingers."

Hattie nodded.

"You think this is the man that killed Rosemary?" Jude asked.

Hattie heard the skepticism, but she didn't fault her. Jude had never understood, perhaps people who didn't see spirits were incapable of understanding the mysteries of the world. Hattie didn't understand them either, but she never doubted their authenticity. *Seeing is believing,* her daddy used to say.

Jude opened her camera bag and slipped the strap over her neck, adjusting the camera before snapping several photos. Hattie watched Jude twist the lens and fiddle with the little dials.

"Why are you taking pictures of it?" Hattie asked.

Jude paused, the lens to her eye.

"To see it better, and I'll take the photo to Grimmel and that detective, Bell. If this guy was local someone will remember him, an injury like that would not be soon forgotten."

"She knew him," Hattie murmured.

"Who?"

"Rosemary. When he opened the cabin door, she recognized him, but she wasn't expecting him."

Jude let the camera dangle against her chest and took a seat next to Hattie.

"I didn't remember this morning and then I saw the painting..." Hattie swept a limp hand toward the picture. "The memory of it returned. I was Rosemary, sitting on the floor of the cabin and the door swung open. For a minute I couldn't see him, it was so bright and then-"

"You felt the murder?"

Hattie frowned searching for the sensations, but they hung at the periphery of her awareness. They floated like tiny black spots behind her eyes and when she turned to catch them they flitted away.

"He was familiar, and I was, or Rosemary was, disappointed. Then she noticed the knife, and she wasn't scared at first. She thought it was a joke, or he was teasing her."

Hattie drifted as she spoke, the room undulated and drifted like it was not made of wood and metal, but water, the colors flowed and seeped. She stared through her apartment into another time and place, a dense forest, sun slanting through a doorway, blood spattering the face of the man above her.

"Here," Jude thrust a glass of tepid water into Hattie's hands. She hadn't heard Jude get up or turn on the faucet. Her hands shook as she lifted the glass, but she drank to appease her sister who looked concerned and perplexed.

"How can this be real?" Jude asked. "I mean, you experienced a murder that happened over thirty years ago. Is there any chance you're...?"

"Making it up?" Hattie asked, setting the water on a little glass coaster, a gift from Gram Ruth.

Jude nodded.

"No, but how do I know? How do I explain this?"

"I guess the best way to know for sure is to follow this," Jude gestured to the painting, "and see if anything comes of it. What's that?" Jude went to the painting and knelt, pointing at a little rounded white shape on the floor.

"A hat. A woman's hat with lace around the rim. Rosemary wore it into the cabin."

Jude bit her cheek and lifted her camera, zooming in on the hat and taking a picture. It didn't look like a hat, only a little white blob, but maybe some detail was tucked in the painting and Jude would catch it later.

"I want to develop these in the dark room today, but we could have dinner later?" Jude asked.

Hattie looked at her surprised. Jude never asked her to have dinner. An occasional breakfast, a cup of coffee, but dinner was usually a time for Jude to go on a date or socialize with her girlfriends. Hattie did not have a single memory of Jude inviting her to dinner.

"Good grief, don't look at me like that," Jude snapped. "I didn't offer you an organ. It's dinner. We can go to Randy's Diner by my apartment."

"I'd like that," Hattie said, folding her hands in her lap and trying to hide the smile growing on her face. "I'm helping with a potluck at the church, but I can ride my bike from there."

Jude rolled her eyes.

"Why not drive your car?"

Hattie shrugged.

"It's too big. I don't like driving it."

Jude sighed and patted Hattie's knee.

"I'd die before I gave up my car. Freedom, Hattie. This is a man's world, but in a car, you can go anywhere."

∼

Jude

JUDE AND CLAYTON spent three hours in the newspaper dark room before returning to his messy desk. Jude's images of Hattie's painting were drying on the line. She had offered Clayton a brief explanation but kept most of the details to herself.

"Thank you, Clayton. I know I give you a hard time, but I'd be lost with you," Jude said, almost putting her hand over Clayton's and thinking better of it.

He looked up from his desk, where he'd been rifling through several newspapers, surprised, a blush turning his freckled face beet colored.

"You're welcome, Jude. And even though you're having a strangely sentimental moment, I won't ask you out. That'd be opportunistic of me."

She grinned and rolled her eyes.

"You're right."

"It was very bold of your grandmother to turn your mother in while hosting her funeral at her own home," Clayton said, shaking his head in disbelief.

"Right? How is it even possible?" Jude muttered, feeling the rage bubbling. She had to stay on task. If she wound back the clock to that horrible funeral and her equally horrible grandmother, fawning over Jude and her siblings, she wanted to puke or worse punch the old woman in her heavily made-up face.

"She knew Sophia had a different name, her hometown was over a hundred miles away, a whole other time, no obituary - only close friends and family," Clayton murmured. "That's how she got away with it."

"But why didn't my dad put a stop to it?" Jude asked. "I mean after he realized Gram had my mom institutionalized, why didn't he blow the whole story up?"

Clayton offered her a sympathetic look.

"Unfortunately, those are questions for your grandmother, Jude. And sooner or later you're going to have to ask them. You know that, right?"

Jude huffed and pulled a cigarette from her purse, lighting it and a second for Clayton which he coughed on at first. He always wanted to smoke with Jude despite his tendency to hack on every inhale.

"I'm not ready to talk with her. I'm afraid what I'll do. And honestly, I want to find my mom first. I want the truth."

"And the trail on your mom has gone cold?"

Jude nodded, taking a drag and leaning back in her chair. Her shoulders and neck ached, and her eyes felt crossed from hours in the dark room.

"I'll make some calls today. Maybe I can help you find her," he murmured.

CHAPTER 28

 eptember 1965
Sophia

"Thank the heavens for you, Kent," Sophia whispered digging through the duffel bag and finding a small change purse with twenty dollars.

She'd found a wool sweater in the bag the night before, and slept in a small grove of apples trees. After piling herself with brush, leaving only a small hole to breathe, she felt warm and safe.

Even if Kaiser searched the woods, he would likely pass her by.

Apple trees held a special place in her heart. Her father had grown them on her childhood farm. She and her bothers had picked them, and her mother baked pies and applesauce from their fruit. Her daddy used to tell her about his own mother, an Irish immigrant, that revered apples as sacred. She insisted on always burying the dead in her family with apples tucked in their coffins. That way, they can get reborn, her father would say with that mischievous gleam in his eye. Afterward he'd make up a story of a young woman who buried her husband with an apple and he came back as a ghoul.

Sophia picked an apple from the ground and sniffed it. The fruit smelled pungent, overripe and on its way to rot. She stood and picked a few from the tree and stuffed them into the bag and ate two before setting off.

It had been ten years since she'd last experienced freedom, and she felt lost in the world. Where did she go for help? If she knocked on someone's door, they'd surely turn her in. At that moment, Dr. Kaiser was likely turning the world against her. The police, the townspeople would all be hunting her, and the sensation was one Sophia remembered well.

She thought back to the day Rosemary died, the angry look on Margaret Bell's face as she stared at Sophia. *The devil's mark*, she'd said, and only later did Sophia learn what she meant - the caul wrapped around Sophia's face at birth. There were stories associated with such a thing and they weren't good ones. Except Sophia's daddy never portrayed it that way. He said it made Sophia special, it was a mark all right, a mark of magic he once told her when tucking her in for bed.

"I could really use your guidance right now, Daddy," she murmured, climbing over a dead tree and scanning the forest for clues as to which way she should travel.

The early sunlight slanted through a tall shimmering maple tree and she turned in that direction. The forest felt safe. Every tree, plant, bug and bird were connected to her life - either her own childhood or the childhood of her children.

After she married Jack, they moved away from the Porter's estate and settled into a creaky old farmhouse on fifty acres of forest that bordered another three hundred acres of state land. In the fall they tapped Maple trees, in the summer she and the kids picked berries for jam and muffins. In winter they strapped on homemade snowshoes that Jack fashioned from the branches of an ash tree and covered with deer hide. Jack liked to joke they had created their own Walden's Pond. He was much more read than she, an intimidating factor when she first met him which he quickly laid to rest. What she lacked in book smarts, she made up in knowledge of the natural world. He read to her from Thoreau, Emerson and Poe. She revealed to him the mysteries each season brought, the edible plants and mushrooms and how to live with the land rather than on it.

Theirs had been a love they had to fight for and neither of them took it for granted. When Gram Ruth first caught them kissing, she sent Jack away to stay with his cousins in New York for two weeks. She put Sophia to work scrubbing the tile floors and dusting the porcelain figures who often watched Sophia with quiet disproving eyes. When Andrew, Ruth's husband, returned from a business trip, he was outraged at Ruth's behavior. He insisted Sophia stop cleaning. He drove to New York and picked up their son. Ruth railed against him. Sophia could hear their yelling through three stories as she slept in a little bedroom on the third floor. Jack would sneak into her room and they would make a canopy with her blankets and lay beneath it listening to the booming voices of his parents. Sophia offered several times to leave, but Jack insisted wherever she went, he would follow so she stayed knowing it would only break Ruth's heart more if she stole her only child.

Sophia kicked at a fallen apple and looked to the sky. The sun had risen, and the temperature climbed. She peeled off her sweater and walked. After years in the asylum, many of them sedentary on Dr. Kaiser's orders, her muscles cramped. She stopped frequently to rest and gulp huge breaths, savoring the damp forest, but most of all the freedom of being outdoors. Not a white wall in sight, no narrow bed and closed door waiting at the end of her day, and most of all, no Doctor Kaiser.

SHE WALKED DURING THE DAY, following the sun. Despite her aching legs, the image of her and Jack's farm was a beacon that drove her forward. It was seventy miles from Traverse City, the home of the Northern Michigan Asylum. A long walk, sure, but she could do it. It would take time following the road from the safety of the forest.

The wildlife delighted her, she stopped at a small stream, cupping the cool water in her hands to drink and looked up to find a spotted fawn on the opposite bank. He stared at her with his black inquisitive eyes and then bounced back into the forest joining several does waiting in the trees. She watched a raccoon climb a tree, squirrels foraging for acorns, and even a fox who streaked past her in a red blur.

When she neared farms, she snuck to their perimeters and snatched a few vegetables for her bag.

She walked for five days before the roads grew familiar. When she found her own road, she lay on the ground and cried, bunching the leaves in her hands and weeping into the soil, reliving a thousand barefoot summer days in the woods.

CHAPTER 29

September 19, 1965
Jude

JUDE KNOCKED on Detective Kurt Bell's door, holding the envelope of photos clutched against her chest. Bell lived in an apartment next to a large courthouse, above a pharmacy.

Jude heard someone inside rustling about.

"Hold on," a voice called.

The door opened, and Kurt stood on the threshold. He'd thrown on a knit shirt unbuttoned, and wore a pair of jeans. He was barefoot, his hair tousled, and several little tissues stuck to his face where he'd cut himself shaving. He scowled when he saw her and stepped from the apartment, closing the door firmly behind him.

"It's inappropriate that you're standing on my doorstep, Miss Porter. Is the press that desperate for a story?"

He touched his face, noticed the tissues, and scrubbed them off, looking more irritated that she had caught him so indisposed.

"Why shave the beard?" she asked. "It looks good on you and I bet the old guys don't think they're getting bossed by a rookie when you're wearing it."

Bell frowned and lifted his eyebrows.

"What can I do for you, Miss Porter?"

Jude, realizing he was not softening anytime soon, pulled a picture from the envelope. She had considered waiting until the next day and going to the police station. The problem was that if she told her story there, other people would hear it, and the snickers would spread around the town in no time. Alone, Detective Bell might at least consider Hattie's painting.

"I may have misrepresented myself the other day," Jude started. "I do work for a newspaper, but I'm not actually writing a story about Rosemary. Sophia Gray, the woman accused of your sister's murder, is my mother."

Bell released a long sigh and pressed his hand to his head rubbing his thumb and forefinger over his temples.

He looked toward the window at the end of the hall and lifted his wrist examining his watch.

"I can give you twenty minutes," he told her.

Jude, relieved, pushed forward, but he stopped her with a hand.

"Not in my apartment. I don't do business here, ever. There's a bench at the courthouse. That'll do just fine." He gestured toward the window. "I'll meet you down there in two minutes."

"Okay, fine, sure," she said, retreating down the steps. The courthouse had a perfectly manicured lawn and in one corner sat an enormous cannon on a foundation of cement and stone. Jude saw a plaque on the side likely naming some general rather than the men who actually wielded the weapon. She took a seat on a bench.

"I'm here. Now tell me why you are," Bell quipped when he arrived moments later with his shirt buttoned, his hair combed and a pair of loafers on his feet.

He was handsome but had the look of man that didn't care much for dating. No ring on his finger, Jude noticed.

"I need to ask you to have an open mind, Detective because I'm going to tell you something that possibly defies your understanding of the world," Jude started, already doubting her ability to convince this clearly hard-headed man that her sister had seen the murderer in a vision.

Bell sighed and looked at her.

"Listen, I've got dinner plans in a half hour so cut the bullshit, Miss Porter."

Jude frowned and bit back her retaliation.

She held a photo out for Bell and he took it, bringing it closer to his face.

"Looks like the silhouette of a man in a doorway. Is this relevant to something?"

"My sister painted this after we visited the cabin where your sister was murdered," Jude explained, hating the story and knowing if she were the one hearing it, she'd laugh out loud. "She has... visions. My mother did too, maybe you heard that. That's how my mom found your sister, she saw..." Jude paused and then spit the words out, wishing she could prove them. "She saw ghosts, and the morning she found your sister, Rosemary appeared to her and led her to that cabin. She panicked and took the knife and ran away."

Kurt snorted and looked her in the eye.

"Really? You showed up at my apartment with a photo of a blurry nothing and a ghost story?"

He stood up, setting the photo back in her lap.

"Listen to me, god-damn-it," she spat, and a rage erupted in her, so hot and acrid she jumped to her feet, ready to scream and claw his face if he didn't give her the twenty minutes he promised.

It was suddenly all too much, her mother being alive, a lifetime of lies, the injustice of the world, poor scared Hattie, and her twin fighting someone else's war.

Bell took a step back, holding up his hands.

"Okay, I'm sorry. Don't-" he paused looking at her balled fists, "do whatever it is you were about to do."

He picked up the photo again.

"Your sister painted this and what? You think it tells us something we didn't already know?"

"That's the man who killed Rosemary," Jude said, her emotion barely held at bay. She poked a finger at the image. "Look at his hands."

Bell brought the photo closer, squinting.

"Three fingers..." he mumbled, his eyes widening for just a moment. Jude saw something pass over his face, dismay perhaps, but then it was gone.

"Did you know him? Was there a local man that had only three fingers? He'd be missing his pinkie and ring finger on the left hand. Hattie said Rosemary knew her killer, she recognized him when he walked into that cabin."

Kurt sighed and ran a hand through his hair, destroying his earlier comb job.

"Have you talked about this with anyone else?" he asked, holding the photo more tightly.

"No, but you recognize him, don't you? Hattie is right."

"Look." Kurt handed her the photo. "There is a person in town with those characteristics, but everyone knew that. Your mother might have inserted that picture into your sister's head for all I know to put the blame on someone else. This isn't evidence, it's just... I don't even know what it is."

"There's more," Jude insisted. She held up the photo and pointed at the little white object on the floor. "This was a hat your sister was wearing. It belonged to your mother. Wide brim with white lace. He took it." Jude jabbed at the man's silhouette. "He took it and has it somewhere in his home."

"How could your sister possibly know that?"

Jude frowned.

"I don't know, Detective, and for what it's worth, I've never bought into this stuff either until now anyway because you know what? It's real. The more I think about the world," Jude waved her hand around, "what does make sense? How are we even here living and breathing? Why do dying people have miraculous recoveries? How do crippled men suddenly stand and walk again? I've always thought it's all laid out clear as day, but that's a lie. We tell ourselves that lie to feel safe, to believe we know what's coming next. You could get hit and killed walking across that street. Poof you're gone. But maybe you're not gone. Most of us believe that, right? That there's something after, and yet we have no room for belief in the mysteries right here with us."

Jude stopped talking. Detective Bell watched her with a mingled sense of wonder and discomfort. He wiped the expression and tapped his watch.

"Time's up," he said.

"Take the picture. Think about what I've said. My number's on the back."

Before he could reply she turned and walked away.

200

HER NEXT STOP was the TV shop. Grimmel stood at a shelf of televisions talking animatedly to an older couple who both stared at the screens enthralled. Jude guessed they'd never owned a TV and were overwhelmed at the sheer idea, let alone the choices.

Jude remembered the first time she saw a television. They had gone to Gram Ruth's for Thanksgiving dinner and there perched on a shining table in the middle of Gram's pristine sitting room was a funny little box with metal horns.

Jude had only been four or five, but both she and Peter had stood with their noses almost pressed to the screen for an hour before their parents dragged them away. It had been their first glimpse of *Howdy Doody*, and Gram had been in rare form allowing them to watch the entire program. Not that anything else was on and even Jude's parents were entranced by the little television though they never purchased one and years later when Gram tried to gift them a television, their father politely refused. Jude and Peter had begged him to change his mind, but he never did. Their mother told them someday televisions would be everywhere, and they'd remember their years without one fondly, which Jude had thought was a load of crap, but now she realized, her mother had been right.

Grimmel smiled and put a hand on the man's shoulder, leading him toward the counter to complete his bill of sale. He had Peter's face, those big sincere brown eyes and though Peter had never sold a thing in his life, he only needed to flash that smile and shine those puppy eyes to turn you into a puddle on the floor. Jude watched Grimmel and yearned for her twin brother. It didn't happen often as an adult, the sense that she was missing, that without Peter she was only a half, but now and then the familiar longing crept in.

Vietnam. He had deployed ten months before and though she received letters every few weeks, she could never think of him without a niggling sense of fear. Men were dying in droves, hundreds, maybe thousands, atrocities reported every day. If she stepped up to Grimmel's televisions she could no doubt find a station reporting on the tragedies happening in Vietnam at that moment.

Grimmel looked up and saw her, his smile growing wide - Peter's smile. She pointed outside and held up her cigarettes, stepping out to the sidewalk for a smoke. She took a few long inhalations, leaning against the brick building, and watching the cars pass slowly down the street.

Grimmel opened the door a few minutes later, the bell tinkling, and ushered out the couple and a large box containing their new TV set. He carried it to their car, helped situate it in the trunk, and returned to Jude.

He gave her a big hug, lifting her off the ground a foot, and then grinned down at her.

"You're back again! I can't tell you how great it is, Jude, meeting you and Hattie. I mean Shirley about knocked me out with a frying pan, I wouldn't stop talking about you two. Spitting images of your mama, the both of you."

Jude smiled, feeling warm at his comment. She had rarely been said to look like her mother, but here was her mother's own brother saying it. Jude almost wanted to cry.

"Grimmel, after we visited the other day, Hattie had a vision," Jude started, digging into her bag for the envelope of photos.

Grimmel nodded, rocking back and forth on his big feet.

"Okay, yeah."

"She dreamed of the cabin, of Rosemary, and I guess dream isn't the right word."

"I understand, Jude. You don't have to break it down for me. I get it." He looked her straight in the eye and Jude sighed, relieved. He got it.

Jude pulled out a photo and held it to him.

He took it, turning it this way and that, holding up a meaty hand to shield it from the light.

"Hattie believes this is the man who killed Rosemary?"

"Yes."

Grimmel leaned closer, squinting and then threw the photo away, catching it fast before the wind caught it and carried it into the street.

"Wow, sorry, that was weird. This guy only has three fingers on his left hand?"

"Yeah."

"You said you met Rosemary's brother, Dale?"

Yes. He directed me to you."

"Did you notice anything unusual about his hands?"

Jude frowned, thinking back, and then opened her eyes wide.

"He wore a glove on his left hand, sheepskin or something. I figured he'd been working when I showed up."

Jude pictured Dale sitting in his chair. He predominantly used his right hand, but Jude had noticed one thing - when he cracked open a can of beer, he balanced it on his knee and used his left hand to prop it in place rather than holding it full on as if he had an injury or...

"Only three fingers," she murmured. "You're telling me, this is Rosemary's brother?" Jude looked at the picture imagining Dale. "But, why?"

Grimmel bit his cheek and shifted.

"Better give me a smoke," he said.

Jude handed him one and lit it.

He took a few puffs, looking thoughtful.

"He was an odd kid. Kinda obsessed with killin' things, animals and what-not. I mean we were boys and there wasn't much else to do so odd ain't exactly the right word, but Tim didn't like him. He told me once if he caught me running around with Dale he'd box my ears, he liked to pretend he was my daddy sometimes."

"Do you think Tim suspected him?"

Grimmel dropped his cigarette and ground it out with his foot.

"Maybe, I mean Tim used to talk about it to me and ma. He'd say the killer's still out there and if we could prove who did it, then Sophia could come home, but my ma used to get pretty worked up. She was afraid if Tim started snooping around, the town would turn their attention back to Sophia and maybe this time they'd find her."

"Shit," Jude whispered.

"What?"

"I gave this photo to Detective Kurt Bell a half hour ago. Dale's brother."

CHAPTER 30

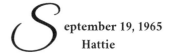 eptember 19, 1965
Hattie

"DON'T YOU LIKE THE ALFREDO?" Damien asked Hattie across the table.

She looked up, caught in a daydream, and then back at her plate. She'd barely taken a bite.

"No, I do, it's great." She wound her fork through the thick pasta and put it to her lips noticing the creamy texture, the slippery noodles, the taste of pepper. He had cooked her dinner, lit candles, poured wine - he watched her with his curious eyes, but Hattie kept drifting.

Jude had left her a phone message that morning. She was returning to Mason and would call later. Hattie had gone for a long bike ride into the country and encountered Damien on her way back into town. He invited her for dinner and though she had intended to spend the evening painting, she said yes.

"You seem far away, Hattie," Damien murmured sipping his wine. "Literally and metaphorically." He grinned and stood from the other end of the long table, coming to sit close to her. "My mom helped me decorate the house. She insisted on a formal dining table even though this is the first time I've used it. Usually it's piled with books."

Hattie blushed and smiled, allowing her blonde hair to fall over her face.

"Gram has a table like this in a big dining room. Jude and Peter called it The Room of Doom." Hattie laughed, grasping her wineglass and holding it so tight the blood in her knuckles disappeared.

Damien reached for her other hand and Hattie started to shrink away and then paused, allowing his fingers to trace her own.

"Let's move, shall we?" he asked.

Hattie glanced at him, his face so easy and relaxed, perfect white teeth gleaming. He had a little mole high on his right cheek. His eyelashes were long and blond like his hair, blond eyebrows, blond hair on his arm. Like me, Hattie thought smiling, weirdly at ease after that small connection - like me.

"Yes, okay."

They stood, and Damien grabbed their plates while Hattie picked up the wine.

His house was large, gleaming wood floors and white walls covered in black and white photographs. He cleaned the common areas, but Hattie detected disarray beyond the observer's eye. A pair of tennis shoes on the stairway, a towel hanging over a closet door.

"I'm always trying to be tidy," Hattie said as she followed him into the sitting area. He laid their food on a long black coffee table that butted close to a mustard colored sofa. Two red arm chairs flanked the couch all facing a bricked fireplace.

"Me too, though I'm not, at all," he admitted.

"Orderliness is next to Godliness," she murmured.

He grinned and shook his head, a lock of blond hair feathering his forehead.

"My mom used to tell me that too, garbage I say. Half the patients I meet have disorders that cause them to clean obsessively. I'd say cleaning is the devil's work, not Gods." He laughed, and Hattie laughed too, though the words made her gasp a little. If Gram heard them she'd hit the roof. "I want to hear you talk," Damien said, settling back on the couch.

Hattie sat stiffly beside him. She'd never been good at dating, and the closeness of Damien made every muscle taut. Her lungs contracted, and she struggled to take her next breath.

"Tell me about your family," Damien urged.

Hattie touched her black skirt, a Jude hand-me-down and pictured her sister who was shorter than her, but stronger times a thousand.

"Jude and Peter are twins," Hattie started, reaching for the handful of solid memories of their lives before that summer, the summer where they lost everything. "Growing up they were so close. Mama and Daddy had me seven years after them, the best surprise, my daddy used to say. But I followed them like a puppy and they ran away from me like a pack of wolves trying to ditch the meek one, the sickly one."

Damien studied her. Hattie felt his eyes so intent on her face she wanted to pick the afghan from the back of the couch and cover her head with it.

"I don't mean it the way it sounds. They loved me. They were just older and different. I was more like Mama. That's what my daddy always said. I lived with my head in the clouds and Jude and Peter were solid. Sometimes my mama would watch them coming across the yard and say here comes Fortress Judy and Peter."

Damien laughed, and Hattie relaxed into the couch, the sound of his laughter enveloping her, chipping away the ice that encased her.

"My mama painted and gardened and told stories. My daddy worked at a rubber factory as a manager, but he didn't have to. They had a lot of money. When my grand-daddy died, I never met him, he left my daddy a fortune, but my daddy liked to work. He wanted a different kind of life than Gram Ruth. He believed in working for a living and taking care of his family, growing your food when you could, darning your own socks. He was real," Hattie said lifting her fingers to the air in front of her where she could see his face and thought if she imagined him hard enough maybe she could feel the stubble on his cheek when he hadn't shaved that morning.

"How did he die?" Damien asked, gently.

"Fell in the barn. Three weeks after my mother died. She didn't die, I realize now, but she did, you know? To us, she died."

"I can't imagine that, not emotionally anyway. Life without a mom or a dad. I talk to my mom every week."

"I can't imagine *that*," Hattie told him. "No, that's not true. I talk to my mom every day, every night, but it's not really her, it's the her I made up. She's..." Hattie touched the emptiness before her, "like a ghost."

"Like the spirits you see?"

Hattie shook her head.

"They're different, more solid than my mom. She's a memory I pretend is near me. They're like… fog early in the morning. I can see them, but if I look too hard, they're not there at all."

"How long have you seen them?"

Hattie looked at her lap and then chanced a glance at Damien. He didn't look critical, not even skeptical, only curious and again she wondered at his interest in her. Why should he care who she was?

"Am I going too far? Sometimes I overstep my bounds, ask too many questions. Occupational hazard," he told her, leaning forward and refilling their wine.

Hattie took another sip. She'd had a glass or two. Her body seemed light, fizzy, like she might float up and away. She set her glass back on the table.

"I don't mind. No one's ever asked. Then again, I don't have a lot of conversations. Jude says I don't talk about things of this world, I'm incapable of small talk."

"And that's a bad thing?" Damien asked, cocking an eyebrow.

"Jude's good at people, talking to strangers. She knows things about the cashier or the waitress within minutes, they tell her stuff because she knows what to say. I'm not good at that. But I know things…" Hattie murmured. "I can see if people are hurt or scared or if they're… mean."

"Mean?" Damien asked, his breath warm as he leaned closer.

"If people are mean they're dark, thick looking. I'm sure this sounds… weird. Does it sound weird?"

"Not weird, unusual, extraordinary. Hattie, could your mom do that? See those things?"

Hattie nodded vigorously.

"Yes, it was like our little secret. Sometimes we'd sit on a bench on the sidewalk in town and just watch people. Like practice, to see if we perceived the same thing."

"And did you?"

"Yes, every time."

"And your mom saw spirits?"

Hattie nodded.

"But I didn't know about Rosemary. She never told me about her."

"It's amazing, Hattie. A gift."

Hattie smiled at him, shy, but the longer she looked into his eyes the more her body seemed to reach out for him. As if their bodies spoke a similar language even when their mouths could not. The skin beneath her clothes grew warm, tingly.

He took her hand and smoothed his fingers across her palm and up over her wrist.

"Can I kiss you?" he asked, leaning towards her.

~

Jude

JUDE STOPPED at PJ's Cafe before starting the two-hour drive home. Grimmel had offered their pull-out couch, practically begged her to take it, but she refused. She didn't sleep well in any bed but her own. Even the three years she lived with Gram Ruth after her parent's deaths comprised sleepless nights tossing on the over-stiff mattress, forever battling an endless supply of throw pillows.

"Coffee, black," Jude told the waitress who set a steaming mug of coffee on her table a moment later.

The diner was dead. It was going on ten pm. Night had arrived and with it the chilly temperatures of late September. Jude had sat with Grimmel and Shirley for three hours pouring over his memories of Dale, the newspaper clippings of Rosemary's murder, and contemplating how they could get the case re-opened. Jude wondered if a message would be blinking on her answering machine from Kurt. He had to have known the most likely suspect was his own brother, but he'd said nothing. He had, however, looked ashen, just for a moment and now she understood why.

Taking out her notebook she flipped through the pages, back to the day she had interviewed Dale. It had been a short and informal meeting, he slammed beers all the while. Dale hadn't revealed much, but that gloved hand told her all she needed to know. She finished her coffee and left a quarter next to the mug before walking into the cool night.

The stars were bright, an endless navy dome punctuated with a thousand pricks of light. She'd last truly seen the stars during her one night with Damien, reveling at their brightness. He had laughed and howled at the moon before they climbed the stairs to the little motel room he'd rented. Jude felt the familiar burst of anger at Damien, almost overshadowed by the hurt beneath it. Of all the times she'd had casual sex she'd never found the infatuation that pervaded her girl-friends' love lives like an invasive species impossible to destroy. Unlike many of her one-night stands, which left the man in her bed heart broken and confused, the tables had turned. It had been Jude sitting around watching the phone, wondering what she had done or not done.

"Why am I still thinking of him?" she growled, flipping her finger at the stupid stars conspiring against her. Those stars had been part of the illusion she bought into that night. What she termed the *love lies* - little bullshit touches that tricked people into believing it was true love when it was just gaseous balls in an indifferent universe.

She thought of Kurt Bell. If he wasn't Rosemary and Dale's sibling, she'd invite him out for a drink. Nothing eased the discomfort of heartbreak like another man's bed, but she couldn't do it. She needed a clear head and the booze and sex that would accompany such a choice would destroy her momentum.

Jude pulled out of the diner and headed for highway 127, letting off the gas as she passed the road that led to her mother's childhood home. It was late, but she had a flashlight and her mother was out there, somewhere. What if she found her way back to that rundown farm-house where it all began?

Jude turned and sped down the road, cranking up her music. The detour was likely a wasted effort, sure, but she hated the thought of going home to her empty apartment, drinking half a bottle of wine and thinking about the message that still hadn't appeared on her machine. As she left the few lights of town behind, the darkness swallowed her little car whole. A half-moon peered from the sky, cut with eerie horror movie clouds.

They reminded her of a hundred trips to the marquee with Peter. Years earlier, they'd gone to see *Invasion of the Body Snatchers* three times. For every new horror film, they bought tickets opening night and sat in the front row scarfing popcorn, watching wide-eyed as the actors raced screaming from whatever creature of the night pursued them. It hurt to think of him, to reminisce, to miss him. *Dr. Terror's House of Horrors* had just opened and each time she passed the theater, she wanted to cry.

He would laugh at her mushiness, but then give her a rib-cracking hug. If he were home, he would be in the passenger seat, hot on the tail of a child killer, desperate to find their mother. He would turn the most serious, heart-breaking moment of their lives into an adventure.

"But you're not here, are you?" Jude grouched.

A flash of black raced from the woods in front of her car and Jude slammed on her brakes, clutching her steering wheel. A black cat passed, pausing on the side of the road to look back at Jude before he disappeared into the forest beyond. Jude breathed and watched the darkness he'd vanished into, swearing he'd had jewels for eyes.

"Fucking Felix," she grumbled, hands shaking as she eased the car forward. "And bad luck to boot."

CHAPTER 31

September 19, 1965
Hattie

HATTIE DIDN'T LOOK AWAY. She stared into Damien's eyes as he got closer and the gray turned to a prism of gold, black, little flecks of light, a gateway. When his lips touched hers, she closed her eyes. The intensity rocked her back. His tongue slid into her mouth and she didn't know how, but her body seemed to understand what to do as she opened her own lips and reached, wrapping her arms around his neck.

He stood, his face splotched with color, his chest rising and falling and leaned down, scooping her from the couch. He carried her up the stairs, and Hattie stared dazed at the shadows dancing on the ceiling, at the soft curls of his blond hair.

When he laid her on the bed, she realized what would happen next, but didn't know how to go about it. She'd never made love before, and felt awkward and terrified.

Before she could curl into a ball and turn away from him, he was leaning over her again, pressing his mouth against hers, pulling her out of her mind and pushing her into her body. He stripped off his shirt, flung it to the floor. His body was hard, contours she imagined on a canvas, an array of light and dark, crevices and hills. She smoothed her hands over tan muscles, a fine blond fuzz coating his chest down to matching dips along his hips to his pants he'd unbuttoned, now shrugged off. And then his hands were on her skirt, not pushing it up, but gently turning her, unzipping it and pulling it over her naked thighs, pale and covered in goosebumps.

She shivered as he pulled up her shirt, took it up over her head and returned his mouth, hot and moist, to her collarbone and shoulders down to her breasts, naked. The sensation as he took her nipple into his mouth forced her up onto her elbows, gasping. He returned to her mouth, kissing her, pressing her legs open, and she glimpsed him for only a second before he slid inside her and she called out - not in pain, or maybe in pain - but also pleasure and need, she needed him to be inside her, needed to snake her arms around him and bury her face in his neck. He was not animal-like as Hattie had often feared men would be. Damien was slow and deliberate, searching her face for signs of discomfort, kissing her, murmuring into her ear she was beautiful, that he dreamed of her every night.

Jude

THE DIRT DRIVEWAY, with its fallen down mailbox, slid into view and she turned in, still shaken from nearly hitting the cat.

"It wasn't Felix," she whispered. Except the previous weeks had offered more than their share of unearthly revelations, which Jude preferred not to contemplate at that moment.

There were no houses next door or across the street. Her mother's childhood home was cloaked in darkness, the grass overgrown, the heavy trees blocking most of the house from view. Pulling down the driveway, she strained toward the window looking for any markings in the dirt, footprints, tracks, but saw nothing.

When she stepped from the car, it was not utter silence that greeted her, but the *night songs* as her mother used to call them. Crickets, tree frogs, cicadas - all indistinguishable from one another - a symphony of insects and reptiles. Jude popped her trunk and rifled through her duffel bag, retrieving her flashlight. She glanced at the smooth black pistol, but left it tucked inside, imagining Hattie over her shoulder scolding her for returning it to her car.

Shining the beam on the ground, Jude crunched over dirt and stone and into dried grass, moving close to the house. She looked at doors and windows, hoping for some evidence that her mother had been there, but it appeared as though no one had walked through the doors in years, decades. Grimmel had told Jude that their mother sold the property and moved two towns over a few years after Rosemary's death.

At the barns, Jude paused, shining her light through the darkened doorways. The woods stretched beyond the last barn, dark and ominous, sheltering a ramshackle cabin where a little girl once died. Against her better judgment, she stepped into the trees, swinging the beam of her light back and forth, lighting trunks and bushes, catching on a pair of glowing eyes, a possum, clinging to a tree.

Now the creatures seemed quieter, the night thicker, and Jude swallowed a lump forming in her throat.

I am not afraid, she thought, frustrated that she needed the mantra, but repeating it in her head, anyway.

Jude usually courted the night. She loved the sensation of moving down a dark sidewalk, heels clacking, with the effervescent thrill of a few cocktails and an evening of flirtation behind her. Unfortunately, tonight she was sober and walking alone through the forest, something Hattie might enjoy, but she did not.

A twig snapped behind her and she spun around, the light weaving through the darkness, but illuminating only the trees, the foliage, the huge darkness beyond.

Jude pressed her hand against her chest, felt the irrational thud of her heart and held the flashlight steady.

I am not afraid.

An owl hooted, and another twig snapped, closer. She moved the beam of her light, feeling suddenly exposed, the single shining thing in a sea of black.

A sharp scratch sounded behind her and Jude turned again, this time flicking the flashlight off as she twisted because she knew that sound. In the distance, not five yards away, a tiny ember glowed. She could not see the silhouette of the person, but already the smell of his cigarette reached her nostrils, released a momentary ache to inhale that smoke, which was quickly buried by terror and a resulting spasm in her abdomen that made her want to puke. The cigarette rose, paused, glowed bright red. A halo of smoke drifted up and dispersed.

Jude froze, not allowing a breath to escape. Why had she left the gun in her car? Idiot, idiot, idiot! *I'm not afraid*, but she was afraid, and her mind scrambled between running as fast as her legs would carry her and lifting the flashlight for a fight. It settled briefly on the possibility that this stranger in the forest was amicable, just a nice old man out for a stroll, but then what nice old man didn't make himself known to a girl alone in the woods?

She stepped away from the glowing ember, leaves and branches crunched underfoot. The ember lowered and the person holding it laughed. It was a dry, humorless sound.

"Runnin'll only drag it out." The man said, and Jude knew the voice, remembered the sound as he drank beer and spoke of his sister - the sister he had murdered.

Jude searched her mind for a plan - crime books she'd read, scary movies, snippets of advice gathered over the years. Keep him talking, they told you, but did that ever work? How many dead women had kept them talking?

"Dale, this will only make things worse for you. Kill me now and you'll likely be facing the electric chair," Jude said, loud, surprised at the confidence in her voice, wishing it would travel to her knees and stop their trembling. She took another step back, wincing at the crunch of leaves.

"They'll never find you. I've learned a lot in my life. You'll just be another cunt who ran off with her boyfriend."

"I don't have a boyfriend," Jude said, taking another step back. "So, there's the first hole in your story."

He laughed, and she cringed as the ember moved closer.

"Why did you kill your sister, Dale?" She took another step back, gentle, muffling the sound with her raised voice.

The cigarette moved up, another plume of smoke rose. Jude realized he couldn't see her. The sound of her voice was giving him her location.

"Because I wanted to," he spat, and his cool tone shifted. He was angry now, and not remorseful as she had hoped.

She turned and ran, zigzagging through the forest, hands in front of her in case she smacked into a tree. Her ears were a tunnel of sound: twigs and leaves crunching, the night songs, and somewhere Dale thundering through the forest behind her. She tried to circle back to the farmhouse but had lost her direction. The woods stretched on and on, she had to be getting close. Her lungs compressed, her thighs burned, and every second she expected to feel his hands on her back.

In front of her, a shape stood out in the darkness. She skidded to a stop staring at that horrible little cabin. She'd get trapped if she went inside so she ducked low, creeping to the edge of the cabin and pressing her back against the outer wall, listening.

Her breath filled the night, ragged, loud and though she strained to hear him, the blood in her ears muffled other sounds.

Breathe, breathe, breathe. She held the flashlight in her hand ready to strike out at anything that moved.

A branch snapped, too close, and she pushed harder against the wall wishing she could disappear into the crumbling logs. Something shifted above her and she stood, ready to step away from the cabin, but a hand shot from the dark window and snatched her hair.

"Ouch," she screamed as Dale's callused fingers plunged into her hair and wrenched her closer to the cabin. She swung the flashlight toward his arm and hit his hand.

He grunted, and she felt the flashlight tossed away. It thudded on the forest floor, and then he had one hand in her hair, the other on her arm, hauling her upward. It hurt. Searing pain raced along her skull where his hands tore at her hair. Her body scraped over the cabin's exterior and she felt the splintered wood dig through her shirt into her flesh. She beat against his hands, his arms, but his grip was unyielding.

"No, no, no," she wailed as her body slid up over the windowsill and he yanked her fully into the cabin. She dropped to the floor, and he kicked her in the head. The impact sent her sprawling to the side, knocking into the wall. Black spots exploded behind her eyes. On all fours, dizzy, and bleeding from the mouth, Jude hunkered lower, covering her head with her hands as he kicked her a second time. The hard toe of his boot connected with her wrist and pain streaked to her shoulder.

He squatted next to her, flipping her onto her back. She slapped at him feebly with her good hand, but he wrapped his large hands around her throat and squeezed. Pulling her knees up hard, she tried to connect with his side, a soft spot maybe, or his head, but her legs bounced off him.

Fire ravaged her throat as her lungs sought air and found only the tightening of his hands.

CHAPTER 32

eptember 20, 1965
Sophia

THE HOUSE LOOKED THE SAME. Set far back from the road, hidden by a line of pine trees six feet taller than when she'd last seen them. The moment she slipped across the road into her overgrown yard, she fell to the ground and wept.

She had not expected lights blazing, her children running through the yard, chased by Jack in his bathrobe as he played Swamp Man - one of their favorite childhood games. Her children were no longer children and her husband was dead, but still the emptiness of her home, the abandoned air around it, made her sob until her ribs hurt. She rolled onto her back, the long grass tickling her arms and neck and stared into the night sky. Not a cloud in sight, but Sophia knew it would storm that night. The currents of electricity buzzed on the air, the hairs on her arms erect as if sensing the oncoming tempest.

She found the back door locked, but when Sophia lifted the planter on the patio, she found their old familiar key, a little silhouette of rust surrounded it. She slid it into the lock and a satisfying metallic click greeted her ears.

"Oh, thank God," she sighed, pressing her head against the door and pushing it open.

She should have practiced caution but didn't. She walked brazenly into her house, steadying her hand on the wall. The darkness did not unnerve her. She slid her hands along the counter opening the junk drawer to the left of the sink and fumbling out a candle and pack of matches. The match lit on her first try, and the candle cast a warm glow over the room.

The coat rack still held Jack's wool coat, a gift from his father for his twenty-first birthday. Next to that hung Jude's rain coat, bright pink, and then a tiny little red coat, Hattie's Christmas coat. Sophia touched each one, leaned her face into the fabric and inhaled their scent. Shoes lay haphazard on the floor, a broken pencil next to a pair of Peter's dirty sneakers. She moved from the mudroom into the kitchen trailing her hand over the yellow counter top, rivulets of dust floating in the slants of moon glow through the window. A little glass kitten sat on the ledge, a gift from Gram Ruth to Jude as a girl. Its tiny black eyes followed Sophia as she gazed around the kitchen, moving with heavy, stiff steps to keep from collapsing onto the wood floor in tears.

The sitting room was identical to her last memory of it, though on that night she'd sat on the sofa with Jack, their hands clasped watching the flames in the fireplace and not talking about what was to come. The next day, Ruth would whisk Sophia away to Andrew's isolated hunting cabin. Jack and the kids would follow in a week.

They were faking Sophia's death. It was a drastic choice, one that terrified Sophia, but Jack believed it was the only way. According to an investigator Ruth hired, the Bell's were out for blood. Sophia would rot in prison if they didn't run.

That night, they sat alone, the kids at Gram Ruth's, the house creaking in her familiar way.

"Cozy in here," Jack said, pulling off his t-shirt, so he sat bare-chested on the sofa.

Sophia smiled, tears pulling at the backs of her eyes.

"Just in case we never see it again," she murmured. "I wanted one last fire."

He pulled her against him.

"In Colorado, we'll have a stone fireplace two stories high. I'll build you a fire every night."

"I love you, Jackson," she told him, nuzzling her head beneath his.

"Forever," he'd said, kissing the halo of her blonde hair as it danced in the firelight.

Ruth's black car arrived early the next morning. It reminded Sophia of a hearse. Sophia kissed Jack goodbye, her stomach filled with wasps instead of butterflies.

"I'll see you on the other side," he whispered into her ear.

It had been a joke, but now, as she surveyed their abandoned home, she realized it had been true. She had died that day, and he had died as well, they just hadn't known it yet.

Jude

JUDE WOKE IN A WHITE ROOM, a white sheet pulled to her waist, a flimsy white gown covering her battered body.

"Hi," Kurt said, giving her a half smile.

He sat in a chair near her bed, his hands clasped in his lap, the knuckles of his right hand split and bruised. His blue knit shirt was bloodstained, and his eye had a purplish tinge.

"Is it possible that I look worse than you?" she asked, lifting a hand to her throbbing throat.

"Considerably," he said, wincing as his eyes trailed from her face to her neck down to her bandaged arm.

"You saved me," she breathed, closing her eyes and calling the memories back to her. The night before had the surreal quality of a bad drug trip, likely thanks to whatever pain killers the nurses administered. She remembered Dale's hands, strong, merciless squeezing and then...

"Yeah," he agreed, rubbing a hand over his face.

"You hurt him? Dale?"

Kurt nodded.

"I put him in a choke hold. He passed out and I cuffed him and left him there. I called for back-up and they took care of the rest. I brought you here."

Jude had a vague memory of babbling as Kurt carried her through the woods.

"How? How did you know where to find me?"

"I didn't," he admitted. "After you showed me that picture, I went to Dale. That was stupid of me. He's my brother, and I assumed you were playing a game. He acted funny, but I didn't think much of it. Later on, I drove back to his house, the house we grew up in, and his truck was gone. I drove around, thinking, and..." he paused as if reluctant to add the rest. "I heard Rosemary speak as if she were sitting right next to me."

"What did she say?"

"Cabin."

"That's how close I came to death," Jude murmured, dumbfounded. What if he had ignored the call of a sister buried thirty years before?

"Don't think about it," he told her, reaching for a cup of water with a straw and stepping toward the bed. He held the cup out and she leaned forward, taking a painful sip.

"About what?" she asked.

"The other possibilities. It's a block against recovery. I know because I've seen enough victims do it. The perpetual cycle of what if? It happened the way it happened, end of story."

She leaned back against her pillows and studied him.

"I'm surprised a detective in Mason, Michigan would have seen a lot of victims. That wasn't meant to be as insulting as it sounded."

He smiled and sat back down.

"I'm getting used to your insults. But it is my line of work after all. I'm not exactly spending my days with old ladies knitting. I don't see a lot of homicide. That's true enough. But accidents, assaults, robberies. Every crime has a victim."

"Except victimless crimes."

"I've yet to see one of those."

Jude might have argued, she loved to play devil's advocate, but her throat hurt; in fact, her whole body hurt, and she wanted to cry.

As if sensing her distress, Kurt spoke. "I called your sister last night."

"Hattie?" Jude asked training her eyes on the little window that showed the pale light of dawn creeping into the sky.

"Yeah. You gave me her number. Not sure if you remember. You were pretty dazed. I left her a message."

"She didn't answer?" Jude asked, surprised. Hattie rarely went out at night.

"I thought I'd call your parents, but you said they were dead. Is that true? Did your mother die in the asylum?" He looked crestfallen as he asked and cast his eyes towards the floor. It wasn't his fault that the town blamed Jude's mother for Rosemary's death, but he shouldered the guilt, anyway.

Jude closed her eyes and shook her head.

"My dad is dead and my mom escaped from the asylum almost two weeks ago."

His head came up.

"Really? And you don't know where she went?"

A tear slipped down her cheek. Kurt pulled a handkerchief from his pocket and stood, but the door opened and Hattie burst in.

Hattie

"JUDE?" Hattie stared at her sister in disbelief. Jude's face was mottled with yellow and purple bruises. Her lower lip was split, both her eyes filled with tiny red cracks, her left arm in a sling. A fiery red ring marked the tender skin of her sister's neck. Hattie stood, speechless, one hand on the door, one foot in the room, the other still rooted in the hall where the world made sense, where her sister did not look like someone had used her as a punching bag.

A man stood near Jude's bed, a hankie in his hand, his eyes studying Hattie. He looked beaten as well, a black eye, bloody knuckles, bloody shirt. The stains stood in sharp contrast to the white room. A slender pole held a bag of fluid steadily drip dripping down to a tube attached to Jude's un-bandaged arm.

"It's okay, Hattie. Come in," Jude croaked.

Hattie started to walk in and then remembered Damien. He hovered in the hall behind her, his hands shoved into the pockets of the slacks he'd pulled on that morning. She'd watched him moving around his room, naked, his body long and lean in the amber glow of his bedside lamp. They'd left his house early; he wanted to take her horseback riding in the mist of dawn, but when she'd stopped at her apartment, she'd heard the message from Kurt and they'd rushed the two-hour drive to the hospital in Lansing, covering the one-hundred thirty miles in record time.

"Damien," Hattie said, and he looked up, his face unreadable. Did hospitals make him uncomfortable too?

"Damien?" Jude rasped.

Hattie turned back to her sister.

"Is he here?" Jude asked, and Hattie stared at the puzzled, and perhaps hopeful, expression on her sister's face.

"Hattie, I..." Damien started, his eyes downcast.

He looked like Jude's dog when he'd chewed her favorite gold pilgrim pumps.

The florescent lights bored down on him. His skin appeared waxy, like a fake person, a man in a wax museum posing as *shame*. Yes, that was the word, he looked ashamed.

CHAPTER 33

eptember 20, 1965
Hattie

THE MAN in Jude's room nudged Hattie out of the way and pushed the door open exposing Damien to Jude. Hattie looked at Jude's raw face, the scratches and bruises, but it was her eyes that held a story. When she saw Damien they opened wider, and lit with a hesitant smile.

"What are you doing here?" Jude asked him, and Hattie heard her attempt to sound angry, overshadowed by the deeper truth - joy. Joy that Damien stood in the hospital hallway.

"Do you know each other?" Hattie asked, wondering at Damien's rigid posture, his eyes that too told a story - not of joy - but regret.

"Of course," Jude whispered, her voice growing fainter each time she spoke. "Isn't that why he's here?"

But Hattie recognized the edge in Jude's voice, the dawning of an idea that a moment earlier had not existed.

"I'll give you some time alone," the man with the beaten knuckles told Jude. He nodded at Hattie and walked down the hall.

"I need to tell you something, Hattie," Damien said, as if he'd finally remembered her, remembered the night before.

"How do you know my sister?" Jude said, lower this time,

venomous. Her eyes had turned to brown slits in her puffy face and her hands held the sheet at her waist like she might rip it in two.

Hattie hung suspended, adrift in a torrent of strange sensations, one moment flying high on the euphoria of the night, and the next crashing, plummeting to the cold, sterile truth of Jude in that big white bed, her skin a million colors. A painting covered in black getting stripped away, Damien's scarlet blush, Jude's narrow eyes, Hattie in the middle, and yet nowhere at all.

Damien moved closer, touched Hattie's elbow, and stepped into Jude's room. He pulled Hattie in after him and shut the door.

Jude watched him with sharp eyes, and her gaze slid toward his hand where he held Hattie's arm.

"I screwed up," Damien told them. He was glancing back and forth at their faces, his gray eyes studying Hattie with each pass. "Hattie," he took her hand in his, squeezed. "Jude and I know one-another."

"You do?" Hattie glanced at Jude who stared at Damien as if fireballs might explode from her eyes.

He shifted to Jude, cringed at her gaze, and continued. "I work closely with several doctors at the Northern Michigan Asylum. It's expected that I seek their guidance for my research. I also need a letter of recommendation. I started working with a doctor a few months ago and recently he asked me for a favor."

Hattie frowned, not following. Jude did not look confused, something like understanding was turning her features.

"That doctor asked me to contact you both."

"Dr. Kaiser," Jude hissed.

Damien looked wearily at Jude as if he feared she might lunge from the bed.

He nodded.

"Dr. Kaiser has been working with your mom at the asylum for a decade. When she escaped, he thought she might go to her children."

"You fucking rat," Jude seethed.

"You knew about Mama?" Hattie asked, her voice trembling. She blinked at him, noticing how the longer she stared the less solid he become, a little blurry, more like a ghost than a real man.

Hattie stepped away, and he released her hand, but his eyes stayed locked on her face. She turned and moved closer to Jude, but Jude stared angrily at Damien.

"I did," he confessed. "I was only meant to speak with you a few times, keep tabs in case your mother made contact, but..."

"But you fucked us instead," Jude said, and the word exploded in Hattie's head. She walked, dazed to a chair and slid down into it, pulling her knees to her chest.

She stared at the white tile floor, the white walls crawling up to the white ceiling. The white blotted out the color of the previous night, the color she felt rising in her cheeks, the color splattering her sister.

Damien moved towards her, squatted, tried to take her hands, but she balled them and stuffed them behind her knees where he couldn't reach.

"I didn't intend it that way, Hattie. You have to believe me."

Hattie didn't look at his face, she focused on that white, empty space. If she stared hard enough, she might disappear into the white abyss, wake up in a room she only vaguely remembered that smelled of her mama. A little paper hot-air balloon hung from the ceiling, a fan whirred on warm nights, and Hattie could curl beneath a quilt with her cat Turkey Legs.

A knock sounded on the door, and a nurse in a white uniform with a white hat perched on her caramel colored hair swept into the room.

"Look at all these visitors, you have," she exclaimed going to Jude's bedside and touching her wrist.

"Get out," Jude snapped hoarsely.

The nurse drew her hand back, shocked.

"Not you," she said. "Them." She nodded her head toward Hattie and Damien.

Jude did not look at her, and Hattie's insides curdled. She wanted to hug Jude and cry and run away all at the same time.

The nurse pursed her lips and nodded.

"She needs her rest. It's been quite an ordeal," she told them.

Damien stood, offering Hattie his hand. She didn't take it but followed him into the hallway.

The man from Jude's room stood near the nurse's station. He stepped forward when they walked out.

"Hattie Porter?" he asked, extending a hand.

She nodded and limply shook his hand.

"I'm Detective Kurt Bell."

Her eyebrows shot up.

"What happened to my sister?" she asked, glancing back at the closed door to her sister's room.

"She was attacked last night and nearly killed."

Hattie sagged to the side and Damien caught her around the waist.

"I'm fine," she murmured, pushing him away. "Because of my painting?" she asked.

"In part, yes. I would like to interview you about that, but I'm sure this has been a tough morning."

He gazed with hard green eyes at Hattie but glanced toward Damien.

"I'm not related," Damien told him. "I'm…"

"A liar," Hattie interrupted him.

He turned crimson but said nothing.

"Do you need help, Miss Porter?" Detective Bell asked, squaring off against Damien who took a step back.

"No, I…" she trailed off. Did she ask Damien to take her home? Stay and wait for Jude to allow her into her room? "I don't feel so well," she murmured, touching a hand to her clammy forehead.

Damien hesitantly reached a hand up and touched the back of her neck.

"You're warm," he said. "Let me take you home, Hattie. You can drive back down this afternoon."

"Is that what you want, Miss Porter? If not, I can arrange a driver for you."

"No," she said, turning toward Damien. "It's okay. I'll be back. I need to… I'm so tired all of a sudden."

∾

Jude

JUDE STARED at the closed door. The pain in her body was miniscule compared to the pain blooming in her chest. A weird hollow sensation landed in her belly coupled with a vice holding her heart hostage so that every beat took an effort she could barely muster. The nurse had given her a sedative and soon she would slip out of the discomfort of her body, the rawness of her emotion, the churning of her mind.

The door opened, and a tiny hopeful flicker ignited within her. Who did she want to walk through? Damien? Hattie? But no, Kurt peeked in, a cup of coffee clutched in one hand.

"May I?" he asked.

She nodded.

"I spoke briefly with your sister, but she wasn't feeling well. I believe she'll be driving back this afternoon."

"My fault," Jude muttered, bunching her sheet in her hand. "I was mean to her. Hattie is delicate."

"Seems that way," Kurt admitted, returning to his seat. "I had the sense I shouldn't say too much, plus she had that fella with her."

"Damien," Jude said his name and a word floated to her lips, but she didn't say it: rejection.

"Is that her boyfriend?"

Jude scoffed, which hurt her throat. She shook her head without answering. On second thought, she didn't know, did she?

"I get the feeling you have a complicated life, Jude," he said.

"These days," she murmured, settling back on her pillows, a heaviness crawling through her limbs.

"I'm going to stay a little while longer if that's okay?" he said.

She closed her eyes and mumbled a sound, but never heard his reply.

CHAPTER 34

*S*eptember 20, 1965
Jude

JUDE WOKE to sun streaming through the hospital window. The chair beside her stood empty, but perched on the corner of her bed was Clayton.

He grinned when she opened her eyes.

"Your Knight in Shining Armor has arrived," he announced.

"What are you doing here?" she asked, smiling despite herself.

Her body ached. She tried to sit up but winced as pain shot through her arm.

"Slow down, Annie Oakley, the nurse on duty looks like a mean one. I don't want her to come in and stick me if you fall out of bed."

He helped her into a sitting position and stuffed several pillows behind her back.

"How did you know?" she asked.

"I called that detective this morning. Bell? I was hoping to put a little pressure on him about your mother's case and he told me what happened. I knew you were tough, but stalking a murderer seems a bit rash," he joked, patting her leg sympathetically.

"I was more prey than predator last night," she rasped. "Can you hand me a drink?" She pointed to the cup of water next to her bed.

"My pleasure."

She took a sip and closed her eyes as the lukewarm liquid flowed down her inflamed throat.

"I feel terrible," she grumbled.

"Well you don't look pageant-ready by any means, but you're still beautiful, Jude. I hope it's okay to say that." Clayton blushed.

She smiled and sighed.

"I appreciate it, Clayton. I don't care all that much right now, but it's still nice to hear. Did you meet Detective Bell?"

Clayton nodded, studying her eyes.

"Handsome guy," he said. "I relieved him of his bedside vigil. He seems rather taken with you."

"Hardly," Jude muttered.

"I had another reason for coming, Jude. And let me preface this by saying we're not doing anything crazy. I just wanted you to know."

"Speak sense, Clayton."

He lifted his leather case from the floor and unzipped it pulling out a single paper.

"I went to the government building in Cadillac and inquired about tax information on the property your parents owned."

Jude stared at him.

"My grandmother must have sold it, right? After my dad died?"

"Well for starters it wouldn't have been hers to sell, without a will it would have passed to your brother, Peter. But that's assuming both your parents had actually died and we know now that…"

"My mother is alive."

"Exactly. And," he laid the document on her lap. "The property is in your mother's name. She owns it."

"I'm not sure I get what that means. It's great, it is, but…."

"That's where she'd go, Jude. To her home, the home she shared with her husband and children."

Jude's eyes opened wide as she gazed at her mother's name on the document - Sophia Anne Porter - her true name.

"We have to go there." Jude pushed the sheet to the floor and started to swing her legs off the bed.

Clayton shook his head, putting a hand on her arm to stop her.

"I already spoke with the nurse. You're approved for discharge after one more check by the doctor. Sit tight and we'll make this happen."

~

SOPHIA

THERE WERE HALF a dozen jars of canned food, but everything else had gone stale. Despite her days eating from the trees she still hungered for fresh food and had woken that morning with the most intense desire for pumpkin sprinkled with sugar and cinnamon.

They'd never grown pumpkins on their own property, but their neighbors, an old couple named Harrison, had dedicated two acres to growing the enormous root vegetables. They donated the pumpkins that didn't sell roadside to the little school for Halloween decorations.

Sophia pulled on a pair of her jeans, standing before the long mirror in the bedroom she'd shared with Jack. The pants hung from her bony waist, and she used one of Jack's belts to cinch them tighter. It felt good to wear her clothes even if her body swam in the familiar fabric. She took the silver brush that Jack had given her as gift and ran it through her blonde hair, still long, but much less full. Lack of nutrition, Kaiser's strange treatments, and jealousy from a handful of asylum patients had all run their course. She braided it and pulled on a ball cap that had belonged to Peter. She smelled it first, inhaling so deep that surely, she could catch some remnant of him.

"Peter," she whispered, fingering the brim of the hat.

The tears wanted to come, but she felt as dry as dust. One night in the house had emptied her well of tears. The photos, smells, clothing, toys. The places she and Jack had made love, the counter where Jude and Peter sat when she baked cookies, the flower garden where she lay with Hattie and watched butterflies. How had she forgotten so much? The house returned it all like a heaping bouquet of flowers waiting on the front stoop - beautiful and fragrant yet filled with thorns. Every single memory hurt. She cried equal parts joy and sorrow, but now this morning, she could not cry. She was left with long sighs and deep creases in her forehead as she studied the remains of her family.

Where were they? Her children? The electricity had been shut off long ago, ten years perhaps. Some of their things were gone, but most of it left behind like collateral damage from a choice she and Jack should never have made. Their first mistake was trusting his mother, but perhaps it went much deeper. She had run from Rosemary's death, a scared child, but the choice changed her, made her into someone who ran away and when faced with the option a second time, she made the same mistake again.

"And I paid with my life and Jack with his," she murmured, sliding her feet into a pair of sneakers she used to wear in the garden. Jack and the kids all had matching pairs. But the kids wouldn't fit anymore, would they?

She closed the door behind her, not bothering to lock it.

~

Jude

CLAYTON AND JUDE pulled to the overgrown driveway. It had once been a clear trail bright with the wildflowers her mother had planted on the edges. Some flowers had grown up the center, weeds filling in the gaps.

"Better not chance it," Clayton said. "We'll get stuck. Just park on the road."

Jude turned off the car and paused with her hands on the wheel. She felt Clayton staring at her but wasn't ready to open the door. It wasn't only the possibility of seeing her mother. If she was honest, her mother felt like a phantom more than a real flesh and blood being. Her childhood home contained a piece of her she had buried long ago. The thought of opening the door, seeing all those familiar things turned her body to stone.

"Are you having second thoughts, Jude? Would you rather I just run and check?" Clayton asked.

Tempting, but she shook her head. She had to go to the house. For ten years she believed Gram had sold it, their things given away, the happiest part of her life a memory.

"No, I have to do it. There have been so many lies. I have to see for myself."

Clayton nodded and got out, walking around to open her door. He offered his hand, but she brushed it aside. She pulled her bag out of the car and slung it over her shoulder. It contained her camera and her gun. This time she wouldn't be caught without it.

They walked down the weeded drive. Jude looked at the flowers and could almost see her mother with her dress bunched around her waist, squatting with Hattie who had to smell and touch every blossom.

"So, this is where the great Jude Porter was reared," Clayton chuckled, but Jude gave him a dry look that silenced him.

She should have been nicer to Clayton, but suddenly she wished he hadn't come. What if she felt the urge to cry? What if her mother was in the house, but the Doctor at the asylum had ruined her? They might find her hunched in a corner eating cardboard and babbling. She inwardly chastised herself for even having the thought.

"Hey, I'm sorry," Clayton said. "Just trying to lighten the mood. I know this is a big deal."

Jude offered him a smile but couldn't say more. They'd come into the yard, nearly as overgrown as the driveway with little bursts of wildflowers. A wave of nostalgia swept over her. Bonfires in the backyard, the tree house their father built still suspended-worse for the wear- from a big oak tree overlooking the garden, the porch swing hanging now by a single cable - its white paint chipped and flaked away. Jude stopped and caught her breath feeling dizzy and sad and warm all over.

Clayton picked his way to the porch, touching a rail and shaking it. It didn't wobble, and he gave her a thumbs up. He walked to the front door and tried the doorknob.

"Locked," he told her.

Jude nodded and blinked at the house. It was closed up - curtains drawn - the air of abandonment hanging unforgiveable. She walked to the back of the house, her eyes eating the details, savoring them, almost choking in her desperation to take it all in. The rock path Peter and her father had made to the back door, digging fat stones out of the forest for weeks, the remnants of a little scarecrow fashioned from straw bales and her dad's old clothes because the deer kept eating their mother's vegetables, memories of Hattie as a baby lying on a blanket in the yard cooing at the birds and the bugs, at their mother's smiling face. Later memories of Hattie as a toddler and then a little girl, dreamy-eyed, always wandering outside with bare feet and that long blonde hair caught with twigs and leaves.

She felt Peter in the familiar trees they'd climbed a million times, in the steep slope of the roof they slid down sneaking out at night, in the second-floor window that had been the play room, where they whiled away afternoons reading, drawing, teasing each other about this girl or that boy at school.

"Ugh," she pressed her face into her hands, not used to the memories or the emotion that accompanied them. She felt like an alien inhabiting her body and realized why she'd always stuffed the feelings down. How did people function with so much going on, all the thoughts and feelings struggling to be at the forefront?

"Are you okay?" Clayton startled her.

She nodded.

"Yep, fine." She swallowed a lump of anguish. "There was a key back here. We'll look for that."

She lifted the heavy pot near the back door, the flowers long dead and gone, but only an outline of a key lay beneath it.

Clayton leaned down and touched his finger to the clean space where the key had been and then smudged the surrounding rust.

"If they took this key a decade ago, this clean spot would not be here," he murmured.

Jude stared at it.

"What do you mean?"

"I think someone recently found the key," he murmured, and his eyes were wide behind his glasses.

Jude moved to the door and tried the knob, it turned, and the door swung in. They stood staring into the kitchen, afternoon sun slanting across the familiar wood floor. A flurry of dirty footprints coated the kitchen floor.

Clayton stepped in, squatted and touched a smudge of dirt.

"It's wet," he said. "Fresh."

∾

SOPHIA

. . .

233

SOPHIA PAUSED at the edge of the woods and stared, disappointed at what was once a thriving pumpkin path. In its place stood a perfectly coiffed yard, green and sparkling. The rows of orange that had once delighted her children had been buried with the years and their corpses likely offered nourishing soil for the useless grass that replaced them.

She sat on a stump and stared into the yard and then at the house beyond. In her time it had been white, but the new owners had painted it violet with dark purple trim. It looked like a house from Alice in Wonderland, one of Hattie's favorite stories as a child. Sophia wondered who live inside now, surely not the Harrison's with their grumpy little dog Seymour who barked ferociously at Jack but loved Sophia and the kids.

"It's all gone," Sophia whispered wondering if she reminded herself enough it would become real. She kept waiting to step back in time to her teenage children, her eight-year-old daughter and her doting husband. Instead, she was like Rip Van Winkle who climbed into the forest and fell asleep for one-hundred years.

She had been asleep for much of the decade that had passed, or unconscious anyway - tied down in dark stifling rooms as medicine and poison were poured into her. She had likely been conscious for much of it, but the trauma of the experiences obliterated her memory of the events. Kaiser had wanted that. He didn't want her to remember because she might tell the orderlies or other patients. If she had no recollection, who could she tell? She simply sounded like another mad woman spouting vague conspiracies committed against her.

"I wonder what day it is?" she said to no one. The house before her was silent and still and she suspected the owners were gone, at work or perhaps on vacation. If she broke into their house, there would surely be a calendar, a working television or radio. She'd slip in and out in two minutes.

"A phone," she muttered as an afterthought. She remembered the phone number of her own home just a few acres away, long ago disconnected, but Gram Ruth's phone would still be turned on. One of the kids might answer and then...

Sophia's hands shook as she tried the doorknob at the back of the house, not because she was breaking and entering, but at the thought of calling the Porter Estate. What if Gram herself answered? What could she possibly say?

Though the exterior of the Harrison's home had transformed the interior was surprisingly similar with new paint and furniture. Gretchen Harrison always had a bowl of the season's fruit in the center of her kitchen table. This household used the table for paperwork rather than eating, an array of mail and open letters lay strewn about. On the floor Sophia saw a tangle of tennis shoes and a raggedy stuffed bear. Hanging on the opposite wall, Sophia spotted the telephone. She moved toward it, repeating the phone number under her breath.

"Stop right there!" a voice said, and Sophia looked up into the barrel of a shotgun.

CHAPTER 35

September 20, 1965
Jude

CLAYTON WALKED OUTSIDE while Jude tore through the house. She ran up the stairs and flung open doors, expecting to find her mother behind every one, but each room lay empty. In her parent's bedroom, Jude found the state-issued clothes on the top of the clothes hamper. She lifted them, touching the fabric like perhaps her mother had gotten lost inside.

"She's alive, and she was here," Jude whispered.

Jude ran back down the stairs, the clothes clutched in her hand, and found Clayton halfway across the yard.

"There are fresh tracks in this grass Jude. Look." He pointed at the flattened grass, some of it already beginning to spring back up.

Jude held up the clothes, not speaking a word, and Clayton raised his eyebrows and then grinned.

"We've got her," he said.

They followed the grass, Jude allowing Clayton to lead, but practically stepping on his heels. In the woods, they lost the tracks, but Jude followed her instincts moving ahead. The Harrisons were their only close neighbors and her mother had been close with Gretchen. She must have gone to them for help. From the woods, Jude watched for the familiar fat orange pumpkins that signaled the edge of the Harrison's property, but a huge expanse of lawn stared back at her. The house looked different too, a strange purple color that reminded Jude of grape bubble gum.

"This is weird," she said, but Clayton was still walking forward following the trail of compressed grass.

"She's inside, has to be." Clayton paused at the back door.

Jude walked to the door and knocked.

Clayton stepped to the side of the house and stood on tip-toe looking in one of the windows. Jude almost told him to stop, thinking they'd look like a couple of perverts peeking in a stranger's windows, but his face had gone pale and he ducked down, slinking back towards her.

"There's a kid in there with a shotgun. I'm pretty sure it's aimed at your mom."

"What?" Jude spun back to the door, ready to burst in.

"Don't," Clayton hissed, grabbing her hand. "If you spook him, he's liable to shoot her, or you."

Clayton moved to the side of the door and pushed Jude out of the way. He leaned close to the door frame.

"My name is Clayton Parker and I know that you're inside with a gun. The woman who broke into your house is not an intruder. She's a patient at a hospital and she was confused and got lost. Please do not hurt her or call the police."

Jude leaned closer to the house trying to hear.

"Whoever you are," Jude called. "You have my mom in there, please don't hurt her."

Another moment of silence passed and then the door opened. The boy with the gun was no older than thirteen, his face had a lucid sheen and his eyes looked glassy.

Sophia stepped behind him, touching his shoulder.

"This is Jared. He's home sick today, and I scared him," Sophia said. "Sit down, honey. I'll get you a glass of water." Jared nodded, mumbled something incoherent, and wandered back to the table.

Sophia stood on the doorstep staring at Jude, her eyes wide.

"Judy," her mom whispered, and Jude rushed forward burying her face in her mother's neck. "Oh, my baby, my Judy-girl."

"Mom," Jude said, trying out the word - not in the past tense - but here and now. "You're real, you're alive..."

∼

DAMIEN

DAMIEN CLOSED the huge text and pressed his face into his hands. His body ached from sitting and his brain buzzed with too much coffee. He'd told Dr. Kaiser's secretary a lie to gain access to his private library.

There he sifted through texts trying to understand Kaiser's obsession with Sophia Gray, but more important some clue that might lead him to the woman. If he could find her, deliver the girls their mother then perhaps Hattie would forgive him. He'd made little progress except for a single letter embossed with an eye within a triangle. It spoke of a meeting with no location specified but referred to the Umbra Brotherhood.

"Damien?" the voice startled him, and he nearly knocked his cup of coffee across the desk. In the amber glow of the lamp he watched Dr. Kaiser emerge from the shadows. He did not wear his customary white coat but had replaced it with a stiff-looking blazer over a high black turtleneck.

"I did not see your request to use my library," Kaiser murmured, his eyes boring into Damien.

Damien stood and stretched, acting casual as he draped his raincoat over the books. He didn't want Kaiser to see he'd been looking into the texts on paranormal psychosis.

"I expected to see you in my office this morning with an update," Kaiser continued, his eyes sliding passed Damien toward the books, mercifully blocked from view. If Kaiser wanted to examine them, he had only to brush the coat aside.

"I'm available now, and I need to stretch my legs. I'll put the books away after," Damien urged, already moving toward the door.

Kaiser lingered, and Damien looked for a diversion. He pulled a pack of mints from his pocket and flung them toward the doctor's feet. Kaiser narrowed his eyes at the fallen mints and then leaned down, plucking them from the floor and taking two long strides to Damien.

He handed them back without a word and Damien opened the box offering one to Kaiser who said nothing, but brushed passed Damien toward the door.

Outside the warm day was subdued by clouds.

"Damien, I sense division in you," Kaiser said, his eyes trained forward. "As if your eagerness to assist me has waned. Have you decided you do not wish to be a doctor?"

Damien felt the words twist in the pit of his stomach.

"No, not at all Dr. Kaiser. There's nothing I want more. My thesis has been consuming a lot of attention, but I promise you, I'm still committed-"

"Because you understand the urgency, do you not? This is not a minor chore I've requested of you. Those girls may hold the key to the whereabouts of a very sick woman. Each day that passes - she or someone else may come to harm."

Damien nodded, overriding his own better sense.

"Yes, and it's been a priority, but I told you the girls have no clue where their mother is. They only just discovered she was alive." The instant the words left his mouth, Damien froze.

Kaiser turned and cast his pale blue eyes on Damien. His smile sent a shiver down Damien's spine.

"They know that Sophia lives," Kaiser said, licking his lips. "And you did not come to me immediately? I am disappointed in you, Damien. Very disappointed."

"Hattie shares her mother's…. neurosis," Damien babbled, searching for some tidbit to appease Kaiser. "She believes she sees ghosts."

Kaiser's eyes widened, and he stood perfectly still. He steepled his hands and put them to his lips, his eyes gleaming as if Damien had just told him he'd won a small fortune. A smile somewhere between pleasure and pain shuddered across the doctor's face and Damien wanted to take it all back. Why had he uttered those words? Hattie's secrets offered to the doctor who wanted nothing more than to imprison her mother for the rest of her life.

"She might have been exaggerating," Damien said trying to put on his professional voice, his doctor speculating voice, but it all came out like a little boy searching for a lie. "I mean she's weird, so I think she plays up the weirdness. Probably heard about her mother's condition and took it as her own. You know how abandoned children are, the trauma reveals itself in strange ways. I've met patients who dress like their dead parent's."

He was still talking, but Kaiser had stopped listening. His lips were pressed into his fingertips, and Damien glanced around feeling deliriously sure that if it were night, Kaiser's face would sprout huge dripping fangs and his hands burst into taloned paws.

"Where is Hattie now?" Kaiser asked, so quietly that Damien barely heard him.

"What?" Damien croaked.

"Where does Hattie live? You mentioned she had left her grandmother's residence," Kaiser continued.

"Why?" Damien asked.

Kaiser narrowed his eyes, and Damien flinched.

"I don't know where she lives," Damien whispered, spreading his hands, sick with regret.

For the first time he saw Kaiser clearly - he was a sick man, a disturbed man, and Damien had just put the monster on the scent of Hattie, beautiful, sweet Hattie.

∼

Jude

"IT'S NOT a good idea to stay here," Clayton announced when they stepped back into Jude's childhood home.

Jude glared at him, ready to argue, but her mother nodded.

"No, you're right." Sophia looked around the kitchen and then her eyes fell again on Jude. She touched her cheek. "I've been dreaming of this moment for so long. Honey, what on earth happened to you?" Sophia put her fingers to the red welt around Jude's throat.

Clayton shifted from one foot to another, and Jude clamped her teeth together to keep from snapping at him.

"Jude, I've got a bad feeling, okay? I think we need to get out of here."

"Clayton, I think we can take five minutes...." And then they heard the voices.

Jude ran to the window and saw two officers picking through the long grass that had once been the driveway.

"No," she murmured, turning to her mother whose face had gone white.

"Out the back, fast. Go through the woods. I'll pick you up down the road," he insisted, shoving them both toward the back door.

"Get rid of those," Jude spat pointing at the state-issued clothes on the kitchen counter.

"Go," he urged.

Jude held her mother's hand, and they fled through the backyard. The police would be near the front door and blocked from view by the house, Jude hoped anyway.

Her mother stayed close, breathing heavily after only a few yards. In the shelter of the woods, they slowed.

"Are you okay, Mom? Can you breathe?"

"I'm out of shape," Sophia whispered, still holding tight to Jude's hand.

Jude squeezed and urged her on, moving deeper into the woods.

"Oh God, what if they question the neighbor boy?" Jude muttered.

"Jared," Sophia breathed. "They won't. House looks empty today, everyone's at work."

They didn't speak as they huddled in a thicket of weeds, close to the ground. Sophia took long slow breaths and when Jude's car appeared, Jude pulled her to her feet and they ran from the trees, climbing quickly into the car, and both lying low as they sped away.

SOPHIA

"Apparently that doctor, Kaiser you said his name was? Called the sheriff here in Cadillac. One of the officers said the man's been so persistent they finally decided to come out and look around," Clayton explained, driving and glancing at Sophia in the back seat.

She lay almost flat on her side and gave him a forced smile. Jude was in the front, sitting low, with one hand sliding awkwardly into the backseat where Sophia held it, stroking her fingers again and again over her daughter's knuckles. She could only see Jude's profile, but marveled at the grown woman who had once been her baby girl.

"We need to print something about that nut job," Jude spat and then caught on the last words as if she might have offended her mother.

Sophia laughed.

"Jude, I'm not a nut job, despite spending the last decade in an asylum."

Clayton and Jude laughed too, and Sophia saw tears pouring down Jude's checks.

"I have so many questions, Mom," Jude whispered, turning in her seat. "How did this happen?"

Sophia pressed her lips together and squeezed her hand.

"I have questions too. Let's get somewhere safe first and then we can talk."

∼

Hattie

THE ASYLUM LOOKED different during the day. Lush green grass, and leaves turning gold as the sun slanted through. Hattie walked to the door she and Jude had entered previously. She paused and looked up at the massive structure noticing a man staring down at her from a window. She could not see his face though he appeared tall.

Inside the entrance, a different woman in a white smock sat behind the table. She glanced up when Hattie entered and adjusted the large spectacles perched on her nose.

"Can I help you?" she asked. The woman looked kind and soft around the edges. Her hair was like heavy mink.

"Umm...," Hattie cleared her throat knowing the words mattered and she had to get them right.

The door behind the woman swung open and a tall dark-haired man in a white coat strode into the room. He was long in the arms and legs and torso. Black hair slicked back from his high forehead, and he looked at her intently from two pale blue eyes.

Hattie had once come upon a bird dying in the forest. She had cradled the robin in her hand and when it passed a film seemed to slip over its eyes. The man before her had similar eyes.

He stared at her as if they knew on another and perhaps they did. Hattie had a terrible time remembering people because she often barely noticed them the first time around.

"Walk with me," he said abruptly.

The man took Hattie's arm, linked it with his own, and nudged her out the door. She caught a fleeting glimpse of the woman at the table watching them, puzzled, but then she shifted her gaze downward and the door swung closed.

"I know why you're here," the man told her, squeezing Hattie's arm.

She allowed him to move her, studying the pale white hand on her arm, those long fingers, skeletal, like the decorations people hung in their windows on Halloween.

"You do?" she asked, troubled. The hair on her arms and neck stood up, and her chest felt tight as if she forced every breath through a pinhole.

"I knew your mother, Hattie."

Hattie stopped and looked into his startling, eerie blue eyes.

"How do you know my name?"

"She told me all about you," he continued, pulling her along again, meandering from the grassy lawn to a forest trail. The leaves blocked the sun, and they walked in shadow.

Hattie should have responded. Gram would have told her she was being rude, speak up, but her mouth had gone dry and like a child she wanted to dig her heels into the dirt and refuse to go any further. She wanted to rip her arm out of the man's grasp and run back to the light of the open lawn. A steady murmur of words she barely heard flowed from his lips Sophia... children... love... spirits... help. She could not hear his message, but she knew the intent beneath it - to lie.

He was stringing together lies all the while watching her with his hungry, dead blue eyes and leading her further into the woods.

CHAPTER 36

*S*eptember 20, 1965
Jude

"This is your home, your very own home," Sophia murmured walking around Jude's apartment touching framed photographs, pressing her hand against a quilt that hung over the back of Jude's sofa, pausing at the book shelf to scan the titles.

Jude watched her mother in silence, repeating *she's alive* again and again in her mind. She had tried twice to call Hattie and even considered driving to her apartment, but a selfish part of her didn't mind that Hattie was out. For a little while she got their mother all to herself.

Sophia turned and moved back to Jude, wrapping her daughter who stood only to her chin in a hug. She rested her head on Jude's, something that took Jude back to her younger years, not that she'd grown much taller since then. She pressed her hands into her mother's back and smelled the familiar soap she'd always used.

"You're so skinny, Mom," Jude said, releasing her and walking to the refrigerator. "I'm not much of a cook, but I have some cheese and salami in here. Would you like a sandwich?"

Sophia smiled and tucked a long blonde hair, loose from her braid behind her ear. Jude could have been looking at Hattie aged twenty years.

"I'm not hungry, Judy. Come sit with me. Let's talk." Sophia went to the couch and sat reaching forward to touch a vase of wilted flowers on Jude's coffee table. They had been roses but now drooped with waxy brown petals soon to release to the table beneath them.

"I've been meaning to throw those out," Jude admitted, remembering how Damien had bought her the flowers during their single night together and in her reverie, she'd planned to press a petal between the pages of a book to preserve it.

"From a boy?" Sophia asked, touching one of the flowers. The petals fell, pooling in a sad little pile next to the white vase.

"Nobody special," Jude said, grabbing the two cups of tea she'd made and carrying them to the sofa. She thought back to that morning in the hospital and cringed.

"You're so grown up," Sophia said, touching Jude's jaw and moving her soft hands up to Jude's short dark hair. "And so beautiful."

Jude forced a smile, never entirely comfortable with such open compliments, and tried not to stare at the bones jutting from her mother's face, at the crude bruise near her right temple, at the way her hands shook when she lifted her mug of tea.

"Can we talk about what happened, Mom? Do you need to rest first?"

Sophia smiled and shook her head.

"I've been asleep for ten years. There's nothing I want more than to be wide awake with you right now. Yes. We both need to talk, there's so much to say." Sophia waved her hand at the air as if all the unanswered questions floated there between them.

"Did you and Daddy plan to fake your death?" Jude asked, thinking back to that long-ago summer, the strangeness of it all, joy followed by heartache.

Sophia nodded, burying her hands in the quilt on Jude's couch.

"It was your grandmother's idea. After I ran into Margaret Bell at the grocery store, we knew she'd be searching for me. Your daddy wanted to run, but Ruth said if we faked my death it would appease the Bell's and if we ran, they might hire someone to find me. I would go away for one week and you kids would believe I had died. I didn't want to, I knew it was wrong, and that it would be horrible for you, my children."

"It was hard," Jude admitted, trying not to examine the memory too closely.

"I panicked, we panicked. We had so much to lose, you three kids, our marriage, this beautiful life. Your father had a lot of money. We could easily disappear, but we didn't want to live in fear of them looking for me."

"But you didn't do it, Mom! Why should you have to run from a crime you didn't commit?"

Sophia's face looked drawn as she spoke.

"Life isn't always fair. They wanted me for Rosemary's murder. A whole town was against me. If I faced them, who knows what they would have done, how they would have destroyed us. Maybe I should have. I've never quite known what the right decision was. But I made the choice, your dad and I, and once it was made, it felt like a big rock rolling down a hill, it just kept picking up speed. I tried to back out the morning Ruth came to pick me up. She was so nice to me. She'd never been nice. She gave me a cup of tea and I just... fell asleep."

"She drugged you?" Jude asked, staring at her mom, incredulous.

Sophia shrugged

"I don't know. When I woke up I was in a little room and there was a man in a chair watching me. He was a doctor, Dr. Kaiser."

"How could they admit you against your will?"

"Asylums are different places. A lot goes on that no one is aware of. Dr. Kaiser took ownership of me that very first day. I received one visit during my time in the hospital from your grandmother. She said that Jack had moved on, he wanted me locked away. He was marrying someone else. The Bell's were satisfied that a murderer had been put away." Sophia started to cry, and Jude took her hands staring at her mother in horror.

"That was a lie. She lied to you," Jude seethed.

"I knew that. I knew Jack would never abandon me. She betrayed him too, her only son. That's how much Ruth hated me."

"She's a witch," Jude snapped, trying to take a drink of her tea, but too enraged to lift the cup without throwing it against the wall.

"I see that temper of yours is still alive and well." Sophia smiled, leaning towards Jude and taking her face in her hands. "Don't let hatred make your choices, Jude. It was a terrible thing that Ruth did, but she had her reasons. We all have our reasons. Now tell me, when did your father die?"

Jude studied her mother's face, feeling the rage giving way to grief. Her voice trembled when she spoke.

"Three weeks after you... were taken. He was in the barn at Gram's and fell."

Sophia nodded pursing her lips.

"Did he suffer?"

"I don't think so. But they never told us much. You had died in an accident and then so did he. I suspected something before he died, though. I saw Daddy smiling the morning of the wake at Gram's. Like he had a wonderful secret he couldn't wait to share with us. I was so lost in my sadness, I never thought to ask him later."

"I can't imagine what it was like for him," Sophia murmured. "I doubt he knew where I was, but he couldn't exactly shout it from the rooftops. We'd faked my death, after all."

"How did you fake your death? Why would anyone believe you hadn't just run away?"

"Your Grandmother had connections. She paid a handful of people off. A policeman said he found the body, a coroner made up an autopsy. We had it all planned, but then..."

"She double crossed you."

"Yes."

"Why? I mean what did she gain?" Jude asked, trying to understand how her grandmother could be so cruel.

"Ruth never wanted me in her home. Your grandpa, Andrew, brought me there. He'd grown up with my daddy and I believe there was a debt between them. I never knew what it was, but when Rosemary was murdered, and the town pointed at me, my mama called Andrew and asked for a favor. He took me in the same night that I found Rosemary's body. I never saw my mother again."

Jude grimaced and shook her head.

"You were a kid, Mom. They couldn't have put you away for long, a detention center for a couple of years at the most," Jude said, exasperated, but also realizing that if her mother hadn't run, Jude would never have existed at all.

"I was thirteen-years-old, Judy. My daddy had died the previous autumn, my mama was trying to keep it together. Jack agreed later that

I should have stayed and faced it. He wanted to meet my family, but I couldn't go back. I was ashamed and... I don't know. I started to wonder if maybe they thought I did it too. Maybe they wanted me gone."

"Mom," Jude sighed and curled up to her mother, such a foreign feeling as a woman who rarely got close to anyone. Her mother, other than Peter, had been the only person Jude ever felt that she could snuggle into, find solace with.

Sophia petted her hair and kissed the top of her head.

Jude started to open her mouth and tell her mother it wasn't true. She knew, she had spoken with Grimmel, Sophia's family had never doubted her innocence, but a knock at the door interrupted her.

THE KNOCKING SOUNDED AGAIN, more insistent.

"Stay in my room, Mom," Jude whispered, pushing Sophia towards her room.

Sophia stared at the door but nodded and hurried from the room.

"I'm coming, I'm coming," Jude yelled. "Don't dent my door or you can pay for it."

She whipped the door open, angrily tucking a strand of hair behind her ear.

Damien stood on her doorstep, his hands shoved into the pockets of his jeans, a twist of blond hair falling across his forehead. Jude felt a surge in her chest at the sight of him, followed immediately by a burst of bright red fury that caused her to slam the door in his face just as he opened his mouth. She stared at the door, fuming, her fists balled at her sides.

It took the better part of a minute and then he spoke.

"I know you're angry, Jude. I deserved that, believe me, I know I did, but I have to talk to you. It's urgent."

Gram had moved from his rug to Jude's legs and he stood obediently beside her, offering a little whine. In a moment he would start to paw at the door.

"What do you want?" Jude snapped.

Another moment of silence.

"I'd rather say it face to face. You don't owe me anything, I get it.

And if you won't open the door, then I'll talk through it, but...." He paused, and Jude heard another door open in the hallway.

"Everything okay out here?" Jude heard the voice of Mrs. Lyon - the woman who lived across the hall with her two small children.

"Everything's fine, Katie," Jude called out. She opened the door reluctantly and offered Mrs. Lyon a tight smile. "This guy's something of a snake oil salesman. I was just telling him to get lost."

Katie Lyon gave Damien a dirty look and backed into her apartment. One of her toddlers tried to stick his head out the door, but his mother pushed him back inside.

"Well don't let him in your apartment, Jude," Katie said, keeping the door open a crack. "Do you want me to call the police?"

Jude watched Damien's eyes open wide, but he didn't try to defend himself.

"No," Jude sighed, shaking her head. "He's the cowardly type, not a threat."

Mrs. Lyon closed her door, and Jude opened hers wider.

"Fine, come in, you've got exactly five minutes and then I want you out."

Damien stepped into her apartment.

"I'm sorry, Jude," he started, holding out his hands, soft smooth hands that she remembered traveling her body.

"You're here to ask my forgiveness?"

"Not exactly," he admitted, stepping further into the apartment. "I'm here because I think I've made a horrible mistake and...."

"And what?" Jude snapped, feeling her throat pulse from the place Dale had squeezed. Jude frowned, letting her hair fall over the side of her face, perhaps masking some bruises.

"I lied when I first met you," Damien went on. "And it was unforgivable."

"Damien," she huffed, glancing towards the closed door of her bedroom. "Get to the point."

"I screwed up that night, Jude. I had too much to drink and..."

Jude laughed and planted a hand on her hip, infuriated at Damien's words. The night had meant absolutely nothing to him. He'd had too much to drink.

"Get out, Damien."

She walked over and shoved him hard. He stood his ground, barely shifting beneath her push.

"I'm worried about Hattie."

Jude narrowed her eyes, the sound of her sister's name on his lips igniting a new bubble of rage within her.

"What about Hattie?" she demanded.

"I told Kaiser that Hattie sees spirits."

"You what?" Jude spit the words more than said them.

"He cornered me and I panicked. I was babbling, not thinking and-"

Jude glared at him, her mind reeling.

"He can't touch Hattie. She's not in the hospital and he can't have her committed for that." Jude wasn't really talking to Damien, but more to herself wondering if her mother could hear their conversation.

"I'm worried about Hattie, Jude," Damien said softly. "I don't know where she lives. I dropped her off at the church this morning. I tried to call her this evening, but-"

"You think I'm going to lead you to my baby sister? You're nuts. Forget your doctorate Damien, you need to join your patients."

He looked wounded by her words, but she played on his guilt. He could not talk back to her; his shame wouldn't allow it.

"Dr. Kaiser doesn't play by the rules," Damien continued. "I didn't know him when I started working with him. I had read some of his publications. He has a brilliant mind. One of my professors spoke very highly of him. I had no idea that he was..."

"What?"

"Twisted, obsessed maybe."

"Obsessed with what? My mother?"

"Yes, but not only your mother. He's obsessed with patients who claim supernatural connections. It's taken me months to realize it. I thought it was simply a focus for his treatment, but I started digging a bit. He requests those patients, the ones that claim to see things. Three have died in his care in the last decade. Three patients, Jude."

Jude opened her eyes wide, studying Damien who looked ready to cry. He was not a man at all, just playing at being one.

"And you gave him Hattie? You really are a coward, Damien."

Damien looked away, at her ceiling, down at the floor. He made a weak attempt at petting Gram, but the dog shifted away.

Jude's bedroom door opened and her mother stepped out.

CHAPTER 37

September 20, 1965
Jude

MRS. BOWERS, a widow for well over two decades, owned the house beneath Hattie's apartment. When Jude knocked on her door, a cacophony of cats greeted her.

"Go on now Fuzz, Beatrix, Marigold - you're going to trip this old lady up," Mrs. Bowers said through the door, and Jude imagined her wading through a sea of cats using a wooden oar to push them aside. She opened the door and two cats raced on to the porch. Despite their urgent escape they immediately dropped into positions of lazy, rolling in patches of sun on the wooden deck.

"Don't mind them," Mrs. Bowers said waving them away and casting her green eyes, tinged with yellow, on Jude. Despite the warm day, she wore a heavy knit sweater, thick corduroy pants and men's slippers.

"Hi, Mrs. Bowers, sorry to intrude. I knocked on Hattie's door and didn't find her. I was wondering if you've talked to her today?"

Mrs. Bowers grinned and held up a length of orange scarf.

"Darning this for little Hattie right now. That slender neck is bound to get a chill. I saw her late this morning. Seemed a bit upset to tell you the truth. Said she was going to Traverse City." Mrs. Bowers cocked an eyebrow that implied scandal and winked. "She's been gone a lot lately, thought maybe she had a beau up that way."

Jude frowned. The only connection Hattie had to Traverse City was the Northern Michigan Asylum.

"What happened to your face, doll?" Mrs. Bowers asked, frowning.

"Clumsy," Jude told her. "Fell down my apartment stairs after a few glasses of wine."

"You independent girls, my goodness," she shook her head and laughed. "I would have been right terrified livin' on my own at your age. Course guess now I do, but after twenty years with Barny I realized I'd have to fend for myself. Snored like a freight train, somebody could'a broke in and murdered me and he never would cracked an eye."

"I've gotta go, Mrs. Bowers. If Hattie comes back can you ask her to give me a call?"

Mrs. Bowers nodded and peeked past Jude to her car where her mother stared out from the front seat, quickly turning her head away. Damien sat in the back, his face grim.

~

Hattie

HATTIE SWAM in a universe of black. No - not swam - floated. She didn't have control of her body, it drifted, soared, fell as if a dozen currents pushed and pulled her first there, now here, but she saw nothing.

She opened her eyes but felt removed from her body as if thinking of opening her eyes involved telling her brain, then racing from her brain to her eyelids to tell them and then back up to her brain to relay they'd heard, but they were so heavy. One lid came up and then the other and the room swam in the same currents of black, occasionally broken by streaks of orange light. Hattie let her head flop to the right and saw a torch lit against a curving brick wall. It reminded her of a pool. Was she sitting in the bottom of a pool?

She gazed for a long time - falling, floating, steadying only to dive again, her body on a strange journey, the room sometimes acting similarly, rolling to the side, righting itself. She lifted an arm, but it didn't move, more than heavy, it seemed to be fastened down. She tried the other and then her legs, all impossibly heavy, unmovable. More flickering light on the ceiling when she looked up, flickering lights when she closed her eyes, and the sound of voices murmuring, some crying.

"Hattie," a clear strong voice broke through the jumble of sensations, a man's voice. She lolled her head to the left and there was the man, the doctor, with his winter blue eyes searching her face. "It's begun to take effect," he said.

He walked to a bag and dug through it. His body seemed to shrink and grow, a monster man with hunched shoulders. Hattie remembered a show that Jude and Peter used to love, *Dr. Jekyll and Mr. Hyde*. When he turned around, the doctor's eyes would have gone from blue to black and he'd be holding a knife.

But no, he turned, stepped toward her, the light played tricks - ghoul's face, man's face, ghoul's face like he was taking off a Halloween mask so fast she couldn't see the flicker of his hand. He held a framed picture. He pushed the photo in front of her, held it too close, she tried to recoil, but her head pressed into the bed and stopped.

Her eyes couldn't focus, the glass reflected firelight, the images within the photo were tiny little particles moving, colored nonsense.

"Water?" she asked him, blinking, slipping into the void, returning some time later. The man stood as if no time had elapsed, his eyes angry, the frame clutched in his hand.

"Look at the photo," he hissed.

She looked, saw a woman in a long dress with a cold smile and colder eyes. It didn't register in Hattie's mind, she swam through the darkness, flickering orange light, the woman's face mean, grinning, sneering.

More sounds, whispering voices, someone was crying. A little girl was crying, and now there were shadows in the room, darting, faster than Hattie's eyes could follow.

"Call her here, call this woman," the doctor snapped, jabbing a finger at the glass frame. "Speak to her! Tell me what she says!"

Hattie blinked, and every blink took hours and catapulted her into a space and time where the world was fluid, darkness and light streaming, pulsing. She tried to focus on the man, so angry, but the shadows grew thicker, surrounded him and then dissipated like bursts of vanishing powder from a magic show.

And then the woman was there, standing just behind the man, long slender arms, but something wasn't right. Her head looked funny and Hattie stared and stared because she couldn't make sense of this woman's strange head. It was not round, but flat on the side and when the woman shifted, Hattie saw the side of her head was caved in, blood matted her hair and stuck to her neck with little bits of white and gray. *Bone and brains*, Hattie thought though she couldn't imagine finding those words on her own.

"You killed your mother…" Hattie murmured, eyelids drooping.

The doctor's eyes flashed, fear, and then triumphant rage. He gripped the picture in his bony hands so hard the glass in the frame shattered. Still, he held it, and blood flowed from his cut fingers and dripped to the floor.

"What does she say?" he screamed into Hattie's face.

"Who?" Hattie mumbled, already losing track of the conversation.

"My mother! What does she say?" He shook the frame at Hattie. She felt a droplet of his warm blood hit her cheek.

The shadows in the room seemed to be shifting closer to the blood, wanting the blood.

One shadow, a young man, darted towards Kaiser and nipped him. Kaiser dropped the frame, spun around, and then stared at his bleeding hand. Had he felt the spirit's bite?

Hattie tried to follow the man's shadow but it disappeared into the darkness. Another shadow darted forward, the woman from the photo. Kaiser yelped and stumbled back, his eyes shifting from anger to terror. His hand was bleeding more now, dark rivulets seeping over his wrists.

SOPHIA

THEY PILED from the car and Sophia ran into woods, ignoring the tremors of anxiety that rose as she spotted the asylum looming in the distance.

"Hattie!" she screamed, pushing through a wall of bushes and searching for the trail Kaiser had taken her down months before.

"Wait, Mom," Jude called, wincing as her arm jiggled in its sling. "Maybe she's in the asylum. She might be talking to a nurse or..."

Sophia shook her head.

"I know, Jude. Dr. Kaiser has her. But I can't remember how to find the hidden doorway."

Damien ran ahead shouting Hattie's name and plunging in and out of a dark grove of trees.

The moon rose, but offered little light, even less through the thick boughs of leaves soon to fall. A half hour went by, and they searched. Sophia realized she'd seen that tree, that stump - they were moving in circles.

"Alice," Sophia shouted, grabbing Damien as he trotted past her. "Go to the hospital and get Alice!"

"Dr. Kaiser's nurse?" Damien asked, bewildered and already shaking his head 'no.'

"It's the only way. She took me there. She can find it again," Sophia said, urgent, shaking him.

Jude appeared, squared off against him, her eyes so filled with anger and hurt that Sophia wanted to wrap her in a hug, but couldn't - there wasn't time.

"I'll expose you, Damien. I'll print the most horrifying story about you imaginable if you don't get that fucking nurse, now! I swear to God I will devote my life to ruining you," Jude spat.

Damien looked between the two women, eyes wide and then he nodded.

"Okay, no, you're right. I'm not thinking clearly. I'll go."

He turned and ran for the hospital.

Jude and Sophia hid in the trees. If Alice saw them, she'd never take them to the secret chamber where Kaiser and his sick group showed off their patients.

Sophia held Jude's hand, watching the trail. After a lifetime of counting seconds, Damien appeared on the path, pulling Alice along.

"Damien, Dr. Kaiser never mentioned that you were aware of the Brotherhood. I'm breaking an oath, I...."

"Alice, I've been here with Dr. Kaiser only once before. He's in danger, I'm telling you. The patient who escaped-"

"Sophia?" Alice hissed.

255

"Yes. She lured him out here. His note was cryptic, but I'm telling you, that's where she took him."

Sophia knew Alice's jaw would be working, sorting through the possibility Damien lied.

"It's this way." Alice picked up her pace.

Sophia and Jude slipped onto the trail behind them and kept their distance. They walked along a patch of old-growth trees, stepped over a tiny creek and hurried up a broad grassy hill. Alice took a sharp left at a wall of bushes. They plunged through, down a hill, and Sophia saw the strange trees from her previous visit. They sprawled along the earth, crawling, rather than raising into the sky.

Alice ducked beneath a large bone-white trunk. Sophia started to follow, but Jude held her back. A dirt mound rose out of the earth, and Alice pushed her hands into a mass of brambles. Sophia heard a click.

"This way," Alice whispered rushing into the tangle of branches.

Damien disappeared behind her. Jude and Sophia followed.

SOPHIA CLENCHED HER EYES SHUT, the sounds of the dead swirled through the tunnels. Dark pools of emotion - pain, anger, despair assaulted her senses. She stopped, put her hand on a wall and whipped it back when a howl of rage burst in her skull.

"Mom, Mom, are you okay? Jude whispered, touching her mom's shoulder.

"Yes, keep going. I'm fine," she said. But the memories of that night were coming back, and worse the cries, shouts and whispers grew louder. The chamber seemed to trap the spirits, to ignite their fury, and amplify their grief. Sophia had encountered many spirits in her life - these were different - angry, hostile, menacing.

"Dr. Kaiser?" Alice called ahead of them.

Sophia heard Dr. Kaiser's voice, shrill.

"Get off me, get away, stop them. You stupid girl, stop them."

Sophia ran, Jude beside her. They charged through the dark tunnel and into the room. The torches flickered from the walls.

Hattie lay on the bed, her face waxen, her blue eyes huge with black dilated pupils in their center.

"LSD," Sophia murmured.

Damien unbuckled Hattie's straps and lifted her from the bed.

Alice hunched over a man in a white coat.

Kaiser.

He was shrieking and flailing at the air, the ground, and he slapped at Alice's hands.

"They're eating me alive," he howled. "The blood, my blood."

Blood gushed from his hand and yes, the shadows seemed to be descending upon him in droves, waves, moving towards that blood.

Jude ran to Hattie and Sophia broke her trance and followed.

"Oh baby," she whispered.

"Mama?" Hattie asked looking at her with huge petrified eyes.

"You're okay, honey. Go," she urged Damien, and they ran from the room, hearing the calls of Dr. Kaiser and the pleas of Alice as they streaked down the tunnel into the dark forest.

EPILOGUE

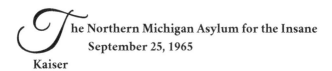

The Northern Michigan Asylum for the Insane
September 25, 1965
Kaiser

KAISER SAT in the hall outside his room. Another patient was sweeping the hallway, occasionally crouching to the floor to brush his hand over the cement as if he'd missed a spot.

A cold sweat popped along Kaiser's brow and he wiped it quickly away lest the patient see his fear.

Dr. Knight paused in the hallway staring at him for a long moment before plastering on one of his placating smiles.

"How are you today, Stephen?" Knight asked squatting down in front of Kaiser.

Kaiser held his hands balled in his lap. He wanted to punch and pummel the doctor. How dare he address him by his first name in front of patients? It was the most terrible breech and an intentional one at that.

"I'm sure you can imagine how I am, Larry," Kaiser hissed. "Where is Alice?"

"She was needed on another floor. How did you sleep last night? Have the nightmares improved?"

Knight spoke to him as if he were a feeble-minded child.

258

"The Brotherhood is very concerned, Stephen. If you were to say something during one of your episodes," Knight trailed off.

"I got you into The Brotherhood, Knight. Me! You were unworthy, most of them are. How dare you threaten me?"

Knight stood up, holding his hands in the air and stepping away as if Kaiser was a wild animal ready to attack.

"Whoa, Stephen. Please calm down or I'll have to call for an orderly. Have you seen the new one who just started? Frank something or other? He's great big." Knight held his arms out wide. "Not the brightest fellow, but strong as an ox."

"Wait," Kaiser gasped, grabbing at Knight's white coat. "You have to get me out of here. She only has power here. Don't you see? This pace," he gestured around wildly, "is a gateway for the dead."

Dr. Knight prised Kaiser's hands from his coat and offered him another of those demeaning smiles.

"Stephen, perhaps it's time for a new treatment," Knight suggested, checking his watch.

"I want to speak with Alice, now," Kaiser bellowed, struggling up from his chair. His body heavy from medication refused to step forward. He collapsed back into his chair.

The patient who'd been sweeping paused.

Kaiser turned his angry stare toward the young man, and he quickly shuffled down the hall.

"I'm afraid that's impossible, Stephen. But do remember what I said. The Brotherhood is not one for taking chances."

Knight walked away, and Kaiser imagined strapping him to the table in the chamber, peeling off his eyelids with a razor sharp scalpel.

The hall stood empty, and soon night would fall. Kaiser shivered and glanced at his cut hand. Already blood had pooled beneath the bandage. No amount of wrapping sufficed. By morning his bed would be soaked in blood.

He blinked down the long corridor, the shadows growing sinister.

She would come for him again as she did every night - his mother, with her smashed-in head and her army of ghosts, ready to take her vengeance.

∾

J.R. ERICKSON

September 27, 1965
Sophia

"He thought you were tucked away, safe and sound in Andrew's little hunting cabin," Gram Ruth said, standing with her back to Sophia.

She had aged in the decade since Sophia had last seen the matriarch of the Porter Estate. Ruth Porter, the woman who had once terrified Sophia, had lost some of her height as arthritis clawed at the weak muscles of Ruth's frame forcing her lower, curling her inward. Her hair had turned from black to silver and though she still pinned it high on her head, the barrettes looked old, tarnished.

Ruth reached forward running her fingers over the china on the foyer bureau, creating smudges she would check later to ensure her housekeeper was cleaning properly. Sophia had seen her do it a dozen times.

The foyer looked as it had that fateful morning thirty years before when Sophia had first stepped foot in the Porter's home and yet all of its grandeur had seeped away. The staircase, once foreboding, the gleaming floors, the statuary more like a museum than a home, looked cold, sterile and most of all - powerless. The woman before her was only a frail old woman, her magic gone.

"And when he went there to find me, what did you tell him?" Sophia murmured, staring at Ruth's pinched shoulders. "How could you do that to him, Ruth? You might have hated me, fine, but your own son, your grandchildren?"

Ruth spun around. Her face too was marked by the years, ruts and grooves around her mouth and eyes, a layer of chalky powder useless against the ravages of time.

She pointed a shaky finger at Sophia.

"You ruined my son, stole him from me. He would have wasted his life on that dreadful little farm you tricked him into buying."

"And now he's dead," Sophia shook her head, more sad than angry.

"You killed him," Ruth hissed, and spittle clung to her thin, painted lips.

"I was trapped in an insane asylum, tortured day and night. How did I kill him, Ruth? Are you sure it wasn't your lies that killed him? Your betrayal?"

Ruth squeezed her hands into fists, breathing heavily, staring at Sophia as if still, after all these years, she would rather see her dead than standing in her house.

"He should have let it go," Ruth spat. "But no, you'd brainwashed him. He couldn't function without you, you saw to that. It wasn't my fault he died in the barn. I didn't push him, he stumbled. I only meant to keep him away from the boxes..."

Ruth stopped abruptly realizing she had revealed a terrible secret.

"You were in the barn when he died?" Sophia asked, having heard the story from Jude, she knew they believed their father was alone, somehow, he fell - end of story. "Jude told me they didn't find him until that evening, Frank found him. You left him there to die?" Now Sophia was angry, her heart pounded against her ribs and her throat filled with rising sobs.

"He was already dead," Ruth shrieked, and she turned back to the bureau picking up a silver pitcher. She reached back with her hand and threw it.

Sophia stepped to the side, and the pitcher crashed to the floor skidding across the slippery marble.

Ruth's bosom, splotched and red, heaved. Her eyes were two angry slits in the fleshy puddle of her face.

Sophia turned and without another word walked from the house. She drove down the long driveway, a fleeting memory of her and Jack kissing beneath the warped oak tree near the entrance. As she watched the Porter Estate fade in the rear-view mirror, she knew she would never see Ruth again.

~

OCTOBER 1965
Jude

"YOU'RE HEALING UP NICE," Detective Bell said, gesturing at Jude's face where the bruises and scrapes had all but disappeared.

"Another month in this," she touched her sling. "And I'll be good as new."

She spoke the words but thought of the nightmares that ripped her from sleep night and after night. In each one she returned to that dank little cabin in the woods and somewhere in the shadows a man waited with a knife.

"I wanted you to know that Dale plead guilty to Rosemary's murder and your attempted murder. There won't be a trial."

Jude sighed, one-part relieved, another part frustrated that she wouldn't get to stare him down in court.

"Good. I hated the thought of my mom having to testify," she admitted.

"We found the bloody hat," Bell said, reaching into his pocket and pulling out a pack of gum. He offered her a piece, but she shook her head. "Dale stuffed it in a trunk in the attic. The proof was right above our heads for thirty years." Kurt shook his head. "I feel like a real ape."

Jude studied his eyes, green orbs of remorse, that watched everything. As they stood near the courthouse, he scanned the streets, the sidewalks, back to her, then off again flitting over the people and the cars passing by.

"The whole thing is way out," she murmured, imaging her parents' farm where, at that moment, her mother was baking an apple pie and Hattie was hanging paper pumpkins in the window for Halloween. "My whole life is different. I'm trying to catch up."

Kurt nodded.

"Since you're trying new things, maybe you'd want to have dinner with me?" He smiled and cocked an eyebrow.

Jude stared at him, surprised.

"Really?"

He nodded, pushed a hand through his dark tousled hair, and shrugged."I understand if it's too weird. Family history and all, but…"

"Yes," she blurted. "In six months."

"In six months?" he exclaimed.

"I'm catching up on a lost decade right now." She shrugged. "Call me in six months."

∼

Christmas Eve 1965
Hattie

. . .

HATTIE SAT cross-legged on a rug by the fire. Her mother wove a needle and thread through popcorn for the Christmas tree, and Jude lounged on the sofa sipping scotch and watching snow fall beyond the window. It had been snowing for two days and they'd rarely left the farm, spending their days sifting through ornaments and crafts from their childhood and watching Christmas specials on television.

Hattie slid her finger beneath the edge of the sealed envelope in her lap and pulled out a sheet of stationary, opening it to Damien's handwriting. He wrote her every two weeks detailing his thesis progress, describing the new Dalmatian puppy he'd taken in, and ending, always, with a paragraph of apologies and hopes that someday Hattie might give him another chance.

She never wrote back, but instead sent him small paintings on the backs index cards. She glanced at her most recent painting, a man's hand with a tiny Hattie nestled inside. Damien would not know it, but it was his hand she painted, remembering the creases and lines in vivid detail, remembering the way his hands cupped her face as he kissed her, and remembering finally, Jude's face at the hospital the following morning.

She set his letter aside and turned to stare into the crackling fire, looking up when someone knocked on the door.

SOPHIA

"I'LL GET IT," Sophia announced, gazing at her two beautiful girls before hurrying to the front door.

She no longer lived with the fear of opening her door. Kaiser, once a doctor, had become a patient at the Northern Michigan Asylum. Damien had written Hattie and told of her of the doctor's hysteria in the days following Hattie's abduction. The man screamed that his dead mother was coming back to take her revenge, and she brought the land of the dead with her.

The knock sounded a second time and when she pulled open the door, a gust of snow blew across the threshold. She looked into the searching eyes of her son, Peter.

"Mom," he whispered, his brown uniform dusted in white, his once shaggy auburn hair cropped close to his head.

Sophia reached forward clutching her son and feeling a sob slip from her throat. Peter stepped into the house and hugged her, lifting his mother from the ground.

"Jude wrote to me. I've been so anxious for my leave, I could hardly stand it. I wanted to surprise you," he whispered. "I can't believe it's you, Mom."

Jude and Hattie hurried from the living room, wrapping their arms around Peter and Sophia. Hattie's tears were quiet while Jude's sobs burst in giant hiccups.

Sophia felt the warmth of her children pressing around her and from the corner of the house, she heard Jack, his voice a whisper in the blowing wind.

"Sophia," he said.

And then she felt him, the spirit of her beloved, as he stepped into their embrace.

ABOUT THE AUTHOR

J.R. Erickson, also known as Jacki Riegle, is an indie author who writes stories that weave together the threads of fantasy and reality. She is the author of the upcoming *Northern Michigan Asylum Series* as well the urban fantasy series: *Born of Shadows*. *Some Can See*, the first book in the Northern Michigan Asylum Series, is inspired by the real Northern Michigan Asylum, a sprawling mental institution in Traverse City, Michigan that closed in 1989. Though the setting for her novel is real, the characters and story are very much fiction.

Jacki was born and raised near Mason, Michigan, but she wandered to the north in her mid-twenties, and she has never looked back. These days, Jacki passes the time in the Traverse City area with her excavator husband, her wild little boy, and her two kitties: Beast and Mamoo.

To find out more about J.R. Erickson, visit her website at www.jrericksonauthor.com.

CPSIA information can be obtained
at www.ICGtesting.com
Printed in the USA
BVHW051215230822
645281BV00006B/147